D0251064

07/2009

WITHDRAWN FROM COLLECTION
OF SACRAMENTO PUBLIC LIBRARY

ONE FINAL FIRECRACKER

★ ONE ★ FINAL FIRECRACKER

by Gregory Maguire

Illustrated by Elaine Clayton

Clarion Books ★ New York

Clarion Books
a Houghton Mifflin Company imprint
215 Park Avenue South, New York, NY 10003
Text copyright © 2005 by Gregory Maguire
Illustrations copyright © 2005 by Elaine Clayton

The text was set in 12-point Garamond Book.

All rights reserved.

For information about permission to reproduce selections from this book, write to
Permissions, Houghton Mifflin Company, 215 Park Avenue South,
New York, NY 10003.

www.houghtonmifflinbooks.com

Printed in the U.S.A.

Library of Congress Cataloging-in-Publication Data
Maguire, Gregory.
One final firecracker / by Gregory Maguire ; illustrated by Elaine Clayton.
p. cm. —(The Hamlet chronicles; v. 7)
Summary: A giant spider and several other odd creatures from the earlier books in
the Hamlet Chronicles return as the small Vermont town celebrates a grammar
school graduation, Miss Earth's wedding, and the Fourth of July.
ISBN 0-618-27480-4 (alk. paper)
[1. Schools—Fiction. 2. Teachers—Fiction. 3. Fourth of July—Fiction.
4. Vermont—Fiction. 5. Humorous stories.] I. Clayton, Elaine, ill. II. Title.
PZ7.M2762Fh 200
[Fic]—dc22
2004020494

ISBN-13: 978-0-618-27480-2
ISBN-10: 0-618-27480-4

QUM 10 9 8 7 6 5 4 3 2 1

For Jonah and Alistair Clayton Boughton
and for Hester Godfrey

Mine eyes have seen the glory of a dragon in the dark.
Like the fireflies of freedom he hath breathed a mighty spark.
With flaming breath his bite is death—and don't forget his bark—
On Independence Day.

Little thing, we hardly knew ya.
Now we're sobbing "bye-bye" to ya.
Graduation: Hallelujah!
It's Independence Day.

CONTENTS

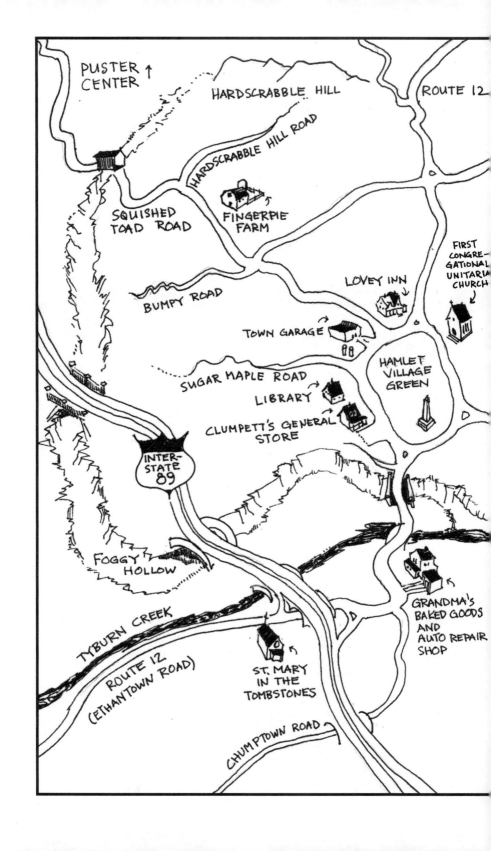

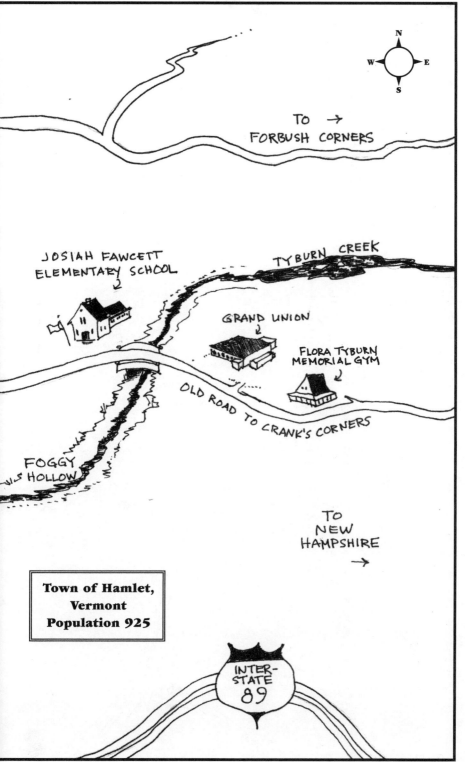

Town of Hamlet,
Vermont
Population 925

Map drawn by author.

1. BEHAVIOR

Putting the telegram aside, Mrs. Tweed remarked mildly to her son, "Looks as if your father is about to blast his way out of prison."

"Trust Dad to get his hands on dynamite," said Thud.

"Don't be rude about your father. His sentence has been commuted."

"Sprung on a legal technicality?"

"In point of fact, he's being released due to uncharacteristically good behavior. Won't it be nice to have him come home again?" She trimmed a bit of azalea stem and replaced the blossom in a cut-glass bowl.

"He's never *been* to our Vermont house before. How can he be coming home?"

"Because his home is his family, Thaddeus, and that means us. I hope you'll be welcoming."

"I'll be welcoming as only I know how."

"That's not very promising." Mrs. Tweed turned her attention to the freesias. "Thaddeus, he's been in jail. It has been no picnic for him."

"No, but he had a picnic committing the felonies that put him there."

"A disrespectful way to put it, but I take your point. He's brought shame to the family. But since he's getting out on good behavior, that's the kind of behavior I want you to greet him with."

"Good behavior?"

"The best."

"How do I do that?"

Mrs. Tweed picked the stem of an heirloom rose and, with fingernails painted roughly the same color as the petals, broke the thorns off, one by one. "You are about to graduate from a school for the first time in your life, Thaddeus. Presumably this means you have learned something. Whatever you have learned, put it to work. If you can think of it in no other way, consider setting your father a good example. Warmth." (Snap a thorn.) "Respect." (Snap.) "Ouch."

"Right," said Thud. "Can I get you a bandage?"

"How kind, Thaddeus," said Mrs. Tweed. "They *did* teach you something at that school."

"I'll bring the aspirin, too, Mom. You're going to need it."

2. THE SINISTER SISTERS

Miss Earth concluded, "Any questions about your final homework assignment of the year, kids?"

For once, her students were speechless—shocked with joy. Each child held a graduation present. The green ticket with gold letters promised to ADMIT ONE to the Sinister Sisters' Circus on the evening of July 2.

"How many Sinister Sisters are there?" asked Fawn Petros. "And how sinister are they?"

"I know the answer to that," said Thud Tweed. "I saw their circus once before, when I spent the summer at a fat farm in the Poconos. The mistress of ceremonies is named Vampyra. Her skin is deathly pale, and her straight black hair is pulled all to one side and falls to her hip. Corpsina, the comic relief, is dumpier. Her red curls flatten on the top and spring out like wings on either side of her head. The Sisters are creepy. I love them."

"They're not really sinister. It's entertainment, that's all," said Miss Earth consolingly. "The greatest show on earth. Your last assignment of grammar school is to come to the circus with me, and enjoy it. You don't have to hand in a written report afterward."

"We couldn't even if we wanted to," complained Sharday Wren. "The circus comes to town on July first. It plays one night only, on July second. And by then school will be out. It's all over."

"I never heard of a bunch of kids who didn't long for summer vacation!" said Miss Earth in a bright tone.

"But Miss Earth," said Hector Yellow, "you're being married the next day! You can't take us to the circus the night before your wedding."

Miss Earth replied, "I can do anything I want. My fiancé will be having a bachelor party with his pals in the town garage, and I have decided I'd rather spend the evening with you. It'll be my last night as a single woman, and who better to celebrate it with than my students?"

"Your *former* students," moaned Anna Maria Mastrangelo.

"Oh, lighten up," said Miss Earth. "I'm not going anywhere."

"But we are," said Anna Maria. "We're going to middle school. Assuming we graduate, that is."

"A safe assumption," said Miss Earth. "Graduation is three days from now. You'd know by now if you were being kept back a year."

There were several sighs. Some were sighs of relief. A few were sighs of regret, from children who wished they could repeat the grade so they wouldn't have to say goodbye to Miss Earth.

Their teacher continued. "I know most of you are coming to my wedding on July third. But on that memorable day, I'll probably be too preoccupied to attend to you as I'd like. Going to the circus the night before seems like a more suitable capstone to our happy time together. It *has* been happy. Hasn't it?"

She looked around. She'd never seen her students with such

long faces. Miss Earth had been their teacher for two years running. Life as they knew it was about to come to an end.

Changing the subject usually helped. Miss Earth said, "Thud,
why don't you tell us a little more about the Sinister Sisters'
Circus?"

Thud Tweed said, "Oh, it's so cool. It has a few wild animals—a lion in a cage, some elephants. Maybe they've got
a gorilla by now. A real gorilla, not a Missing Link." At this
Thud turned and sneered affectionately at Sammy Grubb, who
returned a smile, though wincingly. Some weeks ago, using a
rented gorilla suit, Thud had tricked Sammy into thinking that a
Missing Link in the human evolutionary chain had turned up in
Hamlet, Vermont. Sammy hadn't entirely lived down the shame.

"Also," Thud continued, "the Sinister Sisters have this great
trick just before the final parade. They shoot an audience member out of a cannon. It's so cool."

"Do they ask for volunteers, or do they accept nomina-
tions?" asked Sammy Grubb. "Thekla Mustard would be a good
candidate to shoot out of a cannon. Preferably into New
Hampshire."

"Sammy Grubb, though I intend to go far," said Thekla prim-
ly, "I'll do it under my own steam, thank you very much."

"Class, pay attention," said Miss Earth. "Due to the snow days
we took this winter, our school year is running later than usual.
Our graduation ceremony is on Friday. Saturday night is the Big
Night in the Big Top. Sunday is my wedding, and Monday is the
Fourth of July—not even a week away. It's a packed schedule to
close out a very packed year. So before we're dismissed today, let's
reflect on our time together. I like that phrase of Thekla's, that
she intends to go far. I'm sure you all do. I'm sure you all *will.*"

She went on. "Now, put those circus tickets in a safe place.

5

We need to prepare for change. Imagining change helps it to happen. Can you think up a connection between something that happened to you this year and something you would like to happen to you in the future?"

Hands went springing up into the air. Miss Earth thought: How bracing to see my students so engaged in the possibilities of life!

"Don't just rush forward with your first thought," she said. "Take out a bit of scrap paper and write down several ideas. Put them in order of priority. Choose the most thrilling one to tell us about."

She watched the children scramble to obey. Sunny children in T-shirts and jeans, ribbons and braces, ponytails and earrings—both boys and girls—and a few outlawed rub-on tattoos that Miss Earth decided to overlook this once.

Chin up, she said to herself; you don't know for sure where *you'll* be in the fall. Behind this desk with a new set of students? Or—somewhere else? In any event these children will have flown on toward the rest of their lives. Don't let your lower lip wobble!

"Ready? All right, who would like to start? Yes, Thekla, your hand is up first, as usual. I wonder if you'll ever give anyone else a chance to lead."

Thekla ignored this question as rhetorical. She stood properly by her desk and smoothed down the front of her skirt. "My year has been spent at the helm of the Tattletales Club, whose members are all talented, all wonderful, all girls, all the time. With largeness of spirit, of course, I overlook the short time I was deposed by the *ingrates* and *turncoats* whom otherwise I'm happy to call my closest friends."

Thekla turned her brilliant, somewhat phony smile on the whole class. "With this in mind, I imagine for myself next year a new position. I dream about being the founding head of a new group comprised of the Tattletales and the Copycats. Girls and boys both, together in one club, Miss Earth; that ought to please you. In recognition of your contributions, we could call ourselves the Earthlings. My title, more magnificent than either Chief or Empress, will be—Angel. Angel Thekla. You're all invited to join."

Thekla smiled. She had Miss Earth's attention. Miss Earth had always disapproved of how the boys and the girls in her classroom banded together in separate clubs. This Earthlings notion should please her.

"A noble aspiration," said Miss Earth. "From there?"

In bored voice, studying her fingernails, Thekla recited, "Class president, homecoming queen, a seat in the House, two-term senator from Vermont, chair of some important subcommittees, cabinet member, my party's nominee by acclamation, and beloved president of the United States of America. Perhaps I'll reform the U.N. while I'm at it, as a sort of after-hours hobby."

"What makes you think any boy would join any club you wanted to run, Angel Thekla?" asked Sammy Grubb. "Or live in any country you intended to govern, Madame Dictator?"

Miss Earth looked at Thekla Mustard as if seeing her for the first time—or for the last. How she'd changed! She'd gotten a haircut for the summer and now sported a cap of tight golden ringlets. She was more . . . pert. And almost willowy.

And Sammy Grubb had shot up three inches this year. He looked less like a grubby Little Leaguer and more like a teen heartthrob on the cover of a magazine that sneak-peeked the daytime soap operas.

She brought herself back to earth—back to herself. "Oh, all right, Sammy, since you've volunteered to go next."

Sammy leaned forward on his elbows and looked around. "I've been Chief of the Copycats for all these years, but it hasn't made me want to be chief of anything else. If anything, I've had my fill of clubs. No, my best time this year was hunting for the Missing Link in Foggy Hollow and finding the Flameburper's cocoon. I like the thought of Missing Links. Learning what's the same about different creatures, and what's not. Maybe I'll go into deep-sea exploration to find new species of fish. Or travel to Mars and discover if there are Martians."

"Admirable," said Miss Earth.

Lois Kennedy the Third raised her hand next. Lois was looking more like a kick-butt radical activist than ever. Somewhere over the hills, corporate America had every right to tremble.

Lois asked, "Remember the investigative TV reporter Meg Snoople, who came here last fall when the Siberian snow spiders infested the town? Meg Snoople snoops till she droops. She's my role model. I like spying on people. I want to be like Meg Snoople."

"Perhaps you'll work for the IRS," suggested Miss Earth. "Hector?"

Hector Yellow said, "I enjoyed decorating the church hall when Petunia Whiner gave a charity concert to raise money for the town's new fire engine. I think I'll take art courses, and maybe go into scenic design."

The kids all nodded. That made a lot of sense. Hector had always been the best artist in the class.

"Thud?" asked Miss Earth.

Thud Tweed had transferred to the school in midyear. He had started out a bully, but Miss Earth's exceeding charms had tamed him some. "I've spent my whole academic career bouncing from school to school, since I got thrown out so often," he said. "I'm looking forward to things *not* changing so much this year. To staying in Hamlet and watching things get more and more routine and boring."

"Is there no other ambition you've uncovered in yourself? What's second on your list of priorities?"

"Well, while you were lost in Foggy Hollow, sunk in that coma," said Thud, "I helped your mother make the doughnuts in her Baked Goods and Auto Repair Shop. I thought it was sissy-ish at first, but I grew to like it. Perhaps I'll become a master pastry chef."

"You've continued to lend my mother a hand, for which I'm grateful," said Miss Earth. "I hear you're going to help her make the wedding cake."

"I'm taller than she is, and I can put the top layer on," said Thud proudly. "It's going to be a white feather cake with almond crumble base, red currant smear between layers, double buttercream icing in ivory, satin blue, and—"

"Yum," said Miss Earth. "But enough about all that. Salim?"

Salim Bannerjee was the second-newest child in the class. He had moved to the United States from India almost a year ago. He said, "My dear Miss Earth. I remember when the elephant ghost of Baby Tusker traveled with me from India to London, arriving in Vermont a few months later than I did due to a missed connection. I liked introducing Baby Tusker to the ghosts of mastodons who haunted the hillside. It was gratifying to bring a family together in this way, even if only a ghost family. Perhaps I shall become a lawyer specializing in international adoptions. I'll help waiting families find lonely orphan babies from overseas."

"You have a kind heart, Salim," said Miss Earth. "I've no doubt you'll do much good in life." She had to touch the corner of her eye with her monogrammed handkerchief. "Anna Maria Mastrangelo?"

"I haven't changed much this year," said Anna Maria. "In September I wanted to be a singing nun with my own TV show, and here it is next June, and I still want it."

"Stick to your guns," said Miss Earth.

"Nuns don't have guns," said Anna Maria, though she looked thoughtful, as if this had given her a new idea at last.

Fawn Petros spoke next. She said, "I know I'm not the swiftest arrow in the quiver, Miss Earth."

She waited for her classmates to nod agreement. They didn't. All of them had learned something this year about being kind. So Fawn continued. "I can't imagine the distant future. I can only picture this summer. Maybe I'll start a babysitting service or something."

She was thinking about the four cupids who had come for a visit in February, and how much fun it had been to take care of them.

"You'd be very good at that," said Miss Earth. "I can see the bell is about to ring for recess. I'm not sure we have time—"

The other children chimed in anyway, speaking over each other. Sharday Wren wanted to dance as a Rockette in Radio City Music Hall. Stan Tomaski wanted to work in a used-car shop. Moshe Cohn wanted to go to medical school. Forest Eugene Mopp, the resident Mr. Science, wanted to do anything that involved being outside a lot. Carly Garfunkel wanted to get married and have kids but keep her figure, once she got one. Mike Saint Michael wanted to become a professional soccer player. Nina Bueno wanted to become a firefighter who drove the town's shiny new truck, since sirens made everyone's heads turn to stare and Nina looked good in red.

The recess bell rang. As the kids were lining up, Miss Earth put a hand on Pearl Hotchkiss's shoulder. "What do *you* want?" she asked.

Pearl said, "Miss Earth, I have spent my childhood helping my parents take care of my five sisters, Ruby, Opal, Amethyst called Amy, Beryl, Zirconia, and my brother, Wilberforce. One day they will be able to take care of themselves. At that point I'd be perfectly happy to read for a living."

"Perhaps you'll become a librarian like Mr. Dewey."

"Or a teacher like you," said Pearl. "I've had enough practice, and you are certainly an inspiration." She started to run out the door, little guessing how close to tears she had brought Miss Earth with that compliment.

But then Pearl turned and said, "Miss Earth? You hardly ever give us an assignment without doing it yourself. What do you imagine for yourself next year? I mean, I know you'll be married soon—but anything else?"

Oooh, thought Miss Earth.

She pursed her lips. This very question had been bothering her mightily. What *would* happen to her when she got married? Would she change much? Should she keep the same job? Should she move away, so as to give her life a fresh start, her marriage the room to grow? She just didn't know.

She smiled nicely at Pearl, whom she admired. She said, "That is none of your business, young lady. Run along."

Pearl stood a moment longer. Her expression, perhaps, was one of charity, as if she could imagine the troublesome fog blocking Miss Earth's ability to picture her own future. But before she could think of anything more to say, there was a cry of wonder from the kids in the schoolyard. A huge black-and-white hot-air balloon was wafting fifteen hundred feet overhead. Two women were waving from the basket that hung beneath. The taller one had long dark hair swept to one side. The other looked like a pig in a red wig.

The Sinister Sisters passed overhead, dropping leaflets about the circus. Then the Sinister Sisters drifted wherever the wind blew them, which in this case meant over the Grand Union parking lot.

3. NOTHING IS IMPOSSIBLE

The next morning, before her children arrived, Miss Earth followed her usual routine. She got out the frog food so Kermit the Hermit could have breakfast. She arranged her lesson-plan book and her attendance book neatly on the left side of her desk. On the right side she placed the book she was currently reading aloud to her students—this morning it was *The Incredible Journey* by Sheila Burnford.

Then she went to the computer and turned it on. Since Miss Earth had never traveled far from Hamlet, she had few friends in the distant corners of the globe. But her students had relatives all over. Salim Bannerjee had a grandmother in Bombay. Fern Petros had an aunt in Athens. Nina Bueno had scads of cousins in Bogotá. Thud Tweed had a father in a minimum-security prison in Arkansas. And Anna Maria Mastrangelo had an uncle *rather* high up in the Vatican.

Miss Earth encouraged her students to write to their distant relatives by e-mail. She liked to print out any replies by the time her students arrived.

While the computer was dialing up the Internet service, the school principal arrived in the doorway.

"Hail, Germaine," said Principal Hetty Buttle. "I come in peace." She flashed the intergalactic hand symbol of camaraderie made popular by sci-fi movies, which she adored.

"Hi, Hetty," said Miss Earth. "What can I do for you?"

"Graduation is coming," said Principal Buttle. "Your students will be clearing out their desks for the last time tomorrow. But what about *your* desk? I know your wedding is scheduled for July third. You have a nice little honeymoon planned, no doubt. But what about the fall? Will you be back to take your place at the front of the classroom? I'm late getting the contracts out, I know—the fuss with the Flameburpers, and then our computer conked out. But it still would help me to know your plans."

"Need you assume that just because I'm marrying, I have no professional goals left?"

"I'm asking all the teachers, whether they're marrying or not," said Hetty Buttle. "And I'm asking as a friend, of course."

"Well, whatever I say now, I have the right to change my mind until the contract arrives for signing."

"It's not like you to be evasive," said Hetty Buttle, "nor testy, either. By the tone of your voice, I'm guessing you're not sure *what* you intend to do."

With one hand, Miss Earth opened the windows. With her other, she stacked the milk crates from yesterday's snack time. Sighing, she said, "Hetty, I can't worry about it right now. I'm trying to graduate my students and also to get married to my fiancé. That's all I can manage at the moment. Why don't you tell me about *your* plans? Can you be so certain what you'll be doing come Labor Day this year?"

"I'll be right here, piloting our ship of state through the uncharted universe of the future!" declared Principal Buttle. "Smack in my principal's chair, where I belong."

"I admire your confidence as well as your dedication."

They regarded each other with professional affection. Then the first school bus arrived and they both had to go greet the children. They joined their colleagues—Ms. Frazzle, Mr. Pilsky, Mrs. Messett, Mrs. Amberly, and Mrs. Farmersdottir.

The almost-graduates carefully climbed down the bus steps, holding hands with their kindergarten Little Buddies.

"Of course you can start your own chapters of Copycats and Tattletales," Thekla was saying to a kindergarten boy.

"Or be inventive," Sammy remarked to a little girl. "How about Crybabies and Scaredycats?"

"Isn't that sweet," murmured Ms. Frazzle, putting into words what Miss Earth was herself thinking. "They're becoming humanized, little by little."

"No time for sentimentality—there's work to be done," said Miss Earth crisply, more to herself than Ms. Frazzle. She greeted her own students and ushered them into the classroom.

The sixteen students bustled to their places, and daily chores began. Forest Eugene Mopp, Mr. Science to his friends, headed for the computer to print out any morning e-mails. What he saw made him gasp and say a perfectly foul grownup swear word.

The gabble and rabble subsided at once. Forest Eugene's fifteen fellow students looked up. Miss Earth looked up. Kermit the Hermit looked up.

"What in the name of all that's civil is the matter?" asked Miss Earth, trying to rekindle an atmosphere of gentility in the room.

"The last remaining Siberian snow spider has escaped from the lab at Harvard University," said Forest Eugene.

The room fell into a horrified, gulpy sort of silence.

"Now, class," said Miss Earth in a calm voice, "let's not panic."

"All right," said Forest Eugene, though he made sounds as if he were about to retch with fear.

"At least, not here," said Miss Earth. "Only in an appropriate setting. On your mark. Get set . . ." She threw open the classroom door to the playground. "Go."

The students and their teacher pelted into the bright sunshine and screamed their lungs out. Nurse Pinky Crisp came running from her office to see if it was a case of sudden-onset mass hysteria, the sort often observed during moments of transition like graduation from grade school.

Principal Hetty Buttle, from her spaceship-control-center-themed office, thought grimly, I bet Miss Earth has just mentioned that she's thinking of leaving the teaching profession. What else could cause such pandemonium among her students?

When the students had finished shrieking their shriekies out, they reconvened inside, sitting in a circle on the floor around the reading rocker.

"I don't know what this is all about, but that was a good scream," said Thud Tweed.

"Surely you remember that huge tattered spiderweb in Foggy Hollow?" asked Thekla Mustard. "We told you about the Siberian snow spiders. Last fall, just as school began, a family outing of about seven of them showed up in Hamlet and terrorized the village. One by one they met untimely ends, but the last one survived. Eventually it was relocated to a science lab at Harvard University, under the scrutiny of an arachno-specialist named Professor H.R. Williams. Its poison is unique and potent."

"It's more poisonous than the ghoulish goulash that Mrs. Brill, the lunch lady, makes every Thursday," said Hector Yellow.

"It's more poisonous than Snow White's apple," said Lois Kennedy the Third.

"It's more poisonous than Thekla's breath," said Sammy Grubb.

"It's more poisonous than . . ." began half a dozen other students, but Miss Earth gave them a poisonous look that froze them in midsentence.

"We're neither to monger fear nor peddle prejudice," she said. "But it does seem like a news story to follow. If anyone wants to surf the web and see what else we can learn, I'll grant special permission for ten minutes."

Fifteen of sixteen right hands went poking up for the privilege. Miss Earth chose the one student who wasn't volunteering. "Thud Tweed," she said, "since you weren't here last fall when we had spider visitors, why don't you go to the computer and see what else you can find?"

Grumpily, Thud thumped to the computer console. A few minutes later he gave his report.

"This Harvard scientist guy, Professor Williams," he said, "was carrying the spider in a wire-mesh cage down the hall from one lab to another. The coffee trolley came around the corner. Way too fast. Probably the coffee lady had had too much caffeine and was navigating her trolley above acceptable speeds. Anyway, she crashed into Professor Williams. He dropped the spider cage, and it got all bashed on the floor. A big old hole was torn on one side. But there was no smushed spider. The thing had seen its chance to escape and taken it. Professor Williams thinks the spider must have fled through an open window. But no one knows for sure."

"Thank you, Thud, for that concise and well-delivered report. Any followup questions, people, before we go on with the day's work?"

17

"Will the spider try to make its way back here?" asked Hector Yellow. "I mean, here is where its siblings all met their gruesome ends. Think of *The Incredible Journey*, where two dogs and a cat cross hundreds of miles to return to their homes. Will the spider try that too?"

"Impossible," said Miss Earth. But she really believed that nothing was impossible, except for genuinely tasty gourmet no-fat doughnuts.

At the end of the day, Miss Earth cleaned up her room and hurried to the final faculty meeting of the school year.

"Surprise!" everyone yelled when she walked in. Pink and yellow streamers were draped from the lights, and the staff threw confetti. Mrs. Cobble, the school secretary, bellowed, "It's an engagement party, long overdue!"

Miss Earth's fiancé, First Selectman Timothy Grass, who was affectionately nicknamed "Mayor," stood grinning next to the soft-drink machine. He came over and kissed her as Principal Buttle passed around the party mix. When the staff wasn't toasting Miss Earth, they took turns sucking up confetti with a DustBuster so Jasper Stripe, the janitor, wouldn't have to do it.

"Oh, such commotion!" said Miss Earth, flustered.

She tried to be polite and thank people. She tried to laugh and smile and look perky. She loved Timothy Grass, truly, deeply, really. But she didn't want to turn her love into a stage show to entertain everyone else.

"I wish I could stay and gulp some more fizzy lemonade," she said, "but I promised my mother I'd check out the free-range chickens at Fingerpie Farm. So ta-ta for now, and thanks one and all!" She gave Tim a quick kiss and climbed aboard her Kawasaki 8000 Silver Eagle motorcycle and pulled out of the school parking lot.

It felt good to rush along Squished Toad Road at a respectable and legal speed. The wind whistling past her helmet seemed to clear her mind a bit.

She thought about the missing Siberian snow spider and its whereabouts. Had she been too cavalier about possible danger? *Might* a spider make a pilgrimage back to the place where its siblings had been massacred? Most of the other spiders, such as she was aware of them, had been killed by accident, but the lost spider might not be able to appreciate the distinction between first- and second-degree spiderslaughter.

Nothing is impossible. That was her credo. How well she knew the truth of that! This long year she was finishing had brought such surprises into her life. And she didn't just mean love and romance.

First, at Halloween, Miss Earth herself had been bitten by a Siberian snow spider and nearly died.

Just before Thanksgiving, the ghost of a baby elephant from India had shown up and been adopted by the ghosts of mastodons from the old marble quarry.

Nearer to Christmas, five aliens from the planet of Fixipuddle had crash-landed their spacecraft near Old Man Fingerpie's farm and kidnaped Mayor Grass, thinking he was the real Santa Claus. Happy holidays almost weren't.

As if that hadn't been enough, round about St. Valentine's Day, some adorable cupids were rumored to have been sighted locally, though Miss Earth still wasn't sure if this could have been true.

Then, as spring had approached and the days had begun to lengthen, three genetically manipulated chicken's eggs were discovered in Hamlet. The eggs had hatched into little creatures part lizard, part chicken. Miss Earth's students had called them

Flameburpers because of their occasionally toasty breath. One of the Flameburpers had died—poor Seymour!—but two were still living.

The smaller one, Beatrice by name, was about the height of a medium-sized collie, though she could sit upright and she sported flimsy wings as well as front claws.

The other one, Amos, was tucked away in a cocoon of his own devising. The cocoon was rather large—the heft of your basic compact car. Hamlet residents, though keeping quiet about its whereabouts, nonetheless took turns visiting it where it was hidden in an overgrown recess of Foggy Hollow. They wanted to make sure Amos wasn't morphing into a monster of some sort. They didn't want Amos to break out of his chrysalis and threaten their life, liberty, and pursuit of happiness by exercising his own life, liberty, and pursuit of *them*.

So, yes, Miss Earth had to admit: Nothing was impossible. If all these rare events could occur in Hamlet in a single academic year—and her students could still continue to learn, to grow and thrive—well, it said a lot for public education, if nothing else.

Furthermore, she had to allow that a Siberian snow spider who escaped from a lab some 130 miles away just might be able to make its way overland to the scene of its capture.

And do what? And then what?

Miss Earth shivered. Though she didn't hate spiders, nor did she care to cozy up to one either.

She pulled into the driveway at Fingerpie Farm. Old Man Fingerpie and his wife, Flossie, were in the side yard, weeding their vegetable garden.

"Howdy," called Flossie. "Come to see the Flameburper?"

"No, thank you," said Miss Earth firmly. She knew that Beatrice was still living in a fireproof pen in the Fingerpie barn. But not long ago Miss Earth had become trapped in a spare cocoon made by the other Flameburper, and she wasn't in any hurry to start up a friendship with a member of that particular family.

"I'm just catching up on the health and well-being of your pullets," said Miss Earth. "Remember, we're going to need a mighty lot of them to feed everyone at the wedding."

"We've got it under control," said Flossie Fingerpie. "You wouldn't believe the stink in the henhouse, but everyone's present and accounted for. One hundred forty healthy birds. You know, doing your wedding, Germaine? Plumb cleans us out of chickens. For the Fourth of July barbecue this year, the firefighters got to buy bulk from the Grand Union. We can't supply them this year."

"Barbecued chickens are a Hamlet tradition," said Miss Earth, "but they don't have to be Hamlet chickens for our patriotic crowds to be nourished."

"We run out of charcoal briquets, we can employ that Flameburper back there to cook the birdies," said Old Man Fingerpie. "One of your students is in the barn visiting her, by the way."

"I know my kids are very fond of that critter," said Miss Earth. "I sure hope she isn't still growing anymore. She'll be harder and harder to keep a secret if she does."

"Remind me again why we want to keep her secret?" asked Old Man Fingerpie, whose short-term memory wasn't what it had been.

"She's a mutant. Scientists will do nasty experiments on her if they realize she's still alive and kicking!" said Flossie Fingerpie in a loud voice, as her husband had lost a good deal of his hearing a decade or two ago.

"I'm still alive and kicking; they can do nasty experiments on me," said Old Man Fingerpie. "I don't mind."

Lois Kennedy the Third came out of the barn. "Hi, Miss Earth," said Lois. "Guess what. Beatrice has learned a new trick."

"I don't want to hear about it," said Miss Earth. She wrote out a check and handed it to Flossie Fingerpie. "I have to get home and help my mother with the afternoon cleanup."

"Beatrice has begun to use her wings to help her balance on her toes," continued Lois. "She looks something like a ballet dancer. I mean a lizard-chicken ballet dancer, of course. Especially with that collapsible rack of green feathers up top."

"Delightful," said Miss Earth. "Ta-ta for now." Off she varoomed.

"Have you heard that the Siberian snow spider has escaped from Harvard University?" Lois asked Flossie.

"I didn't know anyone ever escaped from Harvard," Flossie replied. "I'm going out to feed the free-range chickens. Gotta plump 'em up for the wedding."

"I'll stay here and encourage the carrots," said her husband, and he lowered himself into a lawn chair and promptly nodded off.

Reebok, Lois Kennedy the Third's dog and only reliable ally, went nosing about in the weeds by the side of the barn looking for the perfect place to lift his leg. Finding something of interest, he barked a report.

Lois wandered over. "What've you got there, boy, scent of a chipmunk?" she asked. She leaned forward and pawed through the weeds. "Hmmm—I think I know what this is," she said.

She lifted up a strange-looking belt made of computerized circuitry and a kind of enameled leather. "It's one of those alien WordSearch dials!" said Lois. "Perhaps Narr the Fixipuddling left it behind. He never spoke anyway. Do you remember this, Reebok? You wore one for a while, and with its help you could speak English. Did you like that?"

"Bow," said Reebok, noncommittally, and concluded, "wow."

"I wonder if it's still working," said Lois. "You want to try it on again?"

Reebok backed up and whined. He'd had enough of polite conversation to last him a lifetime.

So, since Old Man Fingerpie was in dreamland and Flossie Fingerpie had gone out to the chicken run, Lois turned back and went into the barn.

Beatrice the Flameburper was practicing her pirouettes and jetés, using her wings to correct her balance. When perched on her hind feet, she now stood about two feet tall. The effect of a green scaly lizard-chicken doing something like the Waltz of the Mutants was mesmerizing. A little scary, too.

"Here, duckie," said Lois. "Let me fix this on you."

Beatrice was good-natured. She always responded to Lois's requests, so she tiptoed forward. Then she relaxed into what Sharday Wren, the dancer among the girls, had named the Sixth Position (heels together, toes out, tail flattened on the ground, like a kind of kickstand). Lois had no trouble tightening the WordSearch dial around Beatrice's scaly waist.

"Now," said Lois. "What do you think of that?"

"Help," said Beatrice. "Help!" Her voice was scratchy and gravelly both, as if she'd been a serious smoker for all her young life. "Help!"

"What's the matter?" asked Lois.

"Do you realize what's going to happen to all those chickens?" asked Beatrice.

"Yes, yes," said Lois. "Wedding fricassee is sad, but this isn't

Mission: Impossible. This is a farm. Listen, I have a question to ask you. You remember that cocoon your brother Amos has built around himself? It's awfully large. What should we do when Amos hatches? Will he make trouble?"

"Help," said Beatrice. "And at the risk of repeating myself this early in my career as an orator, I will repeat myself: Help. Help. If you get my drift."

"Help with what?" asked Lois. "You mean, help your brother? Or should we watch out ourselves? Can you clarify?"

"Help those who need help!" said Beatrice, tartly. She was working herself into a state. "I'm *related* to those chickens! I mean distantly, of course, but even so. I can't simply dance around here like a nincompoop ignoring my civic responsibilities—"

Lois didn't find out what Beatrice was proposing to do instead. For just then, Beatrice's stepmother, a dizzy hen named Doozy Dorking, came around the corner of the pen. Doozy saw Beatrice in a silvery girdle, and she ran right up and began to peck at it.

Perhaps Doozy Dorking understood a little English herself now, and had heard Beatrice's cry for help. Perhaps Doozy thought the belt was a noose. Or perhaps she thought Beatrice was being enslaved in a harness. Or maybe she thought it was a cheap glittery show costume, and she disapproved.

In any case, though Lois quickly untied the belt from Beatrice, Doozy kept lunging forward and pecking at it. Beatrice, like any self-respecting teenager, blatted out a little warning flame at her stepmother.

The flare wasn't enough to singe Doozy's eyebrows, had she had any, but a spark fell on the belt. Before Lois could reach for a bucket of water, the little gleaming coil of circuitry began to sputter and spark. It took only a moment for the silver belt to melt into a blackened loop of metallic trash.

"Oh, shoot," said Lois. "That was helpful, Doozy."

Doozy Dorking looked witheringly at Lois, perhaps reminding her that her stepdaughter Beatrice *had* called for help, after all. Then Doozy began to eat bugs for dinner. Like Old Man Fingerpie, Doozy Dorking didn't have a long attention span.

Beatrice struck a pose and twirled, as if portraying *The Suffering of Artists Whose Stepmothers Are Chickens* on some avant-garde stage. "Oh, please," said Lois, as she prepared to say goodbye and leave for the final meeting of the Tattletales before the summer holidays. "I know you're a mutant. I know everyone must march to her own internal drummer. But can't you *try* to be a little more normal?"

Beatrice neither nodded nor shook her head. She just kept dancing, following the beat of her own internal mariachi band.

4. JITTERS

Summer was here. Homework was done forever—well, till September—and the long bright evenings had made parents lenient. So all over town, boys and girls from Miss Earth's class were finishing up afternoon chores and preparing to head out to play.

Only the play wasn't softball, or soccer, or bike riding, or wading in the various streams that coursed down the hillsides. It was the more businesslike play of club meetings. The Tattletales and the Copycats.

Two separate meetings, of course.

Thekla readied her backyard for the final meeting of the year by spreading an old blanket on the grass and making a pitcher of lemonade. When both her parents were out, she wasn't allowed to entertain friends inside, but she had permission to hold club meetings in the yard.

She was alone, so the familiar green shadows of the arborvitae seemed more ominous than usual.

Thekla's father was still at work. Her mother, who was chief volunteer in supervising the cocoon of Amos the Flameburper, hadn't yet returned from her watch. "Eeny meeny miney moe," Thekla sang to herself—loud enough to wake any dozing Siberian snow spiders and scare them away, "catch a spider by the toe. If he hollers, smash him with all 272 pages of the Sunday edition of *The New York Times*. So there."

One by one the Tattletales arrived, on bikes and on foot. All the girls in the class except Pearl Hotchkiss were members. Lois, the last to show up, was in a lather to speak, but Thekla hushed her quiet.

"Girls," said Thekla, "listen up. We're only two days from graduation, and then the Tattletales disband for the summer. We won't reconvene again until the first day of middle school in September, because *some* of us go elsewhere for the season."

Thekla was speaking of herself. The Mustard family always took road trips across America in the summer, stopping at every museum and monument they saw, improving themselves as fast as they could.

"You could appoint a Deputy Empress," said Lois Kennedy the Third. But she spoke without her usual enthusiasm. Long hungry for power, she had recently had a taste of it when she had deposed Thekla for a while. But power hadn't tasted as good as she'd hoped.

Thekla treated that remark with the attention it deserved. She ignored it. "Straighten up, girls, and come to order. Now listen. We graduate in precisely two days—"

"If you're done stating the obvious twice, may I propose a new agenda item?" asked Lois.

Thekla looked across the horizon for a useful wind that might sweep Lois from their midst or, barring that, at least drop a substantial tree limb upon her. "Dear friends and companions of my heart," said Thekla, "and Lois, too, as long as she's here. We all know Miss Earth has invited her students to her wedding. I'm raising the important question of a class gift, which the boys won't think about."

Lois interrupted. "What I have to say is more important than a stupid wedding gift—"

"Aaaaagh!" screamed Nina suddenly. She leaped up and began to flap her arms and slap her neck and ruffle her hair.

"What, what?" cried the other girls.

"I thought it was a spider," said Nina. "I thought it might be— you know. *The* spider."

"The Siberian snow spider, you mean," said Thekla. "Sit down, Nina. That spider is the size of small pound cake by now. It's not going to materialize out of thin air into your thin hair."

Nina seemed hardly comforted.

"If we're thinking of doing something nice for Miss Earth, why don't we get her a new Stephanie Queen book?" asked Fawn Petros.

Miss Earth loved the writing of Stephanie Queen and idolized her fictional heroine, Spangles O'Leary, a movie star-private detective who did environmental protection in her spare time.

"There's a new one out this summer, just in time for beach reading," continued Fawn. "I think it's called *Arrested in Albany*."

Then it was Fawn's turn to shriek and leap up and do a dance. A jitterbug, thought Thekla. We're all jittery. None of us likes change.

"There's no spider on you!" she snapped. "It was a lilac branch bending over in the breeze!"

Fawn sat down again, gingerly. "I wonder if the scent of summertime masks the scent of approaching poisonous spiders?"

"Don't be overly dramatic. There's only one spider left, remember?" said Thekla. "I read that Professor Williams had named it Hubda, after Hubda the Magnificent, the Siberian poetess who described the lore of the snow spider in her epic poem."

"That's a difficult name to call in an affectionate way," said Anna Maria. "Here, Hubda, Hubda, Hubda."

"Nobody says 'Here, Hubda' to a poisonous spider," said Thekla. "Listen, girls, we're losing focus. Is a Stephanie Queen novel a suitable wedding gift?"

"At the circus, maybe we could nominate Miss Earth to be blown out of the cannon," suggested Carly Garfunkel. "Conclude her single life with a bang."

"Enough of this!" said Lois. "May I have the floor, please?"

Before Lois could continue, Sharday exploded into the air. With several years of dance training and gymnastics behind her, Sharday did seven consecutive front flips and finished with a perfect split.

"Hee hee," said Nina, who had been tickling Sharday's neck with a bit of tall grass. "Hubda's moving closer, girls."

"Stop that!" snapped Thekla.

Lois barked, "This is a waste of time! Doesn't anyone want to hear about what Beatrice the Flameburper said to me today? In *English?*"

Now that she had their attention—even Thekla's—Lois recited the story of the afternoon. "Forget wedding gifts," she concluded. "Maybe we ought to be thinking about the happiness and well-being of those poor young chickens who are going to be slaughtered to make Chicken Hamlet for the wedding."

"But how could we save them?" asked Carly.

"And if we did save them," said Thekla, "we'd be depriving the guests of their meal. That's the opposite of a wedding gift. It's a kind of wedding curse."

Not far away, in the tree house in Sammy Grubb's backyard, the boys were having their final meeting of the Copycats Club. It was a good deal less formal than the Tattletales Club meeting. The boys just sat around and whittled with Swiss army knives and sucked the blood out of their nicked thumbs.

After a while, Sammy Grubb asked, "Anybody else feel like being Chief next year?"

Nobody volunteered.

"Maybe we shouldn't have a Copycats Club anymore?" asked Sammy.

No one seemed to have a strong opinion one way or the other.

"What, you're all signed on to Thekla's idea of the *Earthlings?*" asked Sammy, in something close to disgust.

Hector finally voiced their feelings. "Look, Sammy," he said. "Sure, it's a shift. But why get all worked up about it? Change happens."

Thud Tweed, who had finally become a sort of honorary member of the Copycats, snorted. "Look, I'll tell you when change happens. When a mugger comes along and turns you upside down and shakes you to get your cash out of your pockets, that's when change happens. You know, guysters, I'm more interested in the circus. I wish I could be the one to be shot out of the cannon, but I think I'm too big to fit in it."

"It would be cool," said Sammy. "I'd like to try it. But don't you get hurt? Where you do you land? Is there a safety net?"

"The time I saw the show, I couldn't figure it out," said Thud. "Vampyra and Corpsina shoved a kid into the cannon. They crammed his head down with a tool like a plunger. They lit the fuse, and oh, all kinds of noise and fuss. Then there was a big huge BANG and the kid shot out of the cannon. He split the tent and disappeared outside. It wasn't just a trick, either, because the kid came back in the main promenade a few minutes later on the back of an elephant."

"That's the part I'd like to do," said Salim Bannerjee with feeling. "I miss elephants, which we had in India."

"How do you get selected for the privilege?" Sammy asked Thud.

"Well, you have to be in front. A ringside seat. So they can get you in the cannon quickly, before you have a chance to get scared and start screaming for your mommy. Also you have to be small enough." Thud sighed and ate another doughnut. "I don't qualify."

Copycats meetings tended to fizzle out, and this last one of the year was no exception. Salim was the first to leave, as he was expected to read to his younger twin sisters before their beddie-bye time.

He was walking along the road thinking of elephants when a car pulled up alongside him. It was Thekla's mother, Norma Jean Mustard. She was rolling the window down.

"Salim," she said, "you're young and bright, and I'm old and dull. Can you help me? I can't get my cell phone to work. And I'm trying to ring Mayor Grass. Fire Chief Lester Cobble is visiting his sister in Des Moines, and the cocoon in Foggy Hollow has started to smolder. I'm afraid it might burst into flames. I need to find out if the new fire engine has arrived yet, and if they can get it close enough to the ravine to snake a fire hose down there just in case. Quick! What's wrong with my cell phone?"

"Mrs. Mustard," said Salim, "this isn't a cell phone. This is a remote control for a DVD player."

"Oh," said Mrs. Mustard. "No wonder I keep getting a dial tone on the DVD player. Oh well! I better rush on home and call from the land line there."

"Mrs. Mustard!" said Salim. "Would you call my parents and tell them I'll be a little late?"

"You want a lift, Salim?"

"No thanks. I have something I want to do first."

"Suit yourself." She wrenched the steering wheel to the right and jumped her car back onto the tarmac.

Salim didn't like the idea of a Siberian snow spider on the loose any more than the next kid. But he couldn't resist climbing down into Foggy Hollow. By now well-worn paths in the overgrown ravine led straight to the cocoon of Amos the Flameburper, who had been slowly growing and changing inside his self-made pouch for weeks and weeks. Who or what might he be like now?

This far north, spring came late. An air of sweetness filled the evening. In a bower of fresh June leaves, the huge cocoon sat.

Salim made his way up close. It was like a bird's nest that had been woven into a cylindrical basket, completely closed on all sides. Seeping through the fretwork of a thousand browned vines and dead twigs, a faint acrid steam was issuing. It was richer —and warmer to the hand—than it had seemed before.

Salim had once called a Flameburper *friend*. The silly, serious one, named Seymour, who had died tragically young. Salim still missed his little friend, who unlike Beatrice and Amos had never grown larger than a puffball. Seymour had never molted, had never shed his pinfeathers and developed scales and wings and front claws like delicate Beatrice. Seymour had never grown to the size of an all-terrain vehicle, the way Amos was threatening to do. How might Seymour have changed over time? Salim would never know.

Life was all about change. Salim knew this. He had once lived in Bombay, and now he lived in Vermont. He had once been haunted by a ghost elephant named Baby Tusker, and now Baby Tusker was off somewhere else. He had once had a Flameburper named Seymour for a companion, and now he didn't.

And now middle school was approaching. Another change. Why did everything have to change?

Salim Bannerjee stretched out his arms as wide as possible. He hugged as much of Amos's cocoon as he could. He hadn't liked Amos very much. Amos had been a little rapscallion. Still, Amos was poor Seymour's surviving kin. And Salim couldn't wish ill to Seymour's only living brother. "Take care of yourself," he whispered to the Flameburper inside. "Don't roast yourself alive."

That was the message he wanted to send.

Before leaving, he turned and leaned his back against the cocoon. He thought about his other friend, the peripatetic ghost of Baby Tusker, the Indian elephant.

Where are you now? he wondered. Are you happy, off with your adoptive family, haunting some frozen tundra or taiga above the Arctic Circle? Was it hard to leave here? Did you like that change? Do you think of me sometimes? Do you miss me?

Salim let his head fall back. He looked up at the greening branches, and the purpling sky far overhead, and the gray-white smoke issuing from the cocoon. He imagined that the small homemade clouds percolating up from the cocoon were shaped like little wisps of elephants. Ghostly envelopes of elephants, carrying his thoughts, his greetings, his questions off into the stratosphere.

Way, way up, the black-and-white hot-air balloon advertising the Sinister Sisters' Circus floated by.

As Thekla Mustard was picking up the last of the lemonade glasses—making sure no Siberian snow spider had crawled inside one—her mother's car careened into the driveway. Mrs. Mustard got out. "Better come in, Thekla—it's getting late," said Norma Jean Mustard.

Thekla trooped inside after her mother. "How was your day, Mommy?"

"I need to find out when our new fire engine is going to be delivered," said Mrs. Mustard. She grabbed the phone and began punching a number.

"They're hoping to display the new vehicle at the Fourth of July parade," said Thekla. "So it's probably here already."

"I hope so," said Mrs. Mustard. She leaned against the kitchen counter with the receiver against her ear, waiting for an answer.

"You look worried, Mom," said Thekla. Jittery, she thought.

"I suspect Amos the Flameburper is about to hatch," said Mrs. Mustard. "And you know, that's a huge mound of felted material he's wrapped himself up in. If he breathes out fire even once while he starts to emerge, he could immolate himself by accident. It would be horrible."

"You've become attached to that unborn monster, haven't you?" said Thekla.

"I suppose so," said her mother. "Well, you're growing up, Thekla. You don't need me as much as you used to. It's nice to feel wanted by something, even a huge cocooned mutant lizard-chicken slowly cooking itself to life deep in the Vermont woods."

"Not cooking itself to death," said Thekla.

"I sure hope not," said her mother.

"We still don't know if Amos wrapped Miss Earth in a cocoon to protect her from the elements or to store her for his post-emergence supper."

"We may never know. But we have to expect the best of everyone we meet."

"You sound more and more like a teacher."

"That substitute teaching I did when Miss Earth was cocooned must have got to me." Mrs. Mustard hung up the phone. "No one answered, and no phone machine picked up. Where else could Mayor Grass be if he's not at home?"

"Mother," said Thekla, "he's getting married soon. He's probably at Miss Earth's house."

"Of course," said Mrs. Mustard, and dialed the phone again. "Remind me to call the Bannerjees next," she said to Thekla. "Hello? Germaine? It's Norma Jean Mustard. I'm looking for Tim?"

5. LAST DAY OF SCHOOL

When Thekla woke up the next morning, she showered and for the last time dressed in her grade-school clothes. Then she prepared breakfast for her father, who, an older gentleman, tended toward stiffness in the mornings. Since there was no home delivery of newspapers in a town as small as Hamlet, Thekla turned on the little television on the kitchen counter so her father could listen to the morning's headlines, even though the picture was poor.

When everything was ready, she called up the stairs, "Father! I'm about to go to school! Your breakfast is on. Have a good day!"

"Where's your mother?" called Dr. Mustard.

"She's off doing Flameburper monitoring, remember? She thinks the thing is about to bust, or combust."

Dr. Mustard muttered lovingly, "Whatever will she do with herself once the birdy hatches and leaves the nest?" Then he added, "Well, don't forget your lunch, Thekla, and also don't forget to grow in knowledge and wisdom today in school."

"It's a half day."

"Well, do your half day with a full heart."

"Gotcha."

"Thekla Mustard!" Dr. Mustard disapproved of casual language.

"I'm sorry, Father. I mean: Yes, sir."

"I love you, darling."

"I love you too." And she did. Though sometimes she wished she had a father slightly less formal than Dr. Josif Mustard.

Swinging through the kitchen to grab her lunch, Thekla was just about to dash out the door when she heard the sound of a familiar voice on the TV.

It was Meg Snoople, the famous investigative reporter. The one who had come to Hamlet last fall to report on the seven Siberian snow spiders. The same one who had returned in February and aired a live book report by Salim Bannerjee. Now she was speaking furiously at America, poking her finger in the air. Her coif bounced and jounced in sympathy as she spoke.

". . . and I have it from an unimpeachable source that Professor H. R. Williams had never *seen* the coffee attendant before. The franchise that supplies coffee to Harvard says that no coffee trolley is scheduled for a nine-twelve A.M. delivery in the science lab. Furthermore, they insist all the morning personnel are young men newly immigrated from Brazil. They don't have any female employees doing the coffee runs. It was a case of coffee-trolley hijack. So: We turn to Professor Williams."

The camera swerved wildly to catch Professor Williams coming out of a college door. He seemed startled by the camera rushing up to transmit images of his hairy nostrils and blinking eyes. "My goodness," he said.

"What did the mysterious hit-and-run coffee-trolley driver look like? America wants to know!" shrilled the voice of Meg Snoople.

"Why, I hardly saw her," said Professor Williams. "Chesty, I suppose. Blond, though it could have been a wig. Do you suspect hanky-panky?"

"Hanky-panky and *then* some!" barked Meg with professional outrage. "Is there any chance she *intended* to ram your spider cage?"

"Oh, but this spider's bite is usually fatal!" cried the Professor. "If the coffee attendant had purposely plowed into me, that would make her an accessory to murder, wouldn't it? I mean if the spider ever chomps down on some unsuspecting citizen?"

"Where did the attendant go after the accident happened?"

"She disappeared, leaving the coffee trolley untended. I had to help myself to a fresh cup, to steady my nerves."

"I suspect a conspiracy reaching up into the highest corridors of power in the—"

"Please," said Professor Williams. "I'd like to address America, if I may." He turned to the camera and got too close. "Hello, America. How are you? Now listen. If you find Hubda, don't hurt her. Don't smush her with a snow shovel or other heavy implement convenient to hand. She only wants to be loved. And she's the only one of her kind! Hubda, can you hear me? Hubda, are you out there? Come home to Papa! All is forgiven! I'll rent *Arachnophobia* and make cheddar-cheese popcorn."

Meg Snoople began to draw her finger across her throat, signaling to the cameraman to *cut, cut,* this guy is a *nutcase.* But she didn't need to. Professor Williams grabbed her by the collar and said, "May I go now? I have lab results to study." Over his head he flung his briefcase, forgetting it was unlatched. Papers fluttered everywhere as he ran away.

"Another foul crime for the *Breakfast in America* investigative team! We'll snoop till we droop! Now a word from our sponsors, and when we come back, seven ways to stew dande-lion greens." Meg Snoople regained her composure, striking her characteristic pose: one shoulder forward, head reared back, chin up, light dazzling on her gleaming forehead and perfect, adorable, clinically whitened smile.

Thekla shook her head and went to catch the bus. Who in the world might have wanted to liberate the world's last remaining Siberian snow spider?

As he sloshed away at his second bowl of cereal, Sammy Grubb also caught the spider segment on *Breakfast in America.*

He thought about it as he walked to school. He liked to walk when the weather was nice, in case he ran into some screwy bit of the animal kingdom as yet uncataloged, like the Loch Ness monster or a Missing Link. It might seem preposterous, he real-ized, even babyish to believe in such things still. But let's face it: When Siberian snow spiders and mutant chickens both show up in your backyard the same academic year, you should learn to keep your eyes open and expect the unexpected.

Of course, some nervy soul might try to catch sight of the rare Siberian snow spider. Perfectly reasonable. The question was: Who had done it, and why? And was the release of the spi-der back into the wild *intentional?* Was it another job by the Nature's Avengers, the same folks who had kidnaped the origi-nal unhatched Flameburpers from the biotech outfit in Massachusetts?

Nice to have something lively to think about, since other-wise it wasn't shaping up to be much of a Copycats summer. Stan Tomaski went to stay with his father in Cohoes, New York, every August. And Salim's parents were taking the Bannerjee family for a trip back to India, to see Salim's grandmother and

39

great-grandmother and great-great-grandmother, and her mother too if she happened still to be breathing by the time they cleared customs.

Sammy Grubb found himself thinking back to Baby Tusker, that Indian elephant who had died from eating a rotten peanut and whose ghost had followed Salim Bannerjee halfway across the globe all the way to Hamlet, Vermont. What was it about Hamlet that caused such peculiar things to happen here? Was there something in the water? Did ancient ley lines set down by Stone Age settlers play any role?

Or were the Fixipuddlings, who had crash-landed at Old Man Fingerpie's place last Christmas, merely the most recent tour group in an eons-long tradition of intergalactic holiday visitors? Had the shadowy imprint of alien custom subtly altered the event-probability nexus in the space-time continuum around Hamlet?

Or was it just that, with lousy TV reception in the mountains, Hamlet kids read rather more than most, and were therefore more receptive to picking up bulletins from the arcane world than most TV-glutted kids or overworked myopic adults?

He didn't know. In any case, he lost his train of thought about spiders, ghosts, aliens, and mutants once he saw the poster on the side of the Flora Tyburn Memorial Gym. It was twelve feet high and forty feet wide, and a good many of the Copycats were already there, gaping.

The Sinister Sisters' Circus.

"Wow," said Salim. He was pointing to an Indian elephant upon which was perched a young woman of extraordinary balance as well as peculiar taste in clothing, meaning she didn't seem to care much for it at all. "That reminds me of Baby Tusker."

"I was just thinking of Baby Tusker," said Sammy.

"I never get it about clowns," said Stan Tomaski. "Look at

those obvious red noses and the boring floppy feet. Why do they dress up like that anyway? Do they think it's funny? It's not funny, it's stupid."

"And why do they make lions jump through flaming hoops?" asked Mike Saint Michael. "Not very safe for the lion."

"I like the pizzazz, the razzle-dazzle, the sequins and feathers," said Hector Yellow. The other boys looked at him. "I mean, as a concept," he said, "not for my own wardrobe."

Moshe Cohn said, "The circus will still be here packing up when Miss Earth and Mayor Grass get married. It would be nice if the animals could provide some sort of a congratulatory screech-roar-trumpet chorus, wouldn't it?"

They began to straggle on. Because it was the last morning of grade school, they didn't want to miss a minute of it.

The classroom looked strange. The bulletin boards were bare. Kermit the Hermit and a jug of frog food, enough to last ten weeks, stood on a card table near the door. In the picture hanging at the front of the classroom, George Washington seemed almost wistful, as if he were thinking back to his own long-ago student days.

Miss Earth began to take attendance for the last time. "Salim Bannerjee?"

"Here, Miss Earth. We're all here. I've counted us. See? Now, since you're encouraging us to change, why don't we do something different? May we take note of *your* attendance?"

Miss Earth smiled. "Topsy-turvy. Well, why not?"

Soberly Salim said, "All right then. I'll do it. Miss Earth?"

"Present," said Miss Earth. "And while we're on the subject, no presents from kids at my wedding. I hope I've made that very clear."

"Speaking of which," said Lois Kennedy the Third, "who have you invited to the wedding? I mean, besides us?"

"With fancy printed invitations, Mayor Grass and I have invited a few out-of-town friends and family," said Miss Earth. "But Hamlet is so small that I have included local people by word of mouth. Also I put a little notice in the *Hamlet Holler*. The service at Saint Mary in the Tombstones will be simple, and a reception to follow at the Flora Tyburn Memorial Gym. Anyone who is interested may come. But *no presents*," she repeated.

The children liked the idea of attending the biggest wedding of the season. How polite they would all be! The boys would stand straight and stiff like armed guards. The girls would weep, because that was what they thought they should do. Though if it was very funny, they could laugh into their frilly handkerchiefs and everyone would think they were sobbing with high feeling.

Miss Earth read to the end of *The Incredible Journey*. There were some wet eyes in the room. "That's that, then," she said briskly, closing the book with a bang. Then Principal Buttle came in to hand out the last report cards of grade school. "Live long and prosper," she told each student. Celebratory doughnuts and milk were consumed, after which Miss Earth held a raffle to find out who got to take care of Kermit the Hermit over the summer vacation. Pearl Hotchkiss won.

"Great," she said. "One more creature to babysit." Kermit looked insulted and went inside his cave.

"Class," said Miss Earth, "there are only fifteen minutes left, and I have a few final remarks to make. When we meet again tomorrow evening at the Congregational/Unitarian Church for the graduation ceremony, we'll be ready to rock: no time for speeches then. So quickly, put your things away and take your seats."

The desks were about half cleared when the room fell in shadow. Every head turned, even Kermit the Hermit's.

The black-and-white hot-air balloon advertising the Sinister Sisters' Circus was settling down on the lawn just outside Miss Earth's classroom.

"Children, wait," said Miss Earth, but none of the children obeyed. They abandoned their cleanup tasks and ran outside. She followed them.

Close up, Vampyra and Corpsina were not as scary as Thud Tweed's description. Vampyra wore earrings made out of small plastic skeletons. Corpsina's hair was the color of newly harvested cow guts. The sisters were in a stew of excitement.

"Children!" called Vampyra theatrically. "Children of the local community, teachers, anyone! We have alighted here to send a distress signal!"

"We're distressed, all right," added Corpsina. "We're all worked up like nobody's business."

"For two days we've been floating up and down the Connecticut River Valley, advertising the Sinister Sisters' Circus and its arrival in Hamlet, one show only at bargain prices, don't miss it!" continued Vampyra. "But we have set down here not to hand out tickets or promotional brochures—"

"That's good, because we all have tickets anyway," Moshe told them.

"—but to sound an alarm!" Vampyra waved her hands as if trying to dry newly varnished nails. "While floating over that deep and winding ravine that snakes along the edge of your town, we noticed a thin train of white smoke that, as we watched, turned roiling and ugly, charcoal gray—"

43

"—and then, wouldja believe it, a fireball! Right in the woods! Like a small explosion or something! Sheesh!"

"So we landed here at this convenient open grassy space to raise the alarm, lest a forest fire begin to rage in that canyon and consume us all!"

"Sounds like Amos has torched something!" shouted Thud. "I hope not himself!"

"Wait, Thud!" cried Miss Earth, to no avail. Thud began to run wildly around the corner of the Josiah Fawcett Elementary School. His classmates followed him.

"Class dismissed," said Miss Earth in a small voice. "Goodbye, children."

"Who is this Amos?" asked Vampyra.

"A nut case? A firebug? A deep-gully moonshine maker?" brayed Corpsina. "Trouble, I can tell that by the look on your face, Miss Teacher Lady Person."

"I can't talk now," said Miss Earth. "I must ring my fiancé and advise him to sound the alarm for the volunteer fire squad."

And this she did.

6. FIRE IN FOGGY HOLLOW

The alarm—*fire! fire!*—rang out across the center of Hamlet.

Farmers mending fence threw down their tools. Gladys Petros and Olympia Clumpett, who had both done the volunteer firefighter training course, left the Hamlet House of Beauty and Clumpett's General Store, respectively. All the volunteers met at the town garage.

Hamlet's fire department was small, but the town was proud of it. The fire station housed two vehicles. The smaller was usually sent out as first response. Engine Number One was equipped with a pump, and was most useful in conjunction with a pond or a swimming pool.

The second vehicle, Engine Number Three, was the new one—delivered only a day or two ago—and this was its first formal outing. Everyone in town knew that it carried four ladders, wheel chocks, a medical emergency kit, four air bottles, and a large-diameter hose. Oh, was it a beauty, its red paint job shiny as a well-licked cherry lollipop and every steel-bolted plate bright as Mexican silver. It could hold up to eighty thousand gallons of water.

Upon hearing the alarm, many townspeople guessed the same as Thud Tweed and his classmates. Whoever could manage it hurried to join in the effort—bucket brigade if necessary!—to save the Flameburper if he could be saved, or to douse the forest if necessary. Fortunately it had been a wet spring, and the woods were not tinderbox dry. It was unlikely the fire would spread and destroy homes. Still, you liked to be safe and sure.

The kids from Miss Earth's class, having caught the news a few moments before anyone else, were among the first to plunge into Foggy Hollow from behind the Hamlet Free Community Library. (No adults had shown up yet to yell at the kids to stay put.) So the Copycats and the Tattletales, as well as Pearl Hotchkiss and Thud Tweed, went swooping along the paths of the ravine. It didn't occur to them that anything that had produced one fireball might produce a second—and that a ravine made a natural channel through which a fireball might roar.

All they could think of was: *Amos!*

And also, after a moment: *Mrs. Mustard!*—for Thekla's mother was usually keeping watch over the Flameburper's cocoon.

Thud in the lead, they thrashed their way through the woods. The path they took led them past the remains of the spiderweb spun last autumn by the Siberian snow spiders. A harsh New England winter had taken very little toll on the web. Out of their spinnerets those snow spiders had been able to produce something resembling three-ply galvanized steel cord. Eight or nine months later, the web held its spooky shape still. It was a crazed fretwork of hag hair.

The kids smelled the fire first, and they could hear it before they could see it. The scorch and stink of it, the char and chaff of it. The snap and greedy splintery sounds of it, like an army of giant ants chewing through a life-size Lincoln Logs house.

When they came around the last elbow curve of Foggy Hollow and saw the clapping blossoms of cloud and the undulant spikes of flame, they were *really* afraid.

But Amos's cocoon seemed intact. What was burning was the hacked-up remains of the second cocoon, the one in which comatose Miss Earth had been trapped.

"Is Amos still in his cocoon?" screamed Thud in a hoarse screech, over the roar of flames. "We've got to save him!"

"You can't go closer—you're nuts!" yelled Sammy.

"Where's my mom?" bellowed Thekla.

"If his cocoon goes up, Amos will be roasted alive!" Salim was with Thud.

As Salim and Thud began to lunge forward, their classmates jumped them. Fawn tackled Salim easily. Thud was so oversized compared to his classmates that Sammy Grubb was dragged along until Lois, Hector, Moshe, and the rest of the class piled on top and brought Thud down. He was bawling in anger and trying to hit them, but they clung on.

Before he could shake them off, the volunteer fire brigade came crashing down the slope, thrashing through the undergrowth. Mayor Grass led the way, hauling the nozzle of the hose. He was followed by Nurse Pinky Crisp, Hank McManus, Gladys Petros, Father Fogarty, Olympia Clumpett, and Clem Fawcett.

"Where's my mom?" shrieked Thekla.

"She's safe," yelled Mayor Grass. "She ran to get help; she's up top. She's not out of her mind, like you kids. Back up, back away, out of here!"

With the zeal and precision of a well-trained volunteer

corps, which they were, the firefighters positioned the hose and relayed the go-ahead back up the slope. When the water came, it came with a spit and then a gurgling roar. The force was so strong that it took two of them—Mayor Grass and Nurse Pinky Crisp both—to aim the spray.

They doused the crackling, tindery scraps of cocoon first. Then they wetted down the whole area, including the branches of the trees. The water fell to earth in a wide arc, and the kids got drenched.

But when it was safe, they surged forward again, permission granted or no. Mayor Grass met them at Amos's soaked cocoon, and they made their way around to the far side.

There was a hole in the back end about the size of a refrigerator door.

A damp cave yawned inside the cocoon.

It smelled unspeakably foul. But the cocoon was empty. Amos was gone. He had hatched.

The children wanted to follow Foggy Hollow farther to the west and north. Something as large as Amos the Flameburper would be easy to track! But Mayor Grass and Nurse Pinky Crisp and the other firefighters forbade it. So for now there was little to do but climb back up the ravine to the library parking lot.

There, they found a TV camera trained on them. A skeleton crew was finishing a sound check. A lighting assistant had set up some white reflector shields on aluminum frames. Running across the green, where their helicopter had just landed illegally, came the nationally famous investigative reporter and her drop-dead-gorgeous sidekick.

Meg Snoople and Chad Hunkley.

7. SPIES AND SPIDERS

Meg Snoople was a seasoned professional. Whatever had been on her mind up till now was tabled at the sight of smoke-begrimed children and firefighters struggling out of a woodland ravine.

The cameraman intoned in a bored voice, "Live in five . . . four . . . three . . ." and then he held up two fingers, and then one. (A respectable one.)

"I'm Meg Snoople reporting from the idyllic Vermont hamlet called"—here she glanced at a note in her hand—"Hamlet. And though cows in this bucolic wonderland give their milk to make Ben and Jerry's politically delicious ice cream, all is not the pastoral paradise it seems. Here we see young children emerging from a scene of mayhem." She approached Thud, Sammy, and Thekla, who were in the lead, but Mayor Grass gave a stiff jerk of his head to indicate *No talking: Silence!* and the children behaved.

Meg Snoople wasn't cowed. "The children are stunned into apathetic silence by what they've seen. They suffer a syndrome known in medical circles, I believe, as—"

She paused for emphasis just as Olympia Clumpett came clumping by and volunteered, "Yankee taciturnity?"

"Hysterical paralysis," said Meg Snoople firmly. "Who's in charge here?"

"I'm first selectman," said Mayor Grass. He was reluctant to speak but wanted to protect the children from further bother. "I suppose if anyone can answer your questions, I can. Mayor Timothy Grass, ma'am."

"Tim," began Meg Snoople. "I call you Tim because I met you once before. I interviewed you last fall, when your happy town was infested by *Siberian snow spiders*. Can you tell me what's going on here?"

"Oh, little brush fire," said the Mayor vaguely. "Nothing serious."

"Tim, frankly, I'm worried. What were you doing down there with a fire hose? Have you found a new little nest of spider eggs? Has the missing Siberian snow spider come upstream to spawn—so to speak? Come home to roost? Come back for—let me say it softly so as not to scare our youngest viewers—*heinous, bloody, gut-ripping REVENGE?*"

"Oh, we don't think like that," said Tim. "Heavens, no."

"You are an elected official. What do you tell your neighbors when they become deathly frightened of deadly spiders?"

"I usually tell them not to watch so much TV."

Meg Snoople was a bulldog. She wouldn't give in. "Listen, Mayor Grass." (Thekla Mustard noticed she'd reverted to the chillier, more formal title.) "Even if the Siberian snow spider doesn't show up here, it could be stalking some other community. You're the mayor of the only town that's been through this before. What would you say to a cowering, terrified nation, whose fragile sense of well-being has been riven to shreds by this national nightmare?"

"Oh, dearie," said Mayor Grass. He scratched his scalp

through his thinning hair. "I suppose it's best not to accept a dinner invitation from a spider—we all know that old saw— 'Won't you come into my parlor?' said the spider to the fly."

"Are you shirking your civic duty to inform the public?" Meg Snoople appeared about to fly into a rage, though possibly this look was just another professional skill she had.

"Listen," said Tim Grass, looking straight into the camera. "Suppose you're really terrified of spiders. You go to bed shaking and have bad dreams. You wake up to find an eight-foot spiderweb has appeared overnight in your bedroom doorway. In a case like this, probably you should shake out your slippers before you put them on. That's about all I can think of."

"And there you have it," concluded Meg Snoople, turning to look at the camera. "Here in rural Vermont, the prospect of a Siberian snow spider on the loose has terrified sage country folk into imbecility. Stay tuned for all the latest developments in 'SPIDERGATE TWO: Caught in the Web of Revenge?' Now, when we come back, a three-year-old from Topeka, Kansas, recites speeches from Cicero in Latin. Backward. First, a word from—"

"Snoople!" shouted one of her colleagues. It was handsome Chad Hunkley, pointing over her shoulder to something behind his co-anchor.

She turned. Above the tree line, half a mile or so farther west, a pestilential globular cloud of black smoke, roughly ten or twelve feet in diameter, hung in the air above Foggy Hollow. It looked like the result of a small-scale nuclear accident.

"Vermont farmers are hiding something in there!" screamed Meg Snoople. "Oh, what a tangled web we weave! But first, stay tuned for these important messages!" She began to run, and so did the cameramen, Chad Hunkley, Mayor Grass, the volunteer firefighters, and Miss Earth's class.

They all spent the better part of the afternoon crashing through Foggy Hollow. But if that belch of smoke really was the result of Amos the Flameburper exercising his opinions about television journalism, there was no sign of him now. The woods were filled with rotten trees and fallen limbs. They provided an effective blind for a newly rehatched mutant lizard-chicken who didn't care to socialize.

In the end, everyone had to climb out of the ravine and head home for very late lunches or early suppers. There was no further smoke, no noise, no disturbance. In a way, this made people more anxious than ever.

"Something fishy is going on around here. I'll find out what, if it's the last thing I do," muttered Meg Snoople to Chad Hunkley.

"First we better locate ourselves a motel," said Chad Hunkley. "Unless you want to take the crew back to New York tonight?"

"Oh, I don't give up so easily," said Meg Snoople. "I snoop till I droop."

"Well, I'm drooping," replied Chad. He went into Clumpett's General Store. A few minutes later he reappeared with directions to the Widow Wendell's bed-and-breakfast, known as the Lovey Inn.

All over town, Miss Earth's students clomped tiredly into their homes. Had a spaceship been hovering in the stratosphere, and had it been equipped with a special kid-friendly sensor that could home in on such matters, the apparatus would have picked up certain similarities and certain differences in the moods, the tones of voice, the smells of dinner cooking in many different locations.

★★★

Salim Bannerjee groaned when he saw that his father had been laboring over a big mound of chicken parts. The Bannerjees' family restaurant, the Mango Tree, always had a weekend rush on Chicken Korma, Chicken Vindaloo, and the house special, Chicken Bannerjee.

The notion of a huge lizard-chicken on the loose made Salim queasy. All these chicken thighs, these legs, these breasts in damp greasy mounds on the cutting board! "May I have a peanut butter and curry powder sandwich for dinner instead?" he asked his dad.

"We are proud chefs working from the oldest cuisine tradition in the world. We never use curry powder," said his dad. "Except when no one is looking. So my answer is yes."

At Thekla Mustard's house, Dr. Mustard was administering a sip of medicinal brandy to his wife, who was sprawled out on the sofa, suffering a case of jelly limb. "Your mother became overwrought at the sight of Amos's hatching," said Dr. Mustard.

"What did Amos *look* like?" demanded Thekla.

"I saw a claw rip through the casing, an eye peer out, nothing more," said Mrs. Mustard. "I was so taxed with worry that I just keeled over in a dead faint. Amos may never have noticed me. When I came to, the cocoon remains nearby were on fire, so I got myself out of there fast. By the time I reached the library, the fire alarm was already beginning to sound."

"I hope you kept the news of Amos to yourself," said Thekla. "The town is crawling with snoops and spies."

"My little Amos," murmured Norma Jean Mustard. "Has the reading of stories to you in your cocoon paid off? Will you be a solid citizen? Will you be safe?"

"Nature is red in tooth and claw," said Dr. Mustard, shaking his head dubiously. "You can't make a silk purse out of a sow's ear. Can the leopard change his spots?"

"Even given lots of therapy? No, probably not." Mrs. Mustard flumped back onto the sofa with a soft moan. Unpracticed at histrionics, she seemed to be enjoying this. "Oh, my Amos! What next?"

"Earth to Mama," said Thekla, a little crossly. "Relax. You can always find yourself another hobby."

When Pearl Hotchkiss reached her house, she ordered Ruby, Opal, Amethyst called Amy, Beryl, Zirconia, and Wilberforce to come in from the yard. "We're playing inside tonight."

Her siblings protested. The weather was fine! The sun hadn't even begun to set yet! She wasn't the boss of them!

"I am the oldest," she corrected them. "I *am* the boss of you."

She didn't want any of them to be carried off in the jaws of a Flameburper who hadn't eaten in almost three months. But she didn't want to scare them, either. So she said, "Look, I'm going to let you watch *Monsters, Inc.* till Daddy and Mommy get home."

"Whee," they said, and ran inside.

Thud Tweed made his way up the hill to the old Munning Mansion, where he lived with his mother, Mildred Tweed (a.k.a. Petunia Whiner, the famous country-western chantoosie), and a staff of two or three, depending on the season. He'd been here only a few months, and he was still getting used to how the seasons happened in Vermont. There seemed to be six, as far as he could tell: autumn, winter, mud, spring, black fly, and summer.

Late June was the height of black fly season, even on the

manicured lawns around the fanciest house in Hamlet. So all the windows had screens in them.

Thud Tweed doubted that a mesh screen was strong enough to keep out a marauding Flameburper. And in a way he was glad. He liked thinking that Amos might pay a social call. Thud didn't want to be scared out of his socks, of course. But Amos had been his own little friend, those several months back. His first friend in Hamlet, really. And while Thud was getting a little better at fitting in, at having human friends—well, an old mutant friend is something special.

"Thaddeus, darling," said his mother, "come here."

Mrs. Tweed was sitting in a Louis Quatorze chair at her drop-front secretary. She pushed her reading glasses up to the top of her head and, smiling, indicated that her son should take a seat on the Empire sofa opposite. Thud crashed down upon it. Mrs. Tweed winced. But her smile returned.

"Thud," she said, "our deliverance is at hand. Tomorrow your father is being released at last. Mycroft is a good man who made a bad mistake, a silly and stupid and criminal accounting mistake. But he has paid his debt, and liberty is about to be his once more."

"Well, that's the second most exciting thing I've heard today."

Mrs. Tweed didn't ask nosy questions. She continued. "Miss Earth and Mayor Grass have requested that I sing at their wedding on Sunday, and I haven't yet begun to rehearse. So though I'd love to fly to Little Rock and meet Mycroft as he walks through the prison gates, I can't. Would you like to go instead? I can have Harold or Maria Consuelo travel with you."

Thud thought a moment. While he didn't miss his father, he assumed that he did love the man. But Mycroft Tweed was a bigtime industrialist with a finger in a lot of pies in a lot of countries. He had spent most of Thud's childhood off in his private jet, closing deals in Milan, in Buenos Aires, in Durban. He was a foreign entity in Thud's landscape right now.

Meanwhile, Amos was nearby. And might need help.

"No, I think not, Mom," he said. "I'll wait till Daddums comes to see us."

"That should be soon," said Mrs. Tweed. "Doubtless he'll stop off in New York and check on his affairs with his brokers and lawyers, and then he'll whistle up to Vermont and find us waiting with open arms."

Well, waiting, anyway, if not quite with open arms, thought Thud. Of *course* Dad will stop and do business before coming to see us. In Dad's life, Dad comes first.

Fawn Petros ran happily into the Hamlet House of Beauty. Since her mother was one of the volunteer firefighters, and so was her hair salon assistant, Hank McManus, Fawn didn't expect to see anyone in the shop. But a figure was standing by the big old-fashioned minty-blue hair dryer. In the gloom Fawn couldn't tell who it was.

Then the person moved, and said, "Oh my sweetie!"

"Aunt Sophia!"

Fawn flew across the room and gave her favorite aunt a bear hug. "When did you get here?"

"Flew from Athens into Logan Airport, landed yesterday, and I took the Greyhound from Boston to White River Junction today," said Aunt Sophia. "Your dad came to pick me up. Didn't they tell you I was arriving?"

"Yes, but so much happened today that I forgot."

"Well, I'm here for the wedding. After all, Germaine and I

were friends in school from the time we were six. And between you and me, after her former fiancé, Rocco Tortoni, was killed, I never thought she'd get married. But if she's about to tie the knot, well, I want to be here to witness it. And what a good reason to come visit my favorite niece."

"I'm your only niece."

"And you're my only favorite one, too." Aunt Sophia smelled of cigarette smoke. She hugged Fawn again and said, "Your dad has gone to Crank's Corners to pick up a couple of sixpacks. So come on upstairs. I have a surprise to show you while he's gone."

Fawn followed her aunt up the stairs. What surprise? A T-shirt from the Acropolis? A stone from the beach of some famous Greek island she'd never heard of?

Aunt Sophia looked this way and that, then opened the door to the little TV room that doubled as a guest room. The futon was unrolled, taking up almost the entire floor space. On the futon, looking up with a mouth full of peanut butter, was a familiar creature. She was the size of a full-grown house cat, and as her wings churred in delight, she lifted up in the air.

"Rhoda!" said Fawn, and would have covered the little Greek cupid with kisses had Rhoda paused long enough to allow it. "What are you doing here?"

Before Rhoda could swallow her peanut butter to answer, Fawn turned to study her aunt.

"When did you find out about Rhoda?" sputtered Fawn.

Last winter, Aunt Sophia had been shopping in a market stall in Athens. She had found what she'd thought was a cheap imitation of an ancient amphora. She'd mailed it to Vermont, a present for Fawn. But the urn had been genuinely ancient, and for several thousand years it had housed four cupids. Accidentally Fawn had released Rhoda and her three next-door neighbors like genies from a brass lamp. But then Fawn had sent them home by international air mail.

"You asked me to carry the vase to the slopes of Mount Olympus and open it there," said Aunt Sophia. "You never said I had to keep my eyes closed. So when I did what you asked, I met the four cupids you had mailed home. They all went zinging off to find their mother. But a week later, in my apartment near Syntagma Square in Athens, Rhoda showed up at my window."

"Those little boys needed their mom," Rhoda explained. "Kos, Milos, and Naxos are still babies. But I've grown up some. So I asked your Aunt Sophia if I could live with her."

"I agreed," said Aunt Sophia, "on one condition. That Rhoda promise not to try to pierce me with one of her love-potion arrows."

"I *have* only one," said Rhoda. She pulled it from her little quiver and held it up to Fawn. "Normally they come in pairs. But I left the sacred grove without waiting for its double to be ready. So the only way this one will work is if I manage to pin two creatures together with a single arrow point. And while this arrow point is sharp, I don't know if my aim is as good as that."

"Well, don't try it on me," said Fawn. "I love you to pieces already, Rhoda. Slow down your wings and give me a hug!"

Rhoda settled on Fawn's forearm. "I like Vermont now," said Rhoda. "It doesn't seem as cold as it did the first visit."

"This is summer," said Fawn. "Everything is awake again."

"You mustn't tell anyone she is here," said Aunt Sophia. "Your parents would hardly believe it, for one thing. And for another, I suppose she would be considered an illegal alien. I didn't declare her on my customs forms, and she has no passport to be stamped. Homeland Security be stuffed."

"Love knows no national borders!" said Rhoda mockingly, brandishing her little arrow.

"Put that thing back in its quiver," said Aunt Sophia. "I'm a confirmed bachelorette. Don't even *pretend* to shoot anyone with it. Do you hear me?"

Rhoda obeyed. "The truth is," she explained to Fawn, "even though our aim was so poor that our arrows didn't make Miss Earth and Mayor Grass fall in love with each other, they fell in love anyway. I find I have a sentimental attachment to their union. So I wanted to come to the wedding. And I wanted to see you."

She smiled at Fawn, and Fawn smiled back, a sentimental attachment of a different order but just as real, and just as wonderful.

When Sammy Grubb got home, he ran upstairs. His room was pinched between two sharply sloping eaves, and the window's low sill rested almost at floor level. One of Sammy's favorite things to do was drag his blankets onto the floor and lie down on his stomach. He would leaf through comic books or graphic novels, or look at library books like *Monsters from the Deep* and *Aliens R Us.* Whenever he came to a thought-provoking passage, he'd mark his place with a bookmark and balance his chin in his hands. He'd look out the window at the world of Hamlet—the tree house, the used-car parts in the yard, the beginning of Foggy Hollow, the hills that rose beyond it.

He liked to think that the world, if you took the time to look at it, could always, always, *always* show you something new.

It was the main reason to be alive, wasn't it? The main happiness? That the world remade itself, surprisingly, on a daily basis?

Or was that just the main happiness of childhood? He didn't know and he couldn't know, and he wouldn't know until he was as old as Grandma Earth. But judging by how curious, active, and feisty she seemed to be at the advanced old age of whatever she was, Sammy guessed and hoped that the world's daily newness was important to her, too.

Sammy had a professional interest in odd and unique creatures. Maybe it came from having looked at *Where the Wild Things Are* so often when he was younger. He'd always had a feeling there was a special Wild Thing out there, waiting for him.

Sammy couldn't imagine where Amos the Flameburper could have hidden himself. Considering the location of the cocoon, and where the puffball of smoke had later exploded, Sammy wondered if Amos was heading up toward Squished Toad Road. If the Flameburper kept on the track suggested by the ravine's northwesterly direction—away from Sammy Grubb's house, away from the center of town—he'd be nearing Old Man Fingerpie's farm.

Maybe Amos could tell, by smell or some sixth sense, that his sister, Beatrice, was in captivity there? Maybe Amos was going to break her free from her confinement?

Or maybe not. Maybe Amos was simply in hiding, and would double back toward town, now that dusk was finally beginning to settle.

And how had he turned out? Was he reformed, like his buddy Thud? Or had he become a monster aimed at the wholesale destruction of the community?

Sammy kept his eyes trained on the ravine, looking for telltale explosions or little blats of flame like machine-gun fire in comic books. But all he saw was the woods becoming darker.

Black shadows cloaked anything that might be making its way through Foggy Hollow.

Foggy Hollow began at the southeastern edge of town by dipping gently just beyond the Grand Union parking lot. It circled around in a gentle curve toward to the northwest. Twice bridged by the overpasses of the north- and southbound lanes of Interstate 89, where Foggy Hollow was deepest and most impenetrable, the steep cut was also crossed by Squished Toad Road, thanks to a covered bridge that was one of Vermont's most photographed sights. Eventually the ravine grew more accessible as it leveled off at the base of Hardscrabble Hill.

Inside a covered bridge is a good place for a big creature to hide.

And underneath it is a good place, too. Who ever looks under a covered bridge? You can't. You can't see.

Lois Kennedy the Third lived on Squished Toad Road just a few hundred yards northwest of the covered bridge.

She had been to check on Beatrice the Flameburper. She was feeling uneasy about everything. About graduating from grade school. About one hundred forty pullets marked for slaughter for Miss Earth and Mayor Grass's wedding supper. About Amos on the loose.

As she ran through the covered bridge on her way home, she pounded the wooden floorboards extra hard, to make noise, to drum away fear, to keep herself brave.

There was one thing that Lois didn't know about Hubda.

She didn't know that the hatching of the original seven Siberian snow spiders from their long incubation had taken place near a meeting of the Tattletales about ten months earlier. Each little spiderlet was needy, loving, and impressionable. Upon their tiny new-fledged hearts was stamped an image and a longing for the seven schoolgirls called the Tattletales. As it happened, each spider had settled on a different child.

Of the seven, the only spider who had survived was the one that Pearl Hotchkiss had captured in a plastic sandwich bag and brought home as a pet. That was the spider now known as Hubda.

That was the spider that had hitched a ride on the tailpipe of the same Greyhound bus that had brought Aunt Sophia and Rhoda from Boston to White River Junction.

That was the spider now hiding on a strut under the covered bridge in Foggy Hollow.

Hubda didn't have names for things. She didn't know about Flameburpers or investigative reporters on the loose.

Hubda had originally been taken with Nina Bueno, but in the eight months since her captivity at Harvard, she'd changed her spidery mind. Pearl was the one who had captured Hubda with a slice of baloney for bait. Nina? Nina? Who cared about Nina now? Nina was yesterday's news. Hubda now wanted Pearl.

Not all of Pearl. Just a bite. Just a little nip.

Weaving a bed-and-breakfast web for herself under the covered bridge, Hubda didn't know that a fiery-furnace Flameburper was also hunkering down. Twenty-two feet away—on the roof of the same covered bridge. Nor did Amos know that Hubda was nearby. Their paths were yet to cross.

8. GRADUATION DAY

No one slept especially well that night.

The weekday stole into Hamlet more quietly than usual. The school bus didn't belch by. School kids lay awake in their beds, relishing the freedom, feeling funny about it.

As on all days, the future lay tensely coiled, right at hand. It was waiting to happen. It just hadn't happened yet.

At the elementary school, Principal Hetty Buttle pawed around in her files for the graduation speech she had given thirty-two years in a row. Jasper Stripe, the janitor, began to scrape the window frames of the second-grade classroom for repainting. Mrs. Brill, the lunch lady, cleaning out the walk-in fridge, munched on some leftover frozen fish sticks that probably wouldn't make it till next September anyway. Mrs. Cobble, the school secretary, lowered the American flag to take it home for mending and safekeeping. Nurse Pinky Crisp gave herself an eye exam, for fun.

In the classrooms, teachers played loud rock and roll music, and walked around in T-shirts and jeans, and tossed out lots of children's artwork that, let's face it, nobody wanted to look at anymore. And some of the teachers, like Ms. Frazzle, Mr. Pilsky, Mrs. Messett, and Mrs. Farmirsdottir, were sipping mysteriously fizzy drinks and eating peanut brittle at nine in the morning instead of limiting themselves to strengthening coffee.

But Miss Earth eschewed the festivities. She did her work as usual—briskly, no nonsense—and she finished sooner than the others. Rather than chortle a goodbye down the child-free echoing corridors, she slipped out the door of her classroom with Kermit the Hermit and his food supply. She latched the last of her personal items to the back of her Kawasaki 8000 Silver Eagle motorcycle.

Then she roared out of the parking lot.

For the last time?

She still didn't know.

For the past few summers Miss Earth had enrolled in teacher refresher courses. Math fairs, science rallies, geography jamborees. Her favorite was a week-long literature conference, a kind of boot camp for admirers of children's books. There she met other teachers and librarians, and they all went back to being like kids reading for the first time. They read new books, and toasted or trashed them. The colleagues read old favorites, and loved them anew or wondered why they now seemed so stale and stuffy. In any case, the best part of the summer conference was enjoying companionships among professionals, vanquishing the sense of being the last adult reader on the planet.

This summer, Miss Earth wasn't going to the conference. Timothy Grass had said, "Go, Germaine, my honey trove, go! I survived without you for all these years, I can manage one week out of the summer!" But she didn't want to start her married life by taking a solo vacation.

Still, loving to read as she did, she decided to swing by the Hamlet Free Library on the way home. The librarian, Mr. Dewey, had mentioned that a very popular Stephanie Queen novel had finally been returned. (The patron who had kept it out for three years had been using it to prop up his broken milking stool.)

"Here it is!" said Mr. Dewey. "Looks juicy. *Stampeded in Stockholm*. I glanced at the flap copy. Our heroine, Spangles O'Leary, is on her way to accept a Nobel Prize for Persistence from the Swedish Academy. But a jealous runner-up for the same award lets loose in Stortorget, a square in the Old Town in Stockholm, a crazed herd of reindeer with radioactive antlers."

"Where does Stephanie Queen come *up* with such good ideas?"

"What can I tell you? She's a natural."

"Spangles O'Leary is my hero."

"You're mine," said Mr. Dewey.

Miss Earth blushed. "Do I owe any fines?"

"If you did, I would forgive them."

"Mr. Dewey," said Miss Earth. Then she did something that she had rarely, if ever, done before. She giggled nervously. "You're being silly."

"Never more serious," said Mr. Dewey. Miss Earth looked up from her wallet, through which she had been rummaging for her library card. Mr. Dewey's eyes looked—well—dewy.

"Don't say anything you'd regret later," said Miss Earth softly, in case other patrons were lurking behind the standing shelves, eavesdropping for all they were worth.

There was a long silence. A long, long one. Then Mr. Dewey said, "Of course not. It's the Yankee way, isn't it." He stamped

Miss Earth's book and said, "Due in three weeks, Miss Earth. Let me know how you like it."

She fled.

Next, Miss Earth dropped Kermit the Hermit and his summertime food on Pearl Hotchkiss's front porch. But she was afraid her face would still be flaming red by the time she got home. Her mother, known locally as Grandma Earth because of her generally grandmotherly manner, was a keen judge of character and sharp as a tack. Luckily, behind the counter of Grandma Earth's Baked Goods and Auto Repair Shop, Sybilla Earth was too busy thwopping jelly doughnuts into a paper sack to notice her daughter's high color.

"It was a bad season," Widow Wendell was saying in a rush, "a horrible season, really. All the ski traffic went to Stowe or Killington. I was pinching pennies like nobody's business. Then suddenly, KAPOW. Almost every room in my bed-and-breakfast is filled. I'm out of bran muffins—those New Yorkers eat like linebackers. Better give me an extra half dozen of the raspberry crullers."

"Good for your business, good for mine," said Grandma Earth. "Oh, hi, Germy."

"First it was those loony ladies in the hot-air balloon. The Sinister Sisters. They took the twin room. Then that Meg Snoople grabbed the suite, and her co-anchor, Chad Hunkley, took the nice back room over the kitchen. I stuffed the whole camera crew into the attic dormitory—they didn't mind— and thought I was done. What next? A car pulls up at eight-thirty this morning, and it's a dame from out of state—rented car, Florida plates—who says she saw the broadcast last night and is curious about the Siberian snow spider. She wears big dark glasses and a paisley bandanna over her head, so I didn't get a good look at her. She signed the guest register as S. Denim."

"You said a few dozen fresh cinnamon buns?"

"Right. And that's not all. Ten minutes later someone else shows up again. Do you want to know who?"

"If you can tell me in a hurry. I got to replace a Pontiac radiator by lunchtime."

"It was that sneaky guy from Geneworks who was after those little mutant chickadees last spring! Professor Wolfgang something. Einfinger."

"Einfinger! Didn't State Trooper Hiram Crawdad forbid him to come to Hamlet ever again?"

"Bad 'uns never obey."

"And you gave him a room?" Grandma Earth was aghast.

"I can't afford to turn away paying customers, Sybilla."

"What's *he* doing here?" asked Miss Earth, glad for the gossip as a distraction from what had just happened at the library.

"He said he saw the television broadcast last night too. He was curious about that puff of smoke that went blurting up from Foggy Hollow. Maybe he has a scientist's instinct that nothing normal could make a perfect globe of smoke like that. I bet he's here to sniff out the truth and see if one of those Flameburpers survived after all."

"Mercy," said Grandma Earth. "As if we don't have enough going on this week! Oh, by the way, Germaine, Tim called. He left a message with me."

"Yes?" said Miss Earth, preparing to lug her things to her room.

Her mother pursed her lips and smiled and went *smooch smooch* in the air. Miss Earth was embarrassed but, in a funny way, relieved, too.

It turned out to be a fine day. Even so, most kids stayed close to home. They didn't ring each other on the phone. They didn't speed on their bikes to visit each another. No last-minute Tattletales campaign was mounted, no defensive Copycats skirmish resulted. The first of July steamed with an air of soft desolation.

Then the Sinister Sisters' Circus caravan arrived, in three long trucks and four SUVs and a clown car with square wheels. Taped circus music, which like all circus music was distinctly unmusical, blared from loud-speakers. Small black and white helium balloons bobbed from the truck fenders and door handles. Miss Earth's students—and most of the other kids in the town too—came tumbling toward the town green. The excitement of watching a circus tent go up! Of hearing a lion roar! Of seeing an elephant led out of a truck and poop the hugest poop on the planet, right there in front of them! The thrill of it all chased away the graduation blues, at least for a while.

Even Meg Snoople and Chad Hunkley and the camera crew showed up. Meg scowled as if convinced the circus had been brought to town just to distract them. But the spectacle was so interesting that she eventually forgot to be professionally suspicious.

The afternoon wore on, and the blue of the sky began to seem richer. The circus animals were fed and bedded down. The music was turned off after the Clumpetts complained of not being able to hear themselves think. The Sinister Sisters gave away the last of their balloons. The children went home.

Miss Earth's students, with pride and dread alike, brushed

their teeth and changed their underwear, and one or two of the kids even applied deodorant, though it felt stupid to do so.

Anna Maria Mastrangelo was allowed at last to wear dangly earrings.

Sammy Grubb brushed his hair for the second time this year. (The first time was the day school began, last September.)

Fawn Petros cried a little, and her aunt Sophia held her. To cheer Fawn up, Rhoda the cupid said, "I'll come to the graduation ceremony with my arrow, and if I see any two kids sitting extremely close together, touching arms, I'll try to skim them both with a single arrow. That'll liven things up a bit."

"Don't you dare," said Fawn, but she laughed at the notion and felt a little better.

At all their separate homes, the families got into their cars. Everyone sat up stiffly so as not to wrinkle their moods.

In her famous blue nylon dress printed with diagrams of the planets in their orbits, Principal Buttle stood at the doorway. She greeted the students by name. She hugged each one, which was totally embarrassing.

The families and friends took their seats and waved to one another. Everyone was polite and whispery, as if it were a funeral.

The graduates, meanwhile, gathered in a small room to the side. Miss Earth chirped, "Well, gang, this is it! Chins up! Eyes ahead! Smile for posterity!"

Grandma Earth began to squeeze "Pomp and Circumstance" out of the pipe organ. Miss Earth led her children down the center aisle.

Salim Bannerjee waved at his parents and his sisters, Meena and Meera. They waved back vigorously, as if they hadn't seen him in years. His mom wore a midnight-blue sari with mirrors sewn in it. His dad smelled comfortably of dahl.

Nina Bueno bobbed her head at her parents, and the yellow rose fell out of her hair and everyone following her stepped on it.

Moshe Cohn wore his yarmulke even though this was a secular ceremony. Both his grandmothers, the bony one and the padded one, smiled their toothy and crinkled smiles.

Carly Garfunkel winked at her sister, Paula, who had graduated a few years earlier and now thought the whole thing was babyish. But it wasn't.

Samuel Lemuel Grubb, Chief of the Copycats, walked like a military kid, with the straightest bearing in the class. He had taken out his earring because his dad made him.

Pearl Hotchkiss was mortified when her baby brother, Wilberforce, screeched, "Pill! Pill!" That was how he said her name, and Ruby, Opal, Amethyst called Amy, Beryl, and Zirconia all broke up into gales of laughter, and Mr. and Mrs. Hotchkiss could do nothing to shut them all up.

But at least the ice was broken then, so everyone began to relax.

Lois Kennedy the Third wished that Reebok could have joined her baby brother and her parents and her parents' best friends. He'd have run up to her and licked her knees, and everyone would have said "Awwww!" Her father, who with Clem Fawcett and Mayor Grass was one of the selectmen, harrumphed as if he could read her mind and was glad Reebok was safe at home locked on the screen porch.

Anna Maria Mastrangelo couldn't keep herself from folding her hands as if in prayer and lowering her eyes in saintly decorum. Then she bumped into Lois Kennedy the Third in front of her, so she began to walk normally again.

Forest Eugene Mopp, Mr. Science to his friends, wore his biggest pair of tortoiseshell glasses to look especially smart. His mother, the Reverend Mrs. Mopp, was sitting at the front with Father Fogarty and Principal Buttle, ready to intone an invocation.

Thekla Mustard, Empress of the Tattletales, processed with the stately grace of Julie Andrews playing Maria von Trapp getting married in *The Sound of Music*. She took a step and then stopped still, and took a step and stopped still. Before long all the kids from Bannerjee to Mopp were already standing at their places, but those stuck behind Mustard—Petros through Yellow—were all slowed down in the traffic tie-up.

"My little angel," said Dr. Mustard, wiping his glasses. "Would that my sainted mother could have seen this day!"

"Be glad we're here," whispered Norma Jean Mustard, clinging to her husband. "And not eaten up by some marauding Flameburper or other."

Fawn Petros grinned at Gladys and Dimitri Petros and Aunt Sophia. She saw Aunt Sophia's large handbag bulge a little, like a satchel of microwave popcorn punching itself into different cushiony shapes. Rhoda on form!

Michael Saint Michael kept checking under the chairs for a stray Siberian snow spider.

Stan Tomaski felt distinctly weird. Though his parents were divorced, his dad was standing normal as normal in the row right next to his mom and her friend Trish. Was this what grownup life was going to feel like? Queasy does it.

Thud Tweed had never graduated from anyplace before; he'd only been evicted or exiled or fired. Every time his dad thought up a new scheme, either the family pulled up stakes and moved or Thud was sent to a new school. So Thud wasn't used to so much attention from people who had actually begun to know him *personally* rather than from a notice posted in a teachers' lounge. He hulked along and pretended not to be related to his mother or to Harold the chauffeur or Maria Consuelo the cook. The second two weren't too hard, because he *wasn't* related to them, but his mother was an effort. Still, if he thought of her as Petunia Whiner, the famous country-western singer, instead of as plain Mildred Fotheringill Tweed from jolly old England, it was a bit easier. At least his embarrassing father hadn't yet arrived fresh from jail.

As long as Thekla was gumming up the works with her silly pomp, Sharday Wren did some impromptu toework in place, showing off four years of dancing lessons to her parents, her sister Kanesha, and Hank McManus, her dance instructor.

Hector Yellow, who had decorated the room in the Josiah Fawcett Elementary School colors—pumpkin and pine—brought up the rear. It was his job to carry the bouquet of flowers for Miss Earth. They were roses, but since roses come in neither pumpkin nor pine, he had settled on yellow. (He'd put his foot down over the notion of red roses: They would clash.)

Then, at last, they were all in their places, with bright smiling faces. Father Fogarty said a prayer. The Reverend Mrs. Mopp said a prayer. Mayor Grass, as senior selectman of the town, welcomed everyone and thanked Sybilla Earth for the hospitality of Grandma Earth's Baked Goods and Auto Repair Shop, which was supplying doughnuts for the party afterward. Also Clumpett's General Store, for contributing root beer floats.

"Miss Germaine Earth," said Principal Hetty Buttle, "would you like to say a few words?"

Miss Germaine Earth stood up as if to accommodate the request, then shook her head and sat down again.

"Well, then, moving on," said Principal Buttle neatly, and continued: "And that's what this is all about, isn't it? Moving on."

She delivered herself of her familiar and well-loved graduation address. It was all about change being inevitable, but tradition being important, and that's why she wore that same dress every year. The whole universe was open for her students to explore. The parents and families who had heard this same speech at other graduations laughed at all the same jokes. Then Principal Buttle said that if she had the chance, even now, she'd mount a spaceship and fly to the stars! Somehow, they all believed her.

Then it was over. Refreshments, goodbyes, and home.

The family graduation parties were fun. Cakes were cut, presents were presented, hilarity was hilarious. But bedtime came at last, as always it does. And to more than one graduate, the pillows on their beds offered less comfort than usual, turning unseasonably damp, even salty.

9. AMBUSH AT THE COVERED BRIDGE

The first week of July in Hamlet marks two things at the same time.

For one, the Fourth of July is about to be celebrated.

Of course, this is as true in Idaho, Delaware, South Carolina, and Alaska as it is in Hamlet, Vermont. But a Fourth of July celebration in a small town in Vermont has a special feel to it. Every now and then small northeast towns like to display a starchy, let's-show-them-how-it's-done New England attitude toward things. Provincial, yes; fairly obnoxious, agreed; but it's the genuine article just the same. Yankee pride.

So, as in much of the country, bunting is being unwrapped and tacked up. Flags are being run up flagpoles. Cooks are rummaging around for their strawberry shortcake recipes. Hamburgers and hot dogs and beer and soda are selling like flapjacks, and flapjack batter is selling pretty well, too.

In Hamlet, Vermont, the first week of July also sees a sizable influx of flatlanders returning from distant states to spend the next eight or nine weeks in the mountains. So on the Saturday before July Fourth, the Clumpetts usually open up their general store a few minutes early. The truck delivering the Boston and New York newspapers arrives with heavier bundles—the order swells during the summer months. Customers start showing up. *Hi, Betsy!* they say. *Polly, you're looking grand—how was your winter? Anyone seen the Merediths—they up from Georgia yet?*

Sammy Grubb, arriving to buy some milk, knew that a lot of summer residents never got to know the natives. They pushed in and out of the slapping screen door of Clumpett's as if they were the stars of a movie about themselves and Clumpett's were just an old-timey sort of Americana stage setting. *Here's where we spend our summers,* they said, in their perfectly pressed tennis skirts and perfectly polished accents. *Isn't it dear?*

Well, it *is* dear, thought Sammy. That's certainly true. But it's also home, with all the complications of home. A lot of visitors never realize that.

Sammy was polite, though. He waited in line for Olympia Clumpett to ring up his half gallon of milk. Thekla Mustard, in to buy her mom some aspirin, waved at Sammy. But there were too many strangers around for them to call out hellos to each other. Politeness was one thing, but being seen to be friendly outside of school—well, they were hardly ready for *that* yet.

"It's the most amazing thing, Limpy," said Widow Wendell to Olympia Clumpett. "That Professor Einfinger fellow and the Snoople lady are chatting up a storm."

"Romance in the air?" Limpy raised an eyebrow.

"*I've* always wanted to get remarried, but no one ever asks me," groused Widow Wendell. "No, as far as I can tell, they're not talking romance. Einfinger is filling Meg Snoople's ears about the three mutant chicks who hatched here in the spring. He may be convincing her that the return of a Siberian snow spider is less likely than that one of the mutants survived. He's pretty persuasive."

Sammy didn't like the sound of that. Einfinger had been a dangerous man.

Limpy Clumpett remembered that too. "Maybe I should give our friend State Trooper Hiram Crawdad a call," she mused. "Run this Einfinger fellow out of town. He *is* breaking an restraining order, after all."

"Be that as it may, the damage is done," said Widow Wendell. "Meg Snoople and Chad Hunkley are planning to take a camera crew right into Foggy Hollow this morning and see what they can find. Einfinger's going with them."

Thekla Mustard located the bottle of aspirin. She looked at Sammy but didn't say anything. She was listening too.

"There's nothing in that ravine but old beer cans that high-school kids have been littering Vermont with, ever since beer cans and high-school kids were invented," snorted Olympia Clumpett. But Sammy thought: Smart Mrs. Clumpett! She doesn't know who's listening. She's trying to throw nosey parkers off track. The year-round natives knew about two of the Flame-burpers surviving, but why let anyone else in on the secret?

Widow Wendell clucked and headed off. A few other customers bought their eggs and laundry detergent and bread. Just as Sammy got to the head of the line, Bucky Clumpett came in with a bundle of Boston papers. "Howdy, Sammy, how're your folks?" asked Bucky.

"Hi, Mr. Clumpett."

"Well, look at this, won't you," said Bucky Clumpett. He unfolded *The Boston Globe*. "Looks as if some security camera caught a glimpse of that mysterious coffee lady down at the spider lab at Harvard. They've reprinted it in the paper."

Sammy felt Thekla Mustard lunge up and brush past him. "Hmmm," said Thekla. "Curious."

The photo was below the fold. It was about four inches square and showed a woman pushing the coffee trolley, turning to look at the number stenciled on the frosted glass of a lab door. A paperback book stuck out of the pocket of her white service coat. Her hair swung over her face, so her expression couldn't be seen. But it was fairly clear she was not a young Brazilian male. She looked neither young, nor Brazilian, nor male.

"The caption confirms that no one at Harvard ever saw her there before," said Thekla. "Isn't this weird?"

"Are you going to buy the paper or just look at it?" asked Bucky.

"I've seen enough," said Thekla, "and it's very interesting indeed."

When Sammy had paid for the milk, he went out onto the front porch of Clumpett's General Store. He waited there till Thekla emerged.

"What are you doing today?" Sammy asked.

"Going to the circus," she said.

"That's tonight. I mean today. Don't you think we should trail that Meg Snoople and find out whatever she finds out? Amos could be in danger!"

"I think Meg Snoople could be in danger. Or we could. Anyway, Amos is Thud's affair, not ours."

"Thekla Mustard," said Sammy Grubb, "I am appalled at you. We all had a hand in raising up those Flameburpers. Yes, I know Salim and Lois and Thud took care of them first, but we're involved too. *Everyone* is. Look, maybe you're too chicken to throw yourself into the fray, but I'm not. I'll call Thud and have

77

him meet me here in an hour. I'm going back into Foggy Hollow to see what can be seen."

"Remember what happened to Miss Earth!" said Thekla. "She slipped and fell and knocked herself into a coma, and Amos wrapped her up in a cocoon."

"We don't *know* that he was intending to eat her," Sammy reminded her. "Amos might have been protecting her against the bitter cold and the elements."

"Well, he's out and about," said Thekla. "I don't like pairing up with you, Sammy. It sets an ugly precedent, and people might get the wrong idea. But I see I'm going to have to, because we don't have time to call Thud. Look!"

She pointed. Meg Snoople, Chad Hunkley, Professor Wolfgang Einfinger, and three crew members were sauntering across the green and heading for the Hamlet Free Library, there to gain access to the ravine.

"Guess my folks are going to have to do without milk for their coffee today," said Sammy grimly. He went back into Clumpett's and asked for permission to store his milk in the cooler till later. Then he hurried out and rejoined Thekla.

Meg Snoople was dressed for the job. She didn't pause for an instant at the sounds of circus folk preparing for their big show. She didn't stop and drool over the smell of hot pancakes sizzling on a camp stove. She didn't laugh at the little clown car with the square wheels, nor at the clown wearing striped pajamas and big red shoes who stood on the town green and brushed his teeth. She kept her nose pointed forward, and she trundled around the library with a will.

"This is going to be a long day," muttered Sammy to Thekla.

"Well, it's something to do," said Thekla, and Sammy had to agree.

Sammy and Thekla spent the better part of the morning tip-toeing after Meg Snoople and Professor Einfinger and the others. They eavesdropped as much as they could. They heard Einfinger tell the reporters about his boss, Doctor Elderthumb, and the efforts made by Geneworks to splice together genetic material from a blue-toe lizard and a common hen. But the eggs had been stolen by an activist, who had stopped at Clumpett's for some coffee. There, the briefcase of eggs had been hit by lightning. Whatever changes the Geneworks labs had started the lightning had exaggerated. That's where the Flameburpers had come from.

"Unless Amos is deaf, he'll be able to hear those chatterers barking his biography a mile off," whispered Sammy. "They have no idea how to be quiet in the woods."

Thekla whispered back, "I suspect deep down they'd rather not surprise him in the underbrush. They'd rather flush him out into the open. A better story. Hence all their noise."

The party of noisy explorers stopped and examined the spiderweb spun last fall by the seven Siberian snow spiders. Farther on, they came upon the charred remains of Miss Earth's cocoon and the more intact hull of Amos's hatching place.

The camera lights went on. Meg Snoople and Chad Hunkley began to speak in their deep, important voices. "Half of America is going to be crawling all over this," muttered Sammy.

The investigators never did find Amos the Flameburper that day. If they succeeded in crowding him farther northwest up Foggy Hollow, heading toward the more open terrain at the base of Hardscrabble Hill, they couldn't prove it.

Lois Kennedy the Second, the mother of Lois Kennedy the Third, offered to drive her daughter to the village green, where the Sinister Sisters' Circus was preparing to perform. But Lois said she would rather go on foot and ask someone for a ride back. (Squished Toad Road heading townward was downhill.)

Lois, like her friends, had spent a somewhat unusual day— no longer an elementary school student, but not yet used to thinking of herself as a middle school girl, either. She was glad to get out of the house. Happily, she thumped her hightops as she entered upon the old oak floorboards of the covered bridge that straddled Foggy Hollow. It felt good to make a little noise.

Then Lois stopped.

Had something—thumped back?

The covered bridge was a box of purple shadows. The late-afternoon sunshine needled between the weathered planks of the walls. The contrast made it hard to see into the shadows. Was something there?

"Hey now," whispered Lois to herself. She wished that her dog, Reebok, were accompanying her into town.

She thumped her feet again, a little drum roll of six quick stamps.

She thought she heard a scrabble, a rustle, the flex of a bellows, the scrape of a chair.

"Someone taking up residence on the roof of this place?" wondered Lois aloud, in a voice trying to sound brave.

"Or underneath?" she asked in a jolly way.

Something blew against her face. A strand of spiderweb? No, it was her own hair. She was getting spooked by her own hair.

Then she definitely positively undeniably felt the bridge creak and shift, the way it did when a car came along. Only there was no car. No truck, no bike, nobody else but Lois.

Lois and *something else.*

"Hello?" she said. "I'm going to leave right now, okay? Just in case this bridge is haunted, okay? Not that I care. I'll just tiptoe this way. Don't mind me. Toodle-oo."

Something up on the roof scraped along. Heavily.

Mountain lion? And she was trapped! If she left the bridge by either entrance, she'd expose herself to danger. She couldn't run as fast as a mountain lion.

And while she was standing petrified, she was losing time. She might miss the beginning of the circus.

Before too long the sun would hit the lip of Hardscrabble Hill. Dusk would descend. The inside of the covered bridge would grow dark and gloomy. And then what? What?

What was waiting for her out there?

Lois, rarely shy of ideas, was paralyzed with fear.

So she had never been happier in her life than when she heard the purring sound of an approaching car.

It was heading down Hardscrabble Hill from the direction of Puster Center. Lois stood in the middle of the bridge and waved her arms. Cars usually slowed down as they entered the bridge. So did this one.

It was the long black town car driven by Harold, the Tweed family chauffeur. Thud was in the backseat, rolling down the window.

"Want a lift?" he asked.

"Oh, Thud!" said Lois. "My hero!" She leaped into the car, slammed the door shut behind her, and fell against the cool leather upholstery. "Did you see something on the roof of the bridge as you drove up?"

Thud rapped on the window that divided the front seat from the passenger cabin. Harold rolled down the glass and said, "Yes, Master Thud?"

Lois repeated her question. Harold hadn't noticed anything peculiar, he said. But if a mountain lion tried to jump on the freshly waxed Lincoln Continental, Harold McAllister personally would tear that mountain lion limb from limb.

As the car pulled safely out of the covered bridge without further incident, Lois twisted around to look out the rear window. The sun was in her eyes and she had to squint. "Look, Thud, do you see something up there?"

Something *was* there. There was the hulking retreat of a silhouette, all too sun shocked to make out. But whatever was up there didn't want to be seen. It had pulled back to keep as hidden as it could.

"Maybe it's Amos," said Lois. "Maybe Amos crawled up the ravine from where he hatched and is moving along Hardscrabble Hill to the swimming hole in the old quarry."

"I live up that way, too, you know," said Thud. "If it is Amos, maybe he's tracking me down. I hope Mom doesn't take a walk to smell the evening primroses. A huge musclebound Flameburper might cause her to get her knickers in a twist, as she says."

"Should we go warn her?"

"No. She won't be out walking. She's busy planning my dad's special welcome-home supper with Maria Consuelo. Besides," said Thud, "the circus will be starting shortly. I don't want to miss the fanfare."

Soon the wonderful spiked top of the black-and-white circus tent came into view on the Hamlet town green, and Lois forgot to worry about the covered bridge any longer.

10. FRANKENSTELLA IN THE GREAT BEYOND

The Sinister Sisters' Circus was rather a small-scale operation. A one-ring circus. However, what it lacked in scope it sure made up in both dazzle *and* razzle.

A circle of bleachers—racks of seats six rows deep—backed up against the walls of the tent. As the ticket holders found their seats, a Gypsy bagatelle drifted from the audio speakers strung up high around the tent.

The lights dimmed. Drums rolled a drum roll. Vampyra and Corpsina were nowhere to be seen when the clown car with square wheels careened into the central ring. An impossible number of clowns hopped out and fell out and tumbled out, making everyone laugh as they bumped into one another. Next, a strong man strutted in wearing a leopard-skin singlet. He picked up the clown car and shook it up and down, and a last little clown fell out and pretended to screech like a baby. So a big clumsy mother clown with an overgrown mess of curly red hair came lurching up and began awkwardly to kick the strong man in the behind. It was really funny!

The mother clown picked up her baby and put it in a hammock. "Wheee!" cried the baby, who was really some sort of tiny grownup. The mother clown rocked the baby back and forth. But the strong man came and began to tickle her, and she forgot to be careful with the baby. She rocked him so fast that the hammock started to stretch; its cords were all elasticized. The baby went zizzing around in a full circuit, like a swing going up and over and around the top bar of the swing set.

Finally, all went dark. A man's voice announced, "And now, fraidies and gentlemice, your hostesses for the evening: The Sinister Sisters!" Everyone clapped wildly.

A single light came up again, a spotlight in the central ring.

"The Sinister Sisters!" said the voice again. Everyone clapped some more.

"Hello?" said the voice. "Corpsina? Vampyra? You're on, honey dolls."

The mother clown lumbered into the ring. She was carrying the baby clown, burping him and rocking him. She looked around for the Sinister Sisters and then shrugged. She put the clown into a carriage that had appeared out of nowhere and gave it a little kick. It rolled away into the shadows.

Then the mother clown reached down and took off one of her big red shoes. She had a hard time getting it off, and when she did, she shook it as if to remove a pebble.

When she leaned down to put the shoe on again, she recoiled as if in shock. She was pointing at her foot. The spotlight tightened on it.

At the bottom of her clown trouser leg, where there should be one foot, there were two feet, standing very close together.

The clown mother reached down. She located a zipper somewhere near her ankle and began to zip open the side of her clown outfit.

Inside her ballooning right trouser leg were two stockinged ladies' legs.

The zipper went all the way up the side of the costume to the sleeve. And when it was all unzipped, out stepped Vampyra, bowing to the applause. She walked around to the half-deflated clown mother and unzipped the other side of her costume. The clothes fell to the floor, revealing in the other half the red-headed Corpsina, who took off her rubber nose and bit it like an apple and chewed it. They both smiled and waved.

"Welcome to the Sinister Sisters' Circus!" cried the announcer.

For the next ninety minutes, the circus professionals cavorted in a nonstop frenzy of fun. Three elephants came in and sprayed spangly water into a blue light. A lion roared and snapped at peanut butter sandwiches tossed into the air. Vampyra and Corpsina did a magic trick in which Vampyra locked Corpsina in a box and stuck her with swords and sawed her in half. A tightrope walker began a dangerous act, and then the clown baby climbed up the ladder and started to jounce him on purpose. Everyone screamed in terror when the tightrope walker lost his footing, but he bounced safely onto the stomach of a huge clown who had fallen asleep in the ring. (The stomach was an inflated balloon of some sort.) All the while, a busybody sort of music burbled on, and the clowns ran around and behaved clownishly. It was all silly, almost babyish, but somehow it made the kids happy. It felt good to be kids still.

And there was popcorn, and candied peanuts, and soft drinks, and pink clouds of sticky cotton candy, and everyone *ooob*ed and *abb*ed and laughed their heads off.

Finally the music got shimmery and scary and the lights went down again. The announcer's voice said, "And now, maties and gentlehens, our classic finale: shooting a human child out of a cannon!"

Neither Corpsina nor Vampyra had spoken much so far, but Vampyra came forward with a microphone. "This is our signature act," she explained. "Like putting a message in a bottle and sending it out into the unknown seas of the heavens! We need a volunteer. Preferably a child. Children with no known relatives are especially convenient."

She grinned wickedly and went right over to the side where Miss Earth and her former students were sitting in their ringside seats.

"Who would like to be shot into the Great Beyond?" asked Vampyra.

Everyone raised their hands and screamed as if they were loonies on some afternoon game show.

Vampyra continued. "Nothing but a child will do. Someone who believes in the afterlife. Someone willing to take a chance. But who?"

She looked at Thud. "My substantial friend, you'd never fit in the cannon."

Thekla Mustard? "Your clothes are too well ironed. They'd get mussed."

"I don't care!" yelled Thekla, but Vampyra passed on. Lois? Too crabby. Hector? Too timid. Pearl? "You look as if you wouldn't come back," said Vampyra. Fawn? Too lumpy, what with that knapsack she was wearing.

Sammy Grubb?

"Possible. Very possible," said Vampyra. "What's two and two?"

"Four," said Sammy.

"Too smart," said Vampyra. "You, what's two and two?"

"Twenty-two," said Salim Bannerjee.

"That's the ticket!" said Vampyra. She reached into Salim's pocket, and sure enough, his ringside seat was number 22.

"How'd she *do* that?" murmured Lois.

Vampyra and Corpsina helped Salim over the wooden fence and into the main ring. Then the clown car approached, driven by the baby clown. Salim was seated on top of the small car, and he rode—bumpily—in a loose spiraling path around the ring once or twice, until the car pulled up and parked right next to a three-foot-high circular stand. Its sides were painted in silver diamonds and golden lozenges, and a gleaming iron cannon with brass fittings was mounted on top.

The cannon had a wide mouth, and the clown baby held a stepladder as Salim climbed in. Corpsina waddled over to handle the details. "Feet first," said Corpsina. "Wave bye-bye to your chums, chum. You're goin' on a *big* trip! The last big trip! Ha ha ha ha ha!"

Then the lights went down. Salim's head and shoulders were all that was visible.

"Here's your brief, sonny," said Corpsina. "Listen up."

Vampyra explained in her husky contralto. "Many years ago, the first time we tried this trick, we tried it on one of our own family members. To see if it worked. We projected our baby sister, whose name was Frankenstella."

"Was?" asked Salim, a bit nervously.

"*Exactly,*" said Vampyra. "She never came back. So if you meet her in the Great Beyond, tell her we send our love. Our vibrations are sympathetic. Our apologies are copacetic. Our affinities are aligned. Also our creditors are silenced, thanks for asking."

Corpsina interrupted. "Tell the lazy lug she should be good enough to at least to send a note from time to time! Keep in touch! Say hello or something! Being dead is no excuse. Now, sonny, you got any last words of your own?"

In his most polite manner, Salim said, "I wasn't exactly planning on going to the Great Beyond tonight. But do you think I might meet my friend Seymour there? That would make me happy."

"Seymour? *Seymour?* Sonny, you'll *see more* than you can imagine! But don't worry. You look as if you know all about the great cycle of death and birth and regeneration! So long, cannon fodder!" Corpsina laughed maniacally. Vampyra paid no attention, just studied her painted nails—glamorous in black and white stripes.

All the clowns emerged from the shadows. The lion roared and the elephants roared and the strong man beat his chest and roared too. Vampyra and Corpsina hoisted up a long implement like a giant swab for the clearing of giant ears, and they poked it into the mouth of the cannon, pushing Salim down into the barrel.

"Everyone, say bye-bye to your friend!" screamed Corpsina.

"I hope you don't suffer motion sickness," said Vampyra apologetically. To the crowd, she added, "Get ready to hold your popcorn buckets over your heads, just in case."

The drums rolled, the silence fell, the lights grew darker still, except for a spotlight on the very back of the cannon. Corpsina struck a match on her teeth and lit a fuse. The thing sputtered and sparked.

"Oh dear," murmured Miss Earth. "I hope this is not a mistake."

Then—KAPLOW-EEE!

All they could see of Salim's exodus from the mouth of the cannon was a streak of blue light like a dozen shooting stars heading upward all at once. A boom, a searing sound, a ragged caw like the rip of a burlap sack. Then the spotlight swiveled up to the ceiling of the tent. It located the hole that Salim had made when he had shot through, the strips and tatters of ripped canvas still fluttering.

"He'll be hurt!" cried Sammy. "Where will he come down?"

"Oh, my goodness," said Miss Earth. "I *am* shocked!"

"A moment of silence for our dear departed friend," suggested Vampyra.

A violin somewhere played two bars of taps in a slightly whoopsy manner. Then the lights came back up a little. The baby clown was driving the funny car in circles. The strong man chased it until a button holding up his leopard singlet popped, and he had to run and jump into a bucket of water before his outfit fell off. Vampyra and Corpsina took bow after bow as the audience cheered and shouted, "Encore!" The rest of the clowns came out and bowed too, and the lion was brought out once more, and it climbed up on the cannon like a mountain lion on a precipice.

Then two flaps at the back of the circus tent pulled back. Into the big tent came the largest of the three elephants, the one with black-and-white bull's-eye circles painted on her sides.

Sitting cross-legged on the head of the elephant, with a dazed expression on his face, was Salim Bannerjee. He was wearing a sky-blue turban with a huge ruby-colored jewel pinned to the front and a peacock feather jouncing on top. His arms were folded in a magnificent, serene manner.

Everyone screamed and cheered and shouted, "What the—? How'd he do—?"

The elephant circled the main ring and came to a halt. Then the crowd fell silent as Vampyra and Corpsina approached the elephant with a red wooden ladder.

"Well?" asked Vampyra, climbing up. "Any message from our missing Frankenstella?"

89

"I saw no one," said Salim—a little sadly, as if he'd half expected to meet up with his little Flameburper friend in the afterlife. "But I've come back with this." He handed a little wooden box to Vampyra.

"A present from our missing Frankenstella!" shouted Vampyra. She took the box and opened it.

No one could guess the physics involved in what happened next, but out of the little box grew a huge balloon, shaped like a human and almost life-size.

"Frankenstella!" shouted Vampyra. The balloon bobbed. It was white with black markings on it, and it looked like a three-D model of a ghost. "You need a little sunlight, sister! You've gone pale as a ghost!"

She and Corpsina rushed to hug the ghost of their departed sister, but they squeezed Frankenstella too tightly between them. The white balloon slipped through their grasp like a slithery fish in the paws of a seal and bobbed up, eventually disappearing through the hole in the tent.

"What, you have to leave so soon?" cried Corpsina. Vampyra began to wave at the crowd, as if it was they who were leaving. And they were, after the applause ended. The circus was over.

Outside, in the moonlight, you could see the ghost of Frankenstella bobbing in a southwesterly direction, heading toward Rutland.

But, thought Salim on his way home, she was a fake ghost. Circus trickery. Fun, in its way, but disappointing. Only the solid elephant beneath him had been real, and there was no point in forming a friendship with her. The circus tent would be struck by tomorrow morning, probably, and any possible new friend, once again, would only depart.

11. FLAMEBURPERS, UNITE!

The Boykin brothers had a place on the far side of Hardscrabble Hill, closer to Puster Center than to Hamlet. There were three of them: Howard, Woodrow, and Percy. For a fee they would come to your farm with a specially outfitted truck. They would slaughter, bleed, pluck, and truss your chickens and prepare them for the deep freeze if necessary. It was a messy job, and in some ways an ugly one, but they were good at it. When they had a big order—a hundred or more birds—they'd get some Boykin cousins from Crank's Corners to help.

Their busiest season was the Fourth of July, when almost every town in Orange and Windsor counties held chicken barbecues to raise revenue for their local volunteer fire departments. Because of high demand for their services, the Boykin brothers had been forced to schedule the chicken slaughter for the Earth-Grass wedding reception on the very morning of the ceremony. But they had promised they could finish the job at Fingerpie Farm by noon, and they would deliver the birds to the coolers at the fire station. There, as a wedding gift to Mayor Grass, the volunteer firefighters would be lighting the beds of coal. Later, relay teams would rush the roasted chickens across the village center to the Flora Tyburn Memorial Gym, where the wedding reception was to be held.

Howard, Woodrow, and Percy Boykin headed up the hill from Puster Center at about eight in the morning. The day was a bit gloomy, with more long, thin stripes of brown cloud than one would like to see on a wedding morning.

"Rain," said Howard.

"Mess and muck," said Woodrow.

"Little chickens ripe for plucking," said Percy, who liked to pluck chickens, rain or shine.

But when the truck cleared the top of Hardscrabble Hill and started down the other side, they saw that the day's natural gloom was intensified by a cloud of smoke above Fingerpie Farm.

"Snafu," said Howard.

"Trouble and trial," said Woodrow.

"Little chickens ripe for plucking," said Percy, who had a one-track mind.

Howard slowed down when driving across the covered bridge. Dating to the early years of the twentieth century, the bridge was high enough for a horse and carriage and afforded plenty of clearance room for standard automobiles. But the Pluckmobile, as it was called, was a modern vehicle of over-weight proportions. The fit was snug. Howard had to inch forward carefully.

"Spiderwebs," he observed.

"Pinch and poison," said Woodrow.

"Little chickens ripe for plucking," said Percy.

The Pluckmobile squeezed through and rattled along the road. By the time it pulled into Fingerpie Farm, the Boykins could see that the town's firefighters had arrived to keep the Fingerpie barn from burning down. Both pieces had responded to the alarm, and the pumper was busy drawing water from the farm's duck pond.

"Gloriosky!" said Howard, shaking his head at the commotion.

"Stink and smoke," added Woodrow.

"Little chickens ripe for plucking?" asked Percy mournfully.

"Quiet about the little chickens, Percy," said Howard.

The Boykins jumped out of the Pluckmobile. Their Boykin cousins were there, and neighbors had rushed over to help out too. Collapsed upon a stretcher, Old Man Fingerpie wheezed while Dr. Heidi Sternbaum checked his blood pressure and Flossie Fingerpie administered an ancient bottle of smelling salts. Lois Kennedy the Third and her dad, from just up the hill, were heading off a couple of Fingerpie pigs who seemed determined to plunge into the traffic on Squished Toad Road and change its name to Squished Pig Road. Salim Bannerjee kept trying to duck into the barn, and Timothy Grass and Olympia Clumpett were yelling at him to get away.

The Boykin cousins—Buck, Buster, Daisy, and Cecil—helped drag out the heavy hose, while Clem Fawcett adjusted the valves. Between them, Mr. Dewey and Nurse Pinky Crisp supported the nozzle and doused the roof of the barn.

The Boykin brothers ran up to their cousins.

"Accident?" asked Howard.

"Arson," said Buck.

"Flint and fuel?" asked Woodrow.

"Too early to tell," said Buster.

"Something burned down the barn door," said Daisy.

"Little chickens ripe for plucking?" asked Percy.

"Don't worry," said Cecil. "They'll be off in their own chicken yard, out back." Percy smiled.

Mayor Grass struggled into the barn and, after a while, returned and heaved off the air bottle. He gasped to catch his breath, and then he reported to the gathered neighbors, adults and kids alike.

"Don't know *what* in tarnation happened here," he panted. "Might have to get an expert from Montpelier to give an opinion. The fire was worst at the southeast side, where the smaller door is. Think that's where it began."

"I smelled the smoke—I knew it was trouble!" cawed Old Man Fingerpie, who'd come to his senses, or as much of them as he still had. "My daddy's barn burned down in 1928, and I can still remember the unholy stink like it was yesterday!"

"When Old Man hollered, I came running," said Flossie. "The door was just—well, the word that comes to mind is *toast*. A big old gaping hole where the door shoulda been, and the edges of the doorway all flower-petaled with flames."

"It looked like the flaming hoop that the lion in the circus jumped through!" said Lois, and Salim nodded in agreement. "We had just arrived to say good morning to Beatrice and see how she was doing."

"Where is she?" asked Flossie. "Have you seen her?"

They shook their heads. "Didn't get into the barn," said Lois woefully.

Flossie said, "We got the big animals out first—the horses, Nelly and Gus. The cows were in a panic, and one of them had kicked down her stall. They're over in the paddock now, suffering conniption fits."

"The pigs have broken through the lattice underneath the farmhouse porch and are hiding in there," said Lois Kennedy's dad.

"Reebok, our dog, is snarling at them to keep them penned in."

"But where *is* Beatrice?" asked Lois. "Didn't you save her, too?"

"I was soothing the horses, honey," said Flossie.

"Was Beatrice penned in that small galvanized fireproof stall?" said Mayor Grass. "It was empty. One side of it was crushed as if by a battering ram. Something smashed into it, and she escaped."

"Like the Siberian snow spider!" said Olympia Clumpett. "Who is flouncing around New England letting out the freaks of nature? Some sort of addlepated terrorist?"

"Or," said Thud, who had arrived late but was catching on, "maybe she didn't escape. Maybe she was freed."

"By who?" asked Daisy Boykin.

"Or by what?" asked Mayor Grass, looking at the doorway again.

"By Amos," said Thud. "Flameburpers, unite. He came to liberate his sister Beatrice, who was imprisoned in here."

"She wasn't imprisoned!" snapped Flossie Fingerpie. "She was in residence, and we treated her well, and loved her like our own daughter!"

"We never had a daughter," said Old Man Fingerpie. "At least not that I remember. Did we?"

Before Flossie Fingerpie could begin to revive Old Man's memory, the Boykin brothers came around the far side of the barn. They had glum expressions on their faces.

"Catastrophe," said Howard.

"Good and gone," said Woodrow.

"What now? Who?" asked Timothy Grass.

"Little chickens ripe for plucking!" said Percy, starting to sniffle.

They all headed over to see. The Boykin boys were on the money. Whatever had liberated Beatrice had also crashed apart the chicken-wire fence that penned in the chicken run. The whole population of one hundred forty chickens had flown the coop. "Even Doozy Dorking is AWOL," said Flossie.

"What about our wedding dinner?" asked Mayor Grass at last.

The Boykin boys shrugged. If there were no chickens to kill and bleed and pluck and quarter, what was the point of hanging around?

"Sorry," said Howard.

"Godspeed, God bless," said Woodrow.

"No little chickens ripe for plucking," explained Percy, casting a mournful look at his hands and wringing them. They headed back to their Pluckmobile.

"Whatever are we going to do?" wailed Flossie Fingerpie. "We promised the chickens for the wedding banquet!"

"I have a thought," said Lois Kennedy the Third. "It's a long shot. May I use your phone, Mrs. Fingerpie?"

12. GUESTS AND GHOSTS

Lois's big idea had been this. If Miss Earth's former students helped, maybe Salim's father, who was chef at the Mango Tree, could simmer up an emergency wedding vegetable curry. It could supply Timothy Grass and Germaine Earth with a substitute meal to serve at their reception. Mr. Bannerjee was dubious, but he agreed once he heard he would have a work crew to help.

Lois rang Sammy and Thekla to marshal their forces. Sammy Grubb sandbagged the Copycats. Thekla Mustard mustered the Tattletales. Pearl Hotchkiss and Thud Tweed, more or less free radicals, joined in too.

They scrambled about the town begging for every last carrot or tomato or early zucchini to be found in any refrigerator crisper. (It was too early in the season for local vegetable gardens to have produced very much.) "Frozen green beans, too!" Mr. Bannerjee had declared. So frozen green beans, too.

The emergency bicycle brigade crisscrossed the town, delivering conscripted vegetables to the kitchen of the Mango Tree, which had closed its doors to its lucrative Saturday lunch trade because of the crisis.

There, Thekla and Sammy and Pearl were set to peeling potatoes. Fawn and Mike and Stan scraped carrots. Carly and Moshe
rinsed frozen beans in lukewarm water. Sharday and Anna Maria
chopped celery. Nina and Hector and Forest Eugene separated
mushy rutabagas from mushier rutabagas.

On the kitchen CD player, Mr. Bannerjee played a recording
of a cooking raga. This lulled everyone into a sense of culinary
destiny. The air was cloudy with cumin and yellow with turmer-
ic, redolent of fennel seed and peppercorn and coriander all sizzling in a pot the size of a bathtub. Mrs. Bannerjee hurried off
to White River Junction to buy forty pounds of basmati rice.
"Keep your little sisters out of trouble!" she told Salim.

He said to his dad, "Meena and Meera are spitting cardamon
pods in the cumin bucket."

"Take them away!" intoned Mr. Bannerjee dreamily, lost in
the magic of Indian cooking.

"Okay, dad," said Salim, seeing his chance to slip out. Salim
set his sisters up in front of a video of *Hindu Honeymoon*, the
family's favorite Bollywood extravaganza. Then he took the
opportunity of his father's daziness to sneak away unnoticed
with Lois and Thud.

The matter was this. It seemed perfectly clear to Thud and
Lois and Salim, who had known the Flameburpers best, that
Amos the Flameburper must have burned down the door of the
Fingerpie barn. Beatrice had been safely penned into her fire-
resistant chamber. Besides, she couldn't toast a marshmallow at
eighteen inches; her range was limited.

Lois also pointed out that the Fingerpies' chicken run was sit-
uated slightly north of the barn. That morning, she had noticed
that some fencing separating pastures from upland forest
beyond had been smashed. She hadn't mentioned this to the

Fingerpies, who were in too flustered a state to deal. But she'd thought it over and discussed it with Thud and Salim when they had arrived at the Mango Tree with their scavenged ingredients. "I think Amos and Beatrice and Doozy Dorking and the one hundred forty liberated chickens must have headed up into the wilderness of Hardscrabble Hill," she had whispered. "Up near Smugglers' Lookout. Near the swimming hole by the old marble quarry."

"Smuggler's Lookout?" said Thud. "What did they smuggle around here? Triple-X maple syrup?"

By midday, a mild rain was falling—well, hardly a rain, just a thrash of wet wind. A gust of breeze in the roses, a patter of drops on the skunk cabbage. It made sloppy going for Thud, Salim, and Lois Kennedy the Third, poking their way through overgrown meadows and stands of birch and balsam on the craggier side of Hardscrabble Hill.

The track curved below an outcropping of stone in which convenient handholds could be found if you paid attention. The three friends hoisted themselves up onto it. "This is Smugglers' Lookout," said Lois Kennedy the Third. "You can see all of Hamlet below."

She was right. Hardscrabble Hill provided the best bird's-eye view of the center of Hamlet. From northwest of town, you could see how Hamlet worked almost as if reading a map. Even with the trees in full leaf, it was easy to chart the five main roads spoking out of town, leading from the famous Hamlet village green to Forbush Corners, Crank's Corners, Chumptown Falls, Ethantown, and Puster Center. You could make out the sharp cut to the east where Foggy Hollow began, by the Josiah Fawcett Elementary School and the Grand Union parking lot. You could pick out the ravine dipping under the diagonal breezeway of both the northbound and southbound lanes of I-89 and winding around to Squished Toad Road, the covered bridge. You could tell where, a short while later, it lifted itself to ground level at the base of Hardscrabble Hill.

"The air is so clear," said Thud, wonderingly, "it's almost like looking through a telescope. You can make out every building in the center of town."

"There's the Mango Tree. I can smell the curry from here," said Salim proudly.

"And there's the tent—they're taking down the circus tent," said Thud. "Hey, Salim, how did if feel to be shot from a cannon, anyway? Did you really go to the Great Beyond?"

"I wish," said Salim. "It was just the Ordinary Beyond."

"Don't wish too much," said Thud. "You don't come back from the Great Beyond."

"Hindus believe in reincarnation," said Salim. "But I'm only part Hindu, so I'm not eager to experiment with it already. I just miss my missing friends." He was thinking of Baby Tusker and Seymour the Flameburper, both.

"What're we, chopped liver curry?" asked Lois. "Look, just below us. We've climbed high enough to see Ethan Allen Park across from Cormier's llama farm, see? And there's Fingerpie Farm, looking peaceful as anything from this distance. We're so high, we're almost in heaven."

"We *are* almost in heaven," said Thud softly. He sounded peculiar, and Salim and Lois both cast him sharp glances. But before they could tease him for sentimentality, his point was proven. An angel had appeared some thirty feet away, on the edge of the clearing atop Smugglers' Lookout. "Yoo-hoo," cried the angel, flapping its wings.

"I'm having delusions of grandeur," said Lois. "How odd; I

thought only Thekla Mustard suffered that sort of affliction. Look, it's an angel."

"I'm having a psychotic episode," said Thud. "Because I don't even *believe* in angels."

"I'm having a conversion experience," commented Salim, a bit exhaustedly. "It's not enough to be part Muslim and part Hindu, Vermont is turning me part Christian too?"

"You wanted the Great Beyond," said Thud. "Maybe this is your escort service."

"Hey there!" cried the angel. It tried to fly but fell on its face and said a distinctly unangelic word.

"Are you all right?" asked Lois. Angel or no, it seemed to be rather clumsy, and it had bruised its beautiful face. Its hair, a sickly sort of corn-silk yellow, was all crinkly, as if it had stuck the tip of its wing in an electric socket.

"Never better," said the angel. "Though I think I've lost my land legs after all that time in outer space. Excuse my wobbly woozies." It fell down again. "Ow."

"Outer space?" said Thud.

"I don't believe it," said Salim.

"It can't be," said Lois. "*Pimplemuss?*"

"The same!" said Pimplemuss. "Nice to see you again!"

"You've met before?" asked Thud, nearly dumbstruck.

"Yes," said Lois, "but not in angelic form."

"I can't quite get the hang of the wings," said Pimplemuss, flapping them. "They seem to want to go places I don't intend them to go."

"Where are your companions? Are they here too?" asked Salim eagerly.

"Yes," said Pimplemuss, "but they're back at the starship *Loiterbug*. They didn't want to come out until I did a scouting mission and made sure your planet was still more or less safe."

Lois said, "This is fabulous!" Then she remembered her manners. "Thud and Pimplemuss, you haven't met. Thud, Pimplemuss. Pimplemuss, Thud. Pimplemuss is an alien from the planet of Fixipuddle. Thud is a transfer student."

Pimplemuss and Thud looked at each other warily.

"Don't you remember?" said Lois. "We *told* you. Pimplemuss and her four traveling companions were here over the Christmas holidays. Only she wasn't dressed up as an angel then, just a sort of overweight elf."

"I carry it well," said Pimplemuss. "I have big bones."

"Why are you here?" said Lois.

"And why dressed up like an angel this time?" said Salim.

"Oh, am I an angel?" asked Pimplemuss. Her wings drooped. "I have made a mistake. I was trying to be the Ghost of Christmas Past. Remember, your teacher lady read us that story, *A Christmas Carol*? I must have gotten my reference materials mixed up. You can't rely on hard-wired encyclopedias, I tell you. The information dates before you even finish the countdown to liftoff."

"But," repeated Lois, "why are you here, Pimplemuss?"

"Because we were invited," said Pimplemuss.

"To the wedding?"

"What wedding?" Pimplemuss looked at Lois and Salim. "Aren't you two humanettes a little young to get married?"

"Invited to what? Stay on the subject!" roared Thud.

"Lower your voice, you," said Pimplemuss. "Just because you're as big as I am doesn't mean you can speak to a Fixipuddling like that."

"Who invited you back?" asked Lois more sweetly.

"You remember our WordSearch dials," said Pimplemuss. She shifted some folds of white muslin, and sure enough: Around her waist was tied a WordSearch dial. "It allows us to communicate in your language. Well, we must have left one behind by accident. And it began to behave as a sort of walkie-talkie, I guess. Not long ago, we got a broadcast from it. Like an SOS. We couldn't recognize the voice, but the message itself was clear as daylight. It said, 'Help! Help! Do you realize what's going to happen to all those chickens?'"

"But, but," sputtered Salim, "do you mean it was *you* who burned down the door of Fingerpie's barn?"

"Who else?" cried Pimplemuss. "I had a flaming sword. I thought it went with the Christmas Past costume, but clearly I'm out of this galaxy altogether."

"You're out of your mind," muttered Thud.

"Watch it, big boy," warned Pimplemuss. "I'm in no mood. These wings itch, and I don't want to shape shift again until I'm back in the privacy of my own particle shower."

"Can we come and see the others?" said Salim. "I'm in the mood to see some old friends."

"Sure, why not?" said Pimplemuss. She glared at Thud. "As long as you behave. I may not be an angel, but I'm no wilting violet either."

As they turned around and began to traipse through the woods, she answered their questions. The hardest thing to understand was how the aliens could spend six months in outer space, continuing their trip to Fixipuddle, and then do a U-turn and get back to Earth in a matter of several days. Here it was July 3, and Beatrice had belted her SOS into the WordSearch circuitry only four or five days ago.

"Look at it this way," said Pimplemuss. "We took a shortcut."

"That doesn't make sense," said Salim. "Why didn't you just take a short cut home to Fixipuddle, then, and get there already?"

Pimplemuss tried to explain. She got more and more muddled with comments about differential equations and wrinkles in time and seeing eternity in an hour if you spent half a sec thinking about it.

Finally she said, "Well, it's like this. If you have a dream about a place you've never been—say a planet made out of old rubber tires and populated by screaming penguin tooth fairies—then when you wake up, at first you're blotto with shock. But then if someone says, 'Quick, imagine an unlikely planet,' your mind goes to the planet of screaming penguin tooth fairies immediately, because you can already picture it."

"But you already know about Fixipuddle," said Salim.

"Yes," said Pimplemuss, "but we've been galaxy wandering for such a long time that we can't remember it very well. I guess we've been meandering our way home. Frankly, we can remember Earth better. And when we got the distress call, we thought, Those are our friends down there! We'd better go help! And so we did."

"So you *kidnapped* Beatrice the Flameburper and one hundred forty chickens?" demanded Thud. "Intergalactic jail for you."

"We kidnaped no one," said Pimplemuss clippedly. "We invited that strange chickenoid thingy you call—Beatrice?—to come for a stroll through a burning doorway and a smashed fence. A few of her intimate friends implied that they'd like to come along. How could we say no? That would be far too rude."

Lois thought Thud was heading for a showdown with the alien angel. She decided to change the subject. "Well, you're just in time for Miss Earth's wedding," she said. "If you get yourselves all dolled up like wedding guests, you can come and enjoy the festivities."

"Oh, la, what fun!" trilled Pimplemuss. "Narr, Foomie, Droyd, and Peppa will love it!" She began to race through the ferns toward the swimming hole in the old marble quarry. "Look, the *Loiterbug* is hidden behind that stand of trees by the deep sink of water."

But then Pimplemuss stopped. She put the tip of her wing in her mouth and chewed it until feathers came out. "Pfaaah," she said, spitting them out. "A creature I never saw on my previous visit. Is *this* an angel? Should I bow my forehead to the ground, or lead a round of applause, or make a donation to a worthy cause?"

"What are you going on about, Big Bird?" asked Thud.

The kids squinted and peered. Through the slanting bars of light—for the rain had begun to pass over at last—an insubstantial shape was beginning to draw itself together, like a bit of water vapor disguising itself as . . .

. . . as . . .

"A clot of raincloud?" asked Lois.

"A circus elephant?" asked Thud.

"The Ghost of Christmas Yet to Be Believed?" asked Pimplemuss.

But it was Salim who identified it. "Baby Tusker!" he shouted, and lunged forward.

13. REUNIONS

"**G**ee, our local chamber of commerce must spend a bundle on promotional brochures," said Thud wonderingly. "This place is more popular than Disneyland."

Baby Tusker was the same as ever—and why not? Ghosts didn't change, did they? They didn't grow up or get bigger. He was still small—well, small as a young elephant. The champagne-colored, gauze-curtainy look of him hovered like a three-D pencil drawing in the air. You could see trees and the swimming hole right through him. What was *he* doing here too?

He raised his trunk and lowered his head, and if the ghost of an Indian elephant could be said to look bashful, Baby Tusker looked bashful. His trunk reached out to settle on Salim's shoulders, and he nuzzled Salim's ears and tried to ruffle his hair fondly. But his trunk had no material mass, so Salim's hair stayed more or less unruffled, except by the wind.

Salim couldn't speak. The Great Beyond into which the circus cannon had shot him had been the Great Disappointment, really. But here—it was almost the ghost of a ghost, as he had never expected to see Baby Tusker again. It was the Great

Beyond reaching over to *him*, in the shape of an elephant trunk, in the look of an elephant eye.

"Bizarre," said Pimplemuss.

"You're one to talk," said Thud.

She ignored him, continuing, "It looks like a small compressed cloud of galaxy dust."

Lois explained. Baby Tusker had followed Salim all the way from India to Vermont, but Salim and his friends had arranged the adoption of Baby Tusker by a troupe of mastodon ghosts. The new family had then migrated up to the province of Quebec or the Northwest Territories or the North Pole.

"Have you come back for the wedding too?" asked Thud.

Baby Tusker didn't answer.

"Cat got your tongue?" asked Pimplemuss.

"He has no tongue," Lois explained to Pimplemuss, "nor, for that matter, any native tongue."

"That's not true," said Salim, able at last to speak. "Elephants are great communicators. They have shrieks and bellows, and they communicate with ear flappings and stompings, too."

Baby Tusker's ears flapped expressively. But expressing what?

"Oh, why monkey around like this?" barked Pimplemuss. Lois and Salim were beginning to remember about her impatience. The alien fussed with her waistband and removed the WordSearch dial. Large enough to go around Pimplemuss's substantial angelic waist, the WordSearch dial was roughly the same diameter as the root of Baby Tusker's schnozzola. It wouldn't stay in place, of course—Pimplemuss had to hold it in midair with her angelic hands, while Baby Tusker threaded his huge smoky nose through it.

"Can you hear me?" said Salim.

Baby Tusker nodded, but slowly, so Pimplemuss could follow the movement and keep the WordSearch dial more or less in place.

"Why did you come?" said Salim.

The voice of Baby Tusker was surprisingly thick but high—like a tenor with a head cold.

"I was home with my family," he said. "And you know our trunks are very sensitive, like our ears."

"I didn't know," said Salim, "but I'm not surprised."

"Our trunks are like antennae," said Baby Tusker. "I'm not sure if this is true of living elephants, but it's true of ghost elephants. We pick up quivers and vibrations and moods. Usually they're too vague to read, but recently we got a very strong message—all of us. It seemed to be a smoky, charry sort of memory of—well, of me. Floating more or less intact in the stratosphere. Once detected, it was simply a matter of using our capable ears to listen. And I heard your voice."

"You heard my voice?" said Salim.

"You said something like, 'Do you think of me sometimes? Do you miss me? Was it hard to leave here?'"

"I remember thinking that," admitted Salim. "The day before Amos the Flameburper hatched. He was smoking up a packet of puffs into the air."

"Your thoughts may have colored a thought from that creature you call a Flameburper," said Baby Tusker. "The breathy message was like an atmospheric postcard. A cloud of feeling, you might say. Not like anything else on this planet. It delivered your questions to me. So I decided to make an appearance. I'm a ghost; I can do such things."

Pimplemuss began to mug and point. Without her Word-Search dial, she couldn't understand a thing.

"It's okay," said Baby Tusker. "I don't like to talk. I'm shy. Don't make me do it again. But before you give her back her magic talking machine, let me say this to you, Salim."

Lois and Thud pretended not to be listening. Pimplemuss was listening for all she was worth, but she couldn't comprehend a word.

"Stay with me," said Salim. "I beg of you."

"Even ghosts have futures, you know," said Baby Tusker. "I've learned that much since leaving here. I've come back to tell you that: Yes, I miss you, and: Yes, I love you. But the future loves you too, and I'm in the future too. Don't be afraid of what you don't know. That's all the future is—the part you don't know yet."

"Don't leave me again," said Salim. "Just *don't*."

"Even if I'm only in your memory, I'm there, in your future memory, already loving you still. As an Indian acquainted with the idea of *forever*, you should be able to grasp this simple concept."

Baby Tusker withdrew his trunk, and Pimplemuss restored the WordSearch dial to her waist. "What did the little smokeball say?" she asked.

"Sort of the same thing you did," said Salim. "When something is in your memory, you can get there faster." He wanted to hug Baby Tusker. He wanted to tame him and make him a house pet. He wanted to kidnap him.

"I already know that," said Pimplemuss. "Still, he makes a nice sort of friendly fog. Come on. Might as well go say hi to the others."

The starship *Loiterbug* was only a few more yards farther on. It was hidden in a grove of trees, its familiar bulging sides camouflaged with vines and branches.

"Thud," said Lois, "you've never seen the Fixipuddlings in their natural state. They're a little funny looking. Don't scream or anything."

"Are they like giant bugs with humongous fungoid heads?" asked Thud.

"I'll bug *you*," snorted Pimplemuss.

"Hard to describe," said Lois soothingly. "Everything you've ever dreamed of, and more."

The hatch of the *Loiterbug* began to open like a metal mouth. The jaw became a ramp and the overbite a sort of canopy. "You're welcome to come in, but you take us as you find us," said Pimplemuss to Thud. "The others will be glad to see folks they know."

And indeed they were. Four other Fixipuddlings were crowded at the door, waving. Droyd and Peppa, the younger ones, were leaping out of their traveling socks in excitement. Narr, who had never spoken even when equipped with a WordSearch dial, bobbed his beak and covered his eyes with feathery appendages. Foomie, who was not so much male or female as simply Foomie, rubbed Foomie's hair out of Foomie's eyes, which had filled with tears of joy. "A sight for sore eyes," said Foomie, "when old friends meet and greet! Come in, rest a spell, put up your tired tentacles! Or feet, or whatever they're called."

Lois and Salim had been in the *Loiterbug* before, briefly, but Thud never had. He was delighted to explore the splendid central chamber, the bays and banks of equipment, the sleeping quarters below the main deck. "This is cool," he said. "Doozy Dorking and the one hundred odd chickens are down here having a gabfest. *Pee-yew.*"

"Now," said Pimplemuss, "what was that you said about a wedding?"

"A wedding!" Foomie clapped Foomie's handlike append-ages. "Oooh, mercy, I hope we're invited."

"Everyone's invited," said Thud. "Well, aren't they? Didn't Miss Earth say it was an open-house invitation?"

Thus it was, an hour or so later—after a number of experiments on which Salim, Lois, and Thud offered opinions—that the five visiting Fixipuddlings emerged from the particle shower suit-ably disguised as human wedding guests.

Pimplemuss looked like a very tall female state senator, a state senator with partial giraffe ancestry. She had a face like a shoehorn and was dressed in a canary-yellow twin set and pearls, and she clutched a pocketbook with a big clasp shaped like a brass butterfly.

Foomie, the hairiest of the Fixipuddlings, was a bearded old New England salt, in lilac seersucker stripes and a straw boater set at a rakish angle across Foomie's brow.

Narr looked spiffy in a cutaway and spats. He insisted on wearing dark glasses and carrying both a telescope and a mon-ocle, too, which seemed a bit overdone, but he couldn't be dis-suaded.

Droyd and Peppa were done up to look like rather old-fashioned children. Peppa sported a dress resembling a starched pink lampshade, with a pink lacy hem and outsized pink bows, and pink ribbons in her pink hair. Peppa wore a sailor suit and Buster Brown shoes, and he had put on freckles liberally with a frecklestick.

"They look a bit weird," murmured Thud.

"I heard that!" shouted Senator Pimplemuss. "*You* look a bit like an endangered species. Watch out!"

"All eyes will be on the bride," said Lois consolingly.

Pimplemuss made sure to close the ramp of the starship *Loiterbug*. "That Doozy Dorking creature has taken a shine to me," she said. "I don't want her chasing after me at a wedding reception and getting underfoot. She and Beatrice can play fox and chickens with their one hundred forty little friends. That'll keep them amused till we get back."

Baby Tusker walked with Salim, hand in trunk, sort of, given that Salim couldn't really get a grasp. They had tried to convince Baby Tusker to take a turn in the particle shower and see if it could transform him into a wedding guest, but he had refused. So he was just going to have to try to keep hidden on the sidelines.

The sun shifted. The shadows began to lengthen. There was just enough time for the children to run home and get changed into their wedding-guest clothes. Salim had the farthest to go, so he and Baby Tusker took off at a pace. The Fixipuddlings decided to wait for Thud and Lois. They were inclined to take shelter under the covered bridge so no passing driver would see them and offer them a lift to the wedding.

"Don't get spiderwebs in your good clothes, children," said Pimplemuss to Droyd and Peppa. "The underside of this structure is lousy with webs! Don't these humans ever house-clean their planet?" She blew on a fresh web. "Oooh, the spider that wove *this* one! Must be a lalapalooza! Wonder where it is."

14. SPEAK NOW OR FOREVER HOLD YOUR PEACE

By four forty-five, the afternoon had finally turned bright, though the air within the stone walls of Saint Mary in the Tombstones stayed pleasantly dank and musty. The small, west-facing rose window over the altar glowed in vehement greens and blues, royal reds and golds. Their faces speckled with colored stain, guests sat in comfortable silence waiting for the wedding party.

They came in two varieties: human and otherwise.

Grandma Earth usually played the organ for services, but in this instance, as mother of the bride, she had relinquished her seat on the bench for her substitute, Widow Wendell, who at the prospect of another wedding in town was already crying with joy. Or maybe, since it didn't involve herself back at the altar again, rage and frustration.

On either side of the altar loomed two great arrangements of wildflowers—daisies, Queen Anne's lace, cornflowers. By the kneelers, where Miss Earth and Mayor Grass would accept their blessing and pledge their troth, burst an extravaganza of heirloom cabbage roses. Their blooms had been nurtured all spring by cow muck supplied by the generous and helpful cows at Fingerpie Farm.

Yes, it was beautiful. But it was strange—so strange that Miss Earth's former students didn't know whether to laugh or cry, or, if they happened to suffer from allergies to daisies, sneeze.

Thud had been asked to escort Grandma Earth down the aisle. "I've been called a Grandma for ten years or so," said Sybilla Earth in the back of the church, fussing with her only party dress, which she'd had dry-cleaned for the first time this century. "Mostly because of my dropsy chins and cheery ways. I guess I do look the part. But I'll tell you, Thud, if Germaine and Tim give me a grandchild before it's my time to pass to the Great Big Baked Goods and Auto Repair Shop in the Sky, I'll be very happy if said grandchild is half as helpful to me as you have been."

"Oh, go on," said Thud, but he was pleased to hear it.

Farmers had done their evening chores early in order to get gussied up. Merchants had posted CLOSED signs ahead of the normal Sunday schedule. Almost every grownup in Hamlet was there. "It's a good thing there isn't an international jewel thieves' ring casing the town, for this would be a great moment for them to strike," whispered Paula Garfunkel to her sister Carly.

"Who says there isn't? Everyone else comes to town—why not international jewel thieves?" Carly whispered back.

"Nobody in Hamlet wears international jewels, that's why."

"Shhh!" hissed Meg Snoople, who had arrived in church wearing a hat with a brim that seemed broad enough to cast a shadow in three counties at once.

Besides neighbors and friends from Hamlet, the church also welcomed out-of-towners. Fawn Petros's aunt Sophia was there. Chad Hunkley and the rest of the *Breakfast in America* broadcast team squinched over to make room for another guest at the

Lovey Inn, Ms. S. Denim. Stylishly, Ms. Denim wore dark glasses even inside. "Who *is* she?" everyone wanted to know. Even Ernie Latucci, the deejay on the Voice of Vermont, wished he could broadcast a bulletin to find out.

State Trooper Hiram Crawdad noted Professor Wolfgang Einfinger sitting behind a pillar. However, caught up in the spirit of celebration, Trooper Crawdad decided not to make an arrest for Einfinger's violation of a court restraining order.

The Sinister Sisters, Corpsina and Vampyra, came in matching black-and-white striped dresses that made them look like a pair of zebra people. The clowns came too. (The animal trainers stayed away, however, because their smell was strong and they didn't want to distract the congregation.)

Then, of course, there were the nonhuman guests.

Senator Pimplemuss and her entourage sat in a back pew, beaming at everyone. Pimplemuss and Foomie kept spotting students from Miss Earth's class, but the recognition wasn't mutual. The particle shower had done too wonderful a job, and Thud, Salim, and Lois hadn't yet had a chance to whisper the news of the Fixipuddlings' return to their friends.

In a pocketbook roughly the size of a bowling ball carrying case, Rhoda the cupid sat happily. Every now and then Fawn opened the latch and glanced in. Rhoda waved her little hands and wiggled her wings, but she kept her spare arrow in her quiver. There was no need for it here.

Salim couldn't think where to hide Baby Tusker until Lois, who went to Saint Mary's, reminded him of the curtained confessionals in the back of the church. Baby Tusker squeezed inside quite happily. Drifts of grayish smoke leaked out from underneath the hem of the curtain from time to time, but no one seemed to notice.

Present, too, though unbeknownst to anyone else in the room, was Hubda, the last remaining Siberian snow spider. After she'd abandoned her hideout beneath the covered bridge—too much traffic rumbling overhead!—she'd been biding her time inside a box of Fourth of July fireworks stored in the firehouse. But the loud fuss of the volunteer fire alarm ringing—first when Amos's cocoon ignited, and then when the Fingerpies' barn went toasty— had annoyed Hubda. She was in a bad mood. Looking for some peace and quiet, and dreaming sweetly of Pearl, she had made her way into the cool vacant church. She had hidden herself in the shadows of the pulpit, right behind the Good Book itself.

Yes, everyone was present except the two Flameburpers, Amos and Beatrice.

At precisely five P.M., Mayor Grass and his best man, Bucky Clumpett, came out from the sacristy, the room to the left of the altar. Mayor Grass wore a pinstriped tuxedo and was pink and sweating. Father Fogarty and the Reverend Mrs. Mopp followed him and took their places.

Then Jasper Stripe unrolled the white carpet from the back of the church to the front. Meena and Meera Bannerjee, delicious in miniature sky-blue saris, pranced along the newly extended white trail. They sprinkled rose and daisy petals from matching milk pails, then rushed to their parents' pew.

Widow Wendell began "The Wedding March"—not the famous "Here comes the bride, quick, run, and hide" one, but the Mendelssohn that sounds like the music to which a Hollywood star might descend a glamorous staircase.

But it wasn't a Hollywood star, and it wasn't a staircase. It was only Miss Earth, dressed all in white and carrying a spray of orange blossoms.

At first she walked the aisle with her eyes down, but before long she lifted her face, and behind the waterfall of gauzy veil, she smiled blissfully to the right and left. At the front of the aisle, Mayor Timothy Grass beamed with joy. He could hardly keep from rushing forward to take her arm before she had finished arriving. But Bucky Clumpett ground a shoe on Timothy Grass's pants cuff, to keep the groom in his place.

"She's beautiful!" everyone whispered.

Riskily, Rhoda inched herself over the edge of the pocketbook to glance at Miss Earth passing down the aisle. At that moment, Miss Earth's eye swept in her direction. Fawn wondered if Miss Earth saw the cupid. If so, she probably assumed that cupids belonged at weddings, or maybe she didn't believe her own eyes. She neither shrieked nor paled, just kept stepping forward.

Then bride and groom were standing together, hand in hand, and the solemn ceremony began.

Everyone was well-behaved. If a few tears were shed—Mr. Dewey, Grandma Earth, virtually every married woman in the room, and a few unmarried women, too—the tears were silent and the noses were dabbed delicately. No one had to endure the eruption of loud snorting mucousy noises such as might be heard in a hospital ward filled with victims of the swine flu.

When Father Fogarty reached for the Bible to read the Gospel, Hubda the spider did not bite his hand. Well, it wasn't Father Fogarty she wanted. It was Pearl Hotchkiss, though she still couldn't have put a name to her appetites.

When, from the same pulpit, the Reverend Mrs. Mopp delivered an elegant, comic, and touching homily, Hubda again restrained herself. But she was getting agitated. She looked about and spied Miss Earth's bouquet and wondered if she could hide there. Her chance arrived when Miss Earth laid the bouquet down on the pulpit, to free her hands for the vows exchange.

Then came the happy moment. Father Fogarty indicated that Bucky Clumpett should produce the pair of rings.

"Wake up, Old Man," said Flossie Fingerpie to her husband. "The big moment has come!"

"What? Resurrection Day? I'm here, Lord!" cried Old Man Fingerpie with a start.

"So am I," said Miss Earth, cracking everyone up.

"If there is anyone present who knows a reason why this couple should not be joined in marriage," intoned Father Fogarty solemnly, "speak now, or forever hold your peace."

As if shifted by a mild breeze, the door to the sacristy creaked open an inch or two.

Father Fogarty and the Reverend Mrs. Mopp's backs were to the altar, and Mayor Grass and Miss Earth were gazing into each other's eyes. Everyone else in the building was staring at the happy couple. Only the person sitting at the extreme right of the first row was able to see into the sacristy.

That person was Sammy Grubb. He did see. And he could guess immediately what must have happened. Father Fogarty had left the wide sacristy door to the outside open to allow for a flow of air, so Mayor Grass wouldn't pass out with excitement while he waited for his bride. However, through the door, more than a summer wind had ventured in.

In the gloom, piled up on top of each other like three of the four Brementown musicians, were the final three witnesses to the wedding of Miss Earth and Mayor Grass.

Up top, with a look of hysterical glee in her cross-eyed gaze, sat Doozy Dorking, the hen. How had she escaped from the starship *Loiterbug?*

Doozy was perched comfortably on the shoulders of one of her stepchildren, the Flameburper Beatrice.

Who in turn was perched on the shoulders of her own hatchmate, her brother-in-thunder, Amos.

None of them clucked a cluck or hissed a spark to ignite the ceremony. None of them interrupted the wedding. Mayor Grass and Miss Earth got hitched without a hitch, and in another few minutes they were racing down the aisle, while everyone cheered and bawled and sniffled.

All eyes followed them except for Sammy's. He kept watch on the sacristy door, worried that if Father Fogarty turned to go inside and remove his vestments, he might be roasted alive by Amos—the Flameburper—the prodigal son who had come back to the fold.

Amos had changed. In the long months he'd been encased in his cocoon, he'd grown farther—faster—and more different than Beatrice had yet done. Beatrice looked like a crocodile with false Halloween fairy wings, neither pretty nor useful, indeed rather silly.

Amos's development had gone more according to plan. He was, indeed, hardly a Flameburper anymore. His chicken and his blue-toe lizard genes, jazzed up by a lightning strike and baked in a low-heat cocoon for weeks on end, had revised him into a creature never before seen in Vermont. Ever. Not even at the Tunbridge Fair.

If Sammy Grubb could trust his eyes—and he thought he could—Amos had turned into a dragon. An attack dragon or a pet dragon, Sammy couldn't tell, but a dragon just the same.

Sammy, the would-be discoverer of the secret creatures in the hidden folds of the planet, was happier than he'd ever been in his life.

15. AMOS IN ALL HIS GLORY

The congregation flooded out the front doors of the church. Father Fogarty and the Reverend Mrs. Mopp joined the crowd there, as Mr. and Ms. Earth-Grass got ready to duck through clouds of flying birdseed and confetti and bubbles blown from little bottles of soapsuds supplied for the purpose by Aunt Sophia Petros.

Sammy waited till his parents were hemmed in by the congregation departing down the center aisle. Then he slipped away from them. He cornered Thekla and tugged her arm. "What?" she asked, and on seeing his expression, she added to her parents, "You go ahead; I'll be along in a jiffy."

"*What?*" she asked again, when they had escaped the throng. "Are you pursuing me, Sammy Grubb?"

"We have *company,*" singsonged Sammy, putting his finger to his lips.

They reached the front alcove, where Widow Wendell was straightening out her sheet music and sniffling slightly. "Is there a powder room in there?" asked Wilma Wendell. "I'm a fright."

Sammy Grubb knew that lying was wrong—perhaps especially wrong in a church—but he lied anyway. "You look great," he said, "and anyway, the powder room is closed for plumbing repairs."

"Well, I do try my best," said Widow Wendell, "though who notices?"

"I especially admired the chromatic glissando at the end of the trumpet voluntary," opined Thekla, but Sammy pulled her into the sacristy and slammed the door, and bolted it.

It was a risky move. He and Thekla might have been roasted alive as crisply as Father Fogarty or the Reverend Mrs. Mopp might have been. But he took the chance that in some dim recess of their reptilian brains, Amos and Beatrice would recognize their defenders, and hold their fiery breath. Luckily for him, it was a chance that paid off.

For there was a family grouping you didn't often get to see, on the steps of a church or anywhere else, for that matter.

Amos turned to regard them. When he elevated his tapering noggin on the end of his neck, he was nine, ten feet tall. His scaly skin, turquoise as the water around a South Pacific atoll, shimmered with flickers of silver and copper and hot-toaster-coil red. Mighty wings were folded against his sides, with a bulk as of storefront awnings rolled up too hastily. They seemed to be leathern, though several rows of midnight-blue feathers were ranked along the edges. His forelegs ended in surprisingly delicate appendages, partly hand, partly claw, which looked as if sheathed in melon-colored gloves.

His eye was keen, and as mysterious as the eye in a peacock's feather: not kindly, exactly, but not beastly or brutal, as the younger Amos had threatened to become.

Reaching only to his knees, Beatrice the Flameburper looked like a cartoon character. She was adoring and fluttery, and kept trying to use her own slender wings to launch herself up to Amos's cheek and kiss her brother. He did not swipe her away, but neither did he lower his elegant head to meet her halfway.

"Amos!" said Sammy Grubb. "Wait till Thud catches sight of you!"

"Oh, Sammy," said Thekla, "if *anyone* catches sight of Amos! What then?"

"Why are you here?" Sammy asked Amos, as if, in his magnificent evolution, he might have developed the power of human speech.

But if he had done so, Amos didn't reveal it; he kept his own counsel.

"Shoot," said Thekla, glancing out the window. "Here come Forest Eugene's mom and Father Fogarty!"

Sammy's head whipped around. How could he shoo a dragon, a dragonlet, and a comically slow-witted stepchicken out of a holy space where, perhaps, they had taken sanctuary?

He couldn't.

But he had lied before, and he could lie again.

"Don't budge and don't open the door till I say so," he hissed at Thekla. He slipped out and waited to confront Father Fogarty and the Reverend Mrs. Mopp.

"Sammy," said Father Fogarty, approaching, "what are you doing here? I thought you'd be at the reception like everyone else."

"Thekla wasn't feeling well, and I got her to the powder room," said Sammy.

"Oh, poor thing. I'll go see to her," said Forest Eugene's mom.

"She asked if she could be left alone," said Sammy.

"Oh?" Father Fogarty raised an eyebrow. The Reverend Mrs. Mopp looked even more concerned.

"She got sick on her dress," said Sammy. "All over it, and she had to take it off to wash it. She's using the sink in the sacristy."

"Oh, dear," said Father Fogarty. "Well, I can remove my robes here and put them away later, I guess."

"I'll help her, then, and see you at the reception, Father Fogarty," said Mrs. Mopp.

"No," said Sammy, "it's worse than that. Don't go in there. It really stinks. Stinks to high heaven."

"Nonsense, Sammy," said the Reverend Mrs. Mopp. She rapped at the door. "Thekla? May I come in and help?"

"No need," said Thekla in a bright tone. "It wasn't sick so much as excitement. Quite under control now, but I'd rather you let me take care of it myself. Please take Father Fogarty to the reception, and I'll see you there soon."

"Are you quite sure? Nothing embarrasses me—I'm a mother," said Rebecca Mopp.

"I'd prefer it. You'd be doing me a kindness."

Ministers are professionally trained to do kindnesses, so the Reverend Mrs. Mopp and Father Fogarty acquiesced and left. Thekla did sound quite herself, after all: on top of things, articulate, even bossy. "You've become a good friend to her, Sammy," said Father Fogarty as they departed. "Don't think I don't notice."

Have I, wondered Sammy. After all this time? Or am I just pretending, to throw Father Fogarty off the trail?

Then the church was empty at last, and Sammy went back into the sacristy. If Amos had intended to smite them with a blow, he would have done so already. Perhaps he'd just wanted to see Miss Earth become Ms. Earth-Grass. After all, he'd provided her cocoon housing a few weeks ago. Possibly he'd grown fond of her. Stranger things had happened. (Especially here in Hamlet.)

Or maybe, having wakened to find his snack missing, he intended to eat her now? What a horrible way for Miss Earth to end her wedding day: as a human munchie for a puckish mutant blue-toe lizard–chicken dragon! A real bummer.

Sammy knew what he and Thekla had to do. At all costs, Amos and Beatrice had to be kept hidden. But how do you hide a dragon twice the size of a stallion, especially one of whose temperament you aren't sure?

16. MR. AND MS. EARTH-GRASS

The Flora Tyburn Memorial Gym was about a mile away from the church. On the road to Crank's Corners, past the Josiah Fawcett Elementary School, it stood just beyond the Grand Union. It was an older, wood-framed building, with bracketed eaves and large, many-paned windows on three sides. The afternoon having turned so pleasant, a number of folks had previously parked their cars there or in the Grand Union lot and walked to the church for the ceremony. Now they strolled back.

Hector Yellow had done himself proud. With a budget of under forty dollars and a little ingenuity, he had turned the down-at-the-heels auditorium/gymnasium into a pavilion of love.

White swags of crepe paper looped across doorways and window lintels. Tables were decorated with little tea-light candles, twenty per table, which sat in double ranks of ten between the divides of some old-fashioned ice-cube trays he'd found in the basement.

Everywhere, buckets of wildflowers. A jungle of early-summer blooms.

A jug band from White River Junction played in a sprightly fashion as Germaine and Timothy Earth-Grass took their places by the seven-layer wedding cake. There they would meet and greet their guests, namely everyone in the town of Hamlet, Vermont, as well as those outsiders from places like Forbush Corners, Thetford Hill, Puster Center, and the planet of Fixipuddle.

Adults yielded when the former Miss Earth's former students crowded to the front of the line. One by one and two by three, they crowded forward to make feeble jokes, blush, and stammer formal phrases. One by one they leaned forward to sniff the wedding bouquet. Nearly everyone was there, except of course Sammy Grubb and Thekla Mustard, whose absence, in all the excitement, was hardly noticed.

It was lucky that Pearl Hotchkiss didn't come forward yet, either. Pearl had volunteered for cloakroom duty and was stuck for the time being behind a card table. She collected ladies' jackets and gentlemen's sports coats and gave them numbered slips of paper in exchange.

Had Pearl gotten in line and then leaned down to get a whiff of the wedding blossoms, she'd have met Hubda face-to-face. For deep inside the bridal bouquet, slightly overcome by the scent of blossoms but attentive nonetheless, squatted Hubda the Siberian snow spider, waiting patiently for the pheromones of Pearl Hotchkiss to broadcast themselves. Then: The plan of action included a scurrying foray, an attack, and a kiss that, whether Hubda knew it or not, would culminate in a deadly bite of love. And Hubda was in no mood to be shy.

In the meantime, however, there were lots of other interesting and confusing wedding odors for Hubda to analyze and consider.

For one thing, Mr. Bannerjee's invention, Connubial Curry,

was simmering merrily on burners in the industrial kitchen off to one side.

Then there were the various eaux de cologne and after-shave lotions worn by guests. The women stuck to things like Lilac Mist, Lemon Verbena, Attar of Roses, and Persuasion. The men, if they used anything, preferred Hunk Must, Saddlesoap, Essence of Cigar, and Resistance. Some of the perfumes were strong, but then barnyard smells were strong, too, and needed heavy-duty cloaking.

"Oh, you dear, dear thing!" cried the flowery women to Germaine Earth-Grass.

"Congratulations, you're a lucky man," growled the smoky men to Tim Earth-Grass.

Hubda stirred her spinnerets when a certain very peculiar odor approached, a sort of vanilla vinegar.

"I'd like to extend my joy. My liver swells with feeling," said the wedding guest in the canary-yellow twin suit with pearls.

"You must be friends of Tim's," said Germaine. "I don't believe we've met."

"Senator Pimplemuss," said Pimplemuss, doing the best impression of a wedding guest she could manage after extremely rushed advice by Thud, Lois, and Salim.

"And this is—?" The bride turned to Narr.

Pimplemuss's WordSearch dial, whirring underneath her crisp shirtwaist, couldn't locate a word to indicate "husband of a senator." She did the best she could. "This is Señor Narr, my consort."

"A visitor to our fair country," the bride deduced.

"And then some," agreed Pimplemuss. "These are my little . . . sonatinas . . . Droyd and Peppa."

127

Had Ms. Earth-Grass been a bit less excited by her wedding, those names might have rung a bell or two. But she was distracted by so many people, so much to remember! "How lovely you could travel with your family," she said, and turned to Foomie. "And, if you please . . . ?"

"And this," said Pimplemuss, "this is my Foomie."

"Charmed," said Foomie, who was dizzy with high feeling. "May I say, my dear lady, I have rarely experienced such intergalactic tides of goodwill as I perceive are sweeping around you today! It makes the punishing journey very much worth the trouble indeed. The very stars tremble in pleasure! The Milky Way overflows its banks! The moon decides to wane no more!"

"Foomie's emotions tend to run away with Foomie," said Pimplemuss. "Foomie, silence, or I'll clock you."

"Look, Tim," said Germaine brightly, turning to her husband. "Your friends Senator Pimplemuss and her family."

"I'm not her family, I'm her Foomie," said Foomie.

Before Timothy Earth-Grass could mention that he had no recollection of ever meeting the senator or her lovely family, up swept Meg Snoople and Chad Hunkley.

"A surprise to see you both," said Germaine, "but thank you so much for coming to wish us well."

"Something's going on here," said Meg Snoople, "and don't think you can distract me by putting on such an arrant display of wedding bliss!"

"Why don't you have a glass of punch?" said Germaine. "It'll clear your head. Or some curry, which will clear your sinuses? Don't forget to stick around for the cake, too."

"Is that a television camera you have?" asked Tim good-naturedly.

"Everyone takes videos at weddings!" said Chad Hunkley. "Got to record the first dance for posterity, you know."

"Hmmm," said Tim, and gave Bucky Clumpett a look, as if to say, *Watch these two for me, Bucky.*

Next in the receiving line, Wolfgang Einfinger had fallen in step with Professor Williams.

"I am convinced there are mutant chickens nearby," said Einfinger.

"I am convinced there could be a Siberian snow spider nearby," exclaimed Professor Williams. "We must all be wary, but hope. Hubda loves a good party. Perhaps she'll come forward to bestow a blessing of sorts on your union. Congratulations, by the way, you two married people. Stay on your guard."

From behind her dark glasses, the next woman in line said, "I should love to see a Siberian snow spider! How exotic."

"Another friend of Tim's?" Germaine asked her.

"Ms. Denim," said the woman. She didn't remove her glasses. "I just happen to be staying at the Lovey Inn, and my hostess, Widow Wendell, insisted I was invited. *Very* best of wishes."

"Thank you," said Germaine, and Tim added, "And welcome to Hamlet, a fine place to raise children or cows."

Mr. Dewey, next in line, leaned forward and said, "May I get you some punch, Ms. Denim?"

"Call me Suzy," said Ms. Denim. "And yes, you may."

"Her voice rings a bell," said Corpsina, following in the queue. She scowled at Ms. Suzy Denim while Vampyra kissed Germaine Earth-Grass on both cheeks and then Tim, too. "Thanks for letting us tag along."

"Sinister Sisters, you were such help at signaling the fire in Foggy Hollow," said the mayor. "Are your names really Corpsina and Vampyra, by the way?"

"No," said Corpsina. "Actually, my name is Dotty—"

"—and mine is Adele," said Vampyra. "We're Adele and Dotty Coody, from Brooklyn Heights originally. But 'the Coody Sisters' Circus' sounded unsanitary if not downright unsavory."

"But why Sinister Sisters?" said Tim. "Everyone's been wondering. You're not very sinister."

"There are two meanings of sinister," said Corpsina. "One means treacherously dreadful."

"The other," added Vampyra, "means left, as in left-handed."

"Are you left-handed sisters?" asked Germaine.

"No," said Corpsina, "but we are left, all right. Bigtime."

"As in left behind, left high and dry," said Vampyra. "Our dear departed sister left us."

"Frankenstella?"

"Yes. Originally known as plain old Stella. Stella Coody."

"Seems like a funny reason to name a circus. But what devotion you show to your dear departed sister."

"Devotion?" cawed Corpsina. "Frankenstella was the talented one. She left us for greener pastures! Our circus is named Sinister to shame her!"

"Hush, you don't mean that," said Vampyra. "Or not entirely."

But before she could explain further, Ernie Latucci, disc jockey from WAAK, the Voice of Vermont, took the microphone. "Let's get this party rolling! Here to rev our motors, the one, the only Petunia Whiner!"

Petunia Whiner—that is, the social register's Mrs. Mycroft (Mildred Fotheringill) Tweed transformed into a country-western hell-raiser by a ten-gallon, rhinestone-emblazoned white Stetson—came in the side door. She was gunning the engines of the famous Kawasaki 8000 Silver Eagle that Miss Earth had ridden to school every day of her career. She parked the motorcycle at the microphone and hopped off it. Then, in her trademark country-western drawl, she brassed, "For the little lovebirds! Let's put our hands together and make those doozies dance!" She launched into one of her early hits, "Abandoned at the Altar, Do Your Spirits Start to Falter?"

Petunia Whiner was Germaine Earth-Grass's favorite singer. Germaine grabbed Tim, and they rushed onto the dance floor. No one minded that the newlyweds' *pas de deux* was more energetic than suave, though Sharday Wren and her dancing teacher, Hank McManus, did exchange raised eyebrows.

However, the ice was broken. That was what counted. Everyone began to boogie to the hearty foursquare melody. Jasper Stripe went cha-chaing about with Nurse Pinky Crisp. Bucky and Limpy Clumpett sailed by in a foxtrot. Old Man Fingerpie and Flossie Fingerpie attempted a modified Charleston while sitting on folding chairs along the wall. Mrs. Cobble and Mrs. Brill waltzed together in lopsided time. Some of the older parents did the twist. Some of the younger parents did some moonwalking and break dancing.

None of the kids danced except for Sharday, because it was all too embarrassing.

Ernie Latucci noticed. "Well, later on we'll do a conga line," he lectured them humorously. "I'll get everyone here dancing whether they want to or not!"

Just outside the kitchen window, Baby Tusker's talented nose was in ecstasy over the aroma of dinner. "It brings back memories of India, doesn't it?" said Salim. "Baby Tusker, if you stayed with me, you could live in the woods behind the Mango Tree and smell this every day except Monday, when we're closed for business. And I would always be there, Baby Tusker. I would never leave you."

Luckily, the steam of boiling rice was issuing through the screens of the kitchen windows, and whenever Mr. Bannerjee glanced through, he didn't recognize Baby Tusker. He just saw his son, presumably standing alone outside. Salim was having a difficult time with this graduation. All things must pass, but change came harder to some than to others. Mr. Bannerjee, an immigrant, knew this well.

"Salim," called his father, with a cheeriness he didn't exactly feel. "Come inside at once! Time to serve Bannerjee's Connubial Curry!"

"Back away into the forsythia," murmured Salim, and Baby Tusker did. He passed right through the fronds and hoops of the unkempt bushes, imitating a bit of early-evening summer fog.

17. "HITCHED IN HAMLET"

The dinner? A success: steaming heaps of curried vegetables in a coconut-milk-based cream sauce, topped with aromatic almonds and sprigs of late-unfurling fiddlehead ferns culled from Foggy Hollow. Everything was ladled on a bed of basmati rice and decorated with rounds of orange and lemon.

"Best wedding meal I ever had, even including my own, which was Nedick's hot dogs from a Coney Island grease pit," said Old Man Fingerpie. He licked his lips and went for seconds.

"I'll add Connubial Curry to the regular menu at the Mango Tree," promised Mr. Bannerjee to his many admirers. "Also, don't forget we give volume discounts on Tuesday nights."

Sammy Grubb and Thekla Mustard didn't arrive in the hall until the meal was over and the dancing had begun in earnest. Sammy had wanted to lead Amos, Beatrice, and Doozy Dorking away from the church and back up to Smugglers' Lookout, but the chickenish stepfamily wouldn't budge. Perhaps superior olfactory senses helped them sniff out the wedding curry in the atmosphere of Hamlet? It was hard to know. In the end, there was nothing to do but lead them to the gym and hide them in the tennis courts. A helpfully screening bank of cedar trees grew between the gym and the courts, and the courts were closed by now anyway. So the chances of detection were slim.

"Wait here," Sammy had said to the Flameburpers and their stepmother.

"That's an order," seconded Thekla, whose tone of voice communicated her meaning even if English was not a language that the Flameburpers and Doozy Dorking spoke. The creatures appeared to understand, at least at first, and they settled down on the tennis court while Sammy and Thekla made their way into the reception.

Oooh, thought Pearl, seeing them come in together. Thekla with Sammy? Her eyes pricked with sudden tears. She had always had a secret crush on Sammy. She blinked her tears away.

"This place is a zoo," Sammy said to Thekla. "The noise! How do we gather everyone together?"

"We have no time to fool around," said Thekla Mustard. "Leave it to me."

She walked right up to Ernie Latucci and muttered something in his ear. Ernie Latucci shrugged and lowered the volume on Petunia Whiner, who was just launching into to her signature number, "Stick with Your Man!" Petunia Whiner turned and pouted. She wasn't used to having the juice run out while she was in high diva mode.

"Sorry," said Thekla Mustard. "Sorry, Mrs. Tweed."

"Mrs. Tweed? Who in tarnation might *that* sorry critter be?" said Petunia Whiner/Mildred Tweed, to high hilarity.

"Dear Miss Earth," said Thekla Mustard, addressing her former teacher. "Dear Mayor Grass. I mean, dear Mr. and Ms. Earth-Grass." She cleared her throat. Not for nothing had Thekla Mustard governed the Tattletales so wisely and so well for so many years. She knew instinctively how to steer a near catastrophe toward a peaceful landing. "We, your former students and now your friends, know how much you have loved the works of that significant author of superior fictions, Stephanie Queen."

Everyone calmed down to listen. Mr. Dewey sat up straight. He and Miss Earth had always shared a special affection for Stephanie Queen. He glanced sideways at Suzy Denim to see if she showed signs of being a fan, too. He hoped she did. It might prove something of a consolation.

"All year long," said Thekla Mustard, "we have watched you lug about those five-pound novels. *Nabbed in Nairobi. Overcome in Ottawa. Perjured in Parsippany.* Since Stephanie Queen is your favorite writer, and her heroine, Spangles O'Leary, is your favorite heroine, we thought you might enjoy an impromptu wedding present."

Everyone listened, ready to be amazed.

"The former students of the former Miss Earth will soon present a skit called"—here Thekla Mustard paused to think— "'Hitched in Hamlet'!"

Everyone laughed and clapped. When the room fell silent, Thekla said, "Oh. By the way, Copycats and Tattletales and their ilk: We're having an emergency meeting to write and produce such a play. We convene immediately just outside the bike shed. No shirkers. This is an order."

Sammy Grubb thought: You got to hand it to her. She's *good.*

Five minutes later, the Copycats, the Tattletales, Thud Tweed, and Pearl Hotchkiss were gathered by the bicycle shed.

Everyone began to talk at once.

"Guess who's back!" began Salim Bannerjee.

"I can't guess," said Pearl Hotchkiss. "Not Hubda, I hope!"

"I already know," said Fawn Petros, beginning to open her knapsack to reveal Rhoda the cupid at last. "Cross my heart and hope to die."

"Never mind all that!" said Lois Kennedy the Third. "Do you remember the Fixipuddlings?"

"Everyone shut up!" said Thekla Mustard and Sammy Grubb at the same moment.

Thekla and Sammy so rarely saw eye to eye that for them to strike the same note, in the same tone of voice, shocked their friends. An awkward silence followed. Fawn Petros voiced the thought in so many minds. "Has the recent wedding made you two become . . . *romantic?*"

Sammy and Thekla glanced at each other. That three whole seconds passed without either of them vomiting seemed conclusive proof.

"Don't interrupt," said Thekla, blushing. "Sammy, tell them!"

What, wondered Pearl, dreading it. Tell us *what?*

"It's old home week, bigtime," continued Sammy. "Friends, my lifelong hope of finding the Missing Link has been fulfilled. Beatrice has been recovered, and she isn't alone."

Pearl felt a lift in her heart, faint but real.

"Amos?" said Thud. "My little Amos?"

"Your Amos," said Sammy. "But not so little."

There was a rustle of movement in the ground cover beyond the bike shed.

"He's out there. But nobody scream or make any sudden moves," said Sammy. "We haven't been able to keep him away."

"That's just ducky," interrupted Lois. "Because guess what. The Fixipuddlings, who have also dropped by for a visit, came to Fingerpie Farm and liberated Beatrice and the one hundred forty pullets. The pullets are all safe in the engine room of the starship

Loiterbug. At least they were when we last saw them, and since they're not here now, we'll have to assume they're still there."

It was Thekla's turn to interrupt her rival, Lois. "Amos may have located the *Loiterbug* while looking for his sister, Beatrice. Maybe he melted the door open. Anyway, he and Beatrice are *here*—with their stepmother, Doozy Dorking."

Lois interrupted Thekla's interruption. "Doozy has seen Pimplemuss in her original form—you remember what that is like. Nine feet tall, a head with eyes like buttons up its neck, and three baggy legs. A kind of—dare I say it?—a kind of chicken goddess such as the ancient Egyptians might have imagined. Our no-nonsense Doozy has had a mystical experience. She's followed Pimplemuss here, I bet. So Amos and Beatrice, good stepchildren, probably escorted their stepmother in her devotional pilgrimage. Or maybe they just all wanted to come to the wedding."

"*Here?*" said several voices. "Followed Pimplemuss *here?*"

"The senator and her entourage," explained Lois. "Didn't you guess?"

The silence was stunning.

Thud Tweed said, "Look, I know you guys are all slightly nutso. In the nicest kind of way, I mean. But let's face facts. We have a major television personality with a TV camera in the Memorial Gym, and an alien posing as a United States senator, which must be some sort of felony, *and* standing in the wings, just for fun, you tell me, is a giant mutant blue-toe lizard–chicken? Hasn't anyone ever heard the phrase *enough already?*"

"Also Baby Tusker," said Salim, "not to change the subject."

"Also Rhoda the cupid," said Fawn in a small voice.

"Hi, everyone," said Rhoda, waving her single arrow.

"That thing is a lethal weapon," said Pearl, "and it should be confiscated."

Rhoda retorted, "All this wedding stuff, it's putting me in the mood." But she replaced the arrow in her quiver anyway.

"First things first," said Sammy Grubb decisively. "The most important thing to do is get Pimplemuss out of there. Doozy will follow her idol, and then Amos and Beatrice will follow *her*. It'll be a parade of freaks, but it's gotta happen. This place is a powder keg. It's all going to blow sky-high, and on the national news, no less."

"If Einfinger catches sight of Beatrice or Amos, he'll figure out what happened to his little lost eggs," agreed Lois Kennedy the Third.

"But what about your proposed skit—'Hitched in Hamlet'?" asked Thud.

"I just needed to get your attention fast," said Thekla, and grimaced. "But if it comes to that, we'll have to improvise. Time to mobilize, gang. Let's go hustle or muscle that senator from the grand old state of Fixipuddle off the dance floor before the place goes up in fireworks."

But that, alas, was easier said than done.

When the children returned to the gym, Petunia Whiner was just finishing up, "Stick with Your Man!" Senator Pimplemuss and Narr were cutting a fine figure on the dance floor, though Pimplemuss, throwing herself into the proceedings, was hollering "Stick with your Foomie!" This phrase made sense only to the children and the Fixipuddlings.

"Now," cut in Ernie Latucci, "that great gang of kids is back to provide us some surprise entertainment: 'Hitched in Hamlet'!"

Thekla tried to wave him down. Sammy shook his head fiercely. But the crowd went wild, and Germaine and Tim pulled up folding chairs in front of the stage and sat down like a royal couple at a command performance.

The kids crowded offstage. Fawn felt Rhoda twitch inside her backpack. Probably Rhoda wanted to see too. What could it hurt, as long as Fawn stayed in the shadowy wings? She opened the clasps so Rhoda could peer out.

"Oh, well," murmured Thekla, "here goes nothing. Let's do this fast. Salim, you're the public speaker among us. Get us started."

"Ladies and gentlemen," said Salim, "and also visiting aliens from other planets . . ."

Everyone laughed generously.

"A short skit in which Spangles O'Leary, the copper-haired heroine of the Stephanie Queen novels, visits our fair town on the very day that the most beloved teacher in the school—"

"I resent that!" catcalled Ms. Frazzle, the kindergarten teacher.

"—marries the most prominent and important selectman."

"I resent *that!*" catcalled Clem Fawcett, one of the other selectmen.

Thud had been muttering with his mom. She agreed to step back behind a pillar and take off her Petunia Whiner big-hair wig. As Salim was finishing, Thud mounted the wig on Lois Kennedy the Third. "You look like a Muppet with a migraine," he said.

"I love you too, Thud," said Lois dryly. "Let's just get this show on the road, shall we?"

Thekla reached out her arms and said to her former teacher, "May I—please? Just for a moment?" Germaine handed Thekla the bouquet of orange blossoms, unaware that Hubda was crouching inside, still waiting for her moment.

Thekla went and stood by Sammy Grubb.

"And a one and a two!" shouted Salim, pointing to Grandma Earth, who on a portable electronic keyboard had been providing backup to Petunia Whiner. Grandma Earth, almost doubled over in stitches, managed to thump out the opening chords for "Here Comes the Bride."

Forest Eugene Mopp, playing his mother, came forward. "If there be anyone present who thinks these two shouldn't get hitched, squeak now or forever hold your pee!" he said. Everyone guffawed.

Lois, as Spangles O'Leary, lurched forward, an arm dramatically over her forehead as if shielding herself from the glare of spotlights. "Halt! I am Spangles O'Leary, sometime Hollywood starlet and sometime CIA operative committed to liberty and justice and the comedy network for all!"

"Why?" asked Tim/Sammy. "Does it have to do with my betrothed?"

"Yes!" shouted Spangles O'Leary/Lois.

"Is there another who clamors for her heart?" asked Tim/Sammy.

"Yes!" shouted Spangles O'Leary/Lois.

"Who knew?" said Germaine/Thekla, shrugging.

"Who could it be?" shouted Tim/Sammy.

Spangles O'Leary/Lois adjusted her wig and swept her arm toward the room. "Everyone!" she shouted.

"In that case," said Tim/Sammy, "there's only one thing to do."

He grabbed Germaine/Thekla's shoulders and threw an arm around her. Everyone gasped. Was he going to kiss Thekla? Not just *in public*, but *at all?* Quickly, Rhoda fished for her single arrow and fitted it to her bow. She couldn't resist it. If they liplocked, she might be able to pin them with a single missile of love, and confirm their devotion for all time.

Sammy and Thekla never learned how near to romantic danger they had ventured. Luckily, Germaine/Thekla pulled away with a look of horror and shouted, "When in doubt—do the conga!"

Everyone roared with laughter. Grandma Earth picked up the cue and began a saucy bossa nova rhythm that was somewhat at odds with the curried atmosphere, but this was a party and everyone was rocking. The Widow Wendell started the conga line, and the children joined in. Meanwhile, the real newlyweds took a breather on the screened porch off to one side. They had eyes only for each other, so they missed what happened next.

"I love this conga!" bellowed Senator Pimplemuss, grabbing hold of Pearl's shoulder. "Is it some ancient wedding ritual?"

Nurse Pinky Crisp added a snap to the drum line. Mr. Bannerjee began to hand out saucepan lids and wooden spoons for makeshift percussion instruments.

Soon the line snaked across the floor. "When you pass the kitchen doorway," whispered Thud to Pearl, "I'll grab Pimplemuss and whisk her out through the pantry."

But the music, the lights, the candles, the hilarity, the bonhomie—it was all too much. The screened front door burst open and in came Doozy Dorking, squawking in praise, dodging through the conga line, sensing—but not being quite able to find, due to the clever disguise as a senator—her new idol, Pimplemuss.

Behind Doozy Dorking lurched Beatrice the Flameburper. Naturally gifted as a dancer, she joined the conga line. Could Amos be far behind?

Meg Snoople hooted for the cameraman, and the locals, most of them in on the Flameburper cover-up, began to shriek.

18. THE DEADLY BRIDAL BOUQUET

"**I**t's a mutant chicken!" shouted Wolfgang Einfinger. "I *knew* it! Document it, Snoople!"

"A Flameburper!" murmured others in disbelief.

Meg Snoople smoothed down her hair and flecked a bit of clove from her teeth. "Chad! Quick, outside; we go live in five. But let's shoot some archival footage first." Before the wedding guests could take in what was happening, the camera's hot lights blazed on, blindingly. People blinked and the conga line knotted into a traffic tie-up. While Meg Snoople nipped toward the door, the cameraman focused his lens for a close-up of Beatrice the Flameburper.

Beatrice looked alarmed at first. The glare hurt her eyes. She had eyelids to blink, so she blinked, and she squinted.

This made her look unnaturally mean and conniving—not a great way to make a first appearance on national television. But what could she do? She could run for the door, that's what she could do. And that's what she did.

But the damage was done. Proof of her existence was captured on digital video. And the bright lights in the side lot—by the bike shed, not far from the tennis courts where Amos was pacing in the dark—indicated that Chad Hunkley was beginning the broadcast, cutting into prime-time shows all over America with a special evening edition of *Breakfast in America*.

Still, in the Flora Tyburn Memorial Gym, the good people of Hamlet could hardly believe what was happening. "Come on, Pimplemuss!" shouted Lois Kennedy the Third, dragging the alien by the hand. "We have to get out of here so Doozy Dorking will follow!"

"What's going on?" asked Old Man Fingerpie. "Is there a national emergency that requires action in the Senate?"

"But the conga!" said Pimplemuss. "I adore the conga! Besides, I've just learned that the bride flings her bouquet, and whoever catches it is the next to be married! I want my chance!"

Lois didn't stop to argue. She just dragged Pimplemuss away. The other Fixipuddlings, looking longingly back at the wedding cake, followed. Doozy Dorking chased after them, clucking madly, and Beatrice scampered along too, bringing up the rear.

"I thought the senator *was* married, to Señor Narr," murmured Mrs. Cobble.

"I think all this is somewhat screwy, Mr. Dewey," said Suzy Denim. She took a little notebook out of her pocketbook and made a few notes.

"You appear to be very observant," said Mr. Dewey, "and so am I. We have that in common, Ms. Denim. Ms. Suzy Denim. Ms. *Sue Denim*."

Ms. Denim flinched. "What *are* you talking about? Hey, look over there!"

Clem Fawcett, Bucky Clumpett, and Jasper Stripe closed in on Meg Snoople. They didn't do her harm, nor did they threaten her. In a flanking formation, they began to hustle her out of the Flora Tyburn Memorial Gym. "This is a wedding, not a circus, ma'am," said Bucky Clumpett by way of explanation.

"Wait!" shouted Meg Snoople. Everyone paused.

"Something is going on here!" she shouted. "And you're all involved in a cover-up! I demand to know what it is! I demand to know where that funny winged lizardy creature came from—and where it went! *America* wants to know!"

"We believe in liberty and justice for all, but not in taking liberties," growled Clem Fawcett. For a moment it looked as if things were going to get a little ugly.

"Please," said Grandma Earth, coming forward. "Not here, fellows. This is Germaine's big day!"

"I'll explain," said a voice. Everyone turned.

It was Vampyra. She and Corpsina had been whispering hotly. Corpsina nodded vigorously even before her sister began to explain.

"That little lizard thing is a character in our circus performance," said Vampyra. "Are we guilty of bad taste? Guilty as charged—but nothing, nothing more treacherous than that, Meg Snoople. We arranged to let the creature loose here as a publicity stunt, to help us promote our next show."

"You're lying. You can't fool me. You already had a show in Hamlet," said Meg Snoople. "You never do two shows in the same town!"

"It's a free country, ain't it?" Corpsina reminded her. "We got the right to change our minds if we want. And we feel like having another show. Tomorrow night. You're all invited!"

"I don't believe it!" snapped Meg Snoople. "It's a cover-up!"

"You're delusional," said Mr. Bannerjee. "It's not your fault. It's the curry. It'll do that sometimes."

"And now, if you don't mind," said Clem Fawcett. Meg Snoople and her cameraman were ushered firmly out of the building. There they discovered that the senator, her family and entourage, the chicken who seemed to have lost her mind over her congressional representative, and the strange apparition known as Beatrice had all disappeared in the nighttime.

"Doesn't matter, Chad," said Meg Snoople, straightening her clothes. "By tomorrow morning every TV viewer in America will have seen footage of that creature—what was it called?—a Flameburper. Its fifteen minutes of fame are just about to begin, *big*time."

Back in the Flora Tyburn Memorial Gym, folks were trying to recover a sense of celebration. Before long, it began to seem rather funny. But Corpsina and Vampyra, the Sinister Sisters, had never seen Beatrice the Flameburper before. Nor had they a reason to be collaborators in a local cover-up. What had they meant, she was part of their circus?

Lois Kennedy the Third had to know. So she went up and asked them.

"That selectman fellow said that this was a wedding, not a circus," said Corpsina. "I agreed. I don't know who or what that funny winged creature was, but I never like it when people gang up and do the bully routine. It gets my dander up."

"Well, *are* you going to have another show tomorrow night?" asked Lois.

"We hadn't planned to," said Vampyra. "But what with the wedding festivities and all, we've haven't finished taking down our tent. We're not due in Stowe for four days yet. So we'll see. Perhaps we can be of use.

"Besides," she continued, "this is a town where everything seems to come out of the woodwork. So just maybe we'll have a little surprise ourselves to offer. I'm getting a hunch. I'm like that. Psychic."

"You better get your funny friends to go along, though," said Corpsina, "now that we've put our clown butts on the line."

Ernie Latucci had recovered the microphone. "Well, that's a story straight out of Stephanie Queen," he said, "but our own wedding couple is still the main attraction, folks. Now the new bride will toss her bouquet for all the eligible bridelettes-to-be. Ladies and girls, maidens and maids, come forward for the traditional toss of the bridal bouquet."

"Oh, no," said Germaine Earth-Grass, approaching from the porch. She shook her head. She hadn't planned to indulge in this silly custom. But everyone was clapping, so reluctantly she went against her better judgment. She collected her bouquet of orange blossoms from Thekla Mustard and went to one end of the hall.

"I never knew how tempting a wedding could be!" said Rhoda, leaning out of Fawn's oversized pocketbook. "So many opportunities!" She poked Fawn in the hip. "Look. I could zing your town librarian, Mr. Dewey, and that woman he's chatting too. They're so close, they're almost touching."

"If Mr. Dewey is about to fall in love with Ms. Denim, or whatever her name is," said Fawn, "let it happen naturally." She put the heel of her palm on Rhoda's head and pushed her down into the purse. "Give it a rest, Rhoda. I'm busy right now."

All the girls in Fawn's class rushed forward to make up a throng of maybe-married-next-ers. Lois, Thekla, Pearl, Nina, Carly, Anna Maria, Sharday. Fawn joined them. Meena and Meera Bannerjee darted up front. Around the edges, the older unmarried females gathered. Paula Garfunkel, Kanesha Wren, Widow Wendell, Nurse Pinky Crisp, Ms. Frazzle, Principal Buttle. Even the out-of-towners, the Sinister Sisters, and Aunt Rhoda Petros loitered nearby.

The bride took her place with her back to the crowd and made several practice swings.

"Countdown to Loveland! On the count of ten! Ten! Nine! Eight!" shouted Ernie Latucci.

"Seven!" shouted the crowd. "Six! Five! Four! Three! Two! One!"

They all began to cheer as Germaine Earth-Grass flung her beautiful bouquet up in the air.

It turned over and over. It seemed to hang at the topmost point of its arc, higher than the basketball hoops that were all pulled up flat against their backboards to make room for balloons and streamers.

With every eye in the room upon it, the bouquet gave up its secret stowaway. A huge clot of spider—it was spider, it was nothing but spider, it had to be Hubda, a spider that large!—began to tumble through the air.

Everyone screamed. The bride thought the noise was because of the excitement of her bouquet launch. She was already turning to sit down on the chair and hoist her skirts above her pretty ankle so Tim could take the garter off her leg.

Quick as a bee stings, Rhoda whipped her single arrow out of her quiver, aimed, and fired. She missed the falling Siberian snow spider. The arrow made an arc across the room. It split the plastic model of a happy married couple on top of wedding cake. The separate partners each fell backward with a flop into the icing as if trying to make solitary snow angels.

Widow Wendell had been married once before, and she ought to have been able to control herself. But she couldn't. Even at the risk of being bitten by a poisonous spider, she had been compelled to lunge for the flowers. Taller than the schoolgirls, Widow Wendell reached the bouquet first. Later, folks were charitable and said she was trying to get the bouquet to use it as a bat and drive the spider away from Pearl Hotchkiss, toward whom Hubda was falling, falling, even appeared to be swimming . . .

At any rate, that's what Widow Wendell achieved. Maybe because the spider was trailing threads, her descent was slowed like a parachutist's, and the flowers landed first. Widow Wendell caught them and swung at Hubda. The spider was caught full in the face by a cushion of orange blossoms and went ricocheting back toward where she had come from.

Germaine Earth-Grass, who had turned to look for Tim, didn't see the spider missile.

The spider landed on her ankle and took a healthy bite.

"My darling!" cried Timothy Earth-Grass.

"My daughter!" cried Grandma Earth.

"You and your ilk again? Oh, shoo," said Ms. Earth-Grass calmly, looking down at her ankle. A small dot of blood, red as a Valentine's rose, bloomed against her alabaster skin. But she wasn't fussed. The excitement and pleasure of the day had put a mighty calm upon her. Or maybe she was finding it restful to be a married woman.

Before anyone could smack her a second time, Hubda darted across the dance floor and into a mousehole in the baseboards.

Dr. Heidi Sternbaum and Nurse Pinky Crisp came crashing through the crowds to Germaine's side. There they were met by Professor Harold Williams from Harvard University.

"That was Hubda! I'd know her anywhere! Is she all right?" he asked.

"Who, the spider, or me?" said Germaine.

"Last time you were bitten, your ears turned green and

swelled up, do you remember?" said Dr. Sternbaum. "Fortunately I never come out without my stethoscope." From her beaded purse she yanked this helpful instrument and fixed it to her head.

"Speak to me!" cried Tim.

"I *am* speaking," said Germaine. "You're getting all worked up for nothing, Tim. Don't you remember? I've already been bitten once before—last Halloween. Thanks to the earlier exposure, I've probably developed enough antibodies to protect me this time."

Everyone paused and held their breaths.

"You're one smart cookie," said Professor Williams. "You may be right. If Hubda was going to bite only one citizen of Hamlet, you are the safest one to bite. How smart of Widow Wendell to swing the spider your way!"

"And I can cook," said Widow Wendell, primping to beat the band. But Professor Williams only had eyes for Hubda. He ran over to the baseboard and put his nose to the mousehole, crying, "Hubda, it's daddykins! Come to dada!"

"I could run home and fetch my cat, Dogfood," said Hector Yellow.

There was no need. Just then Meg Snoople ran lurching back into the Memorial Gym. "A wicked spider the size of my fist just scurried out of a drain spout! Probably the Siberian snow spider! I chased after it screaming, and I tried to thwack it with my makeup kit. I mean my purse." Her shoulders drooped. "I didn't get it. It disappeared into some bushes. What a story *that* would have made if I had. Daytime Emmy for sure."

"Well, as long as no one has been harmed, why not have some cake now?" asked Tim. "We'll skip the garter hoist. Undignified."

"Just in time," said Fawn to Rhoda. They had sidled cakeward and retrieved Rhoda's misspent arrow before anyone else found it.

Mr. Bannerjee came forward to the cake that Grandma Earth and Thud had baked. He noticed the split couple and quickly corrected the display. He glued the figures back together with a little extra curry sauce. Curry adds spice to everything, including marriage, he thought, and took a moment to smile across the room at his own wonderful wife.

The wedding party of Miss Earth and Mayor Grass—the new Earth-Grass family—continued in the traditional ways. There were no further interruptions of cupid, spider, ghost, alien, mutant, visiting circus personnel, or media personality. The dancing proved lively, the cake scrumptious; and the happy couple whooped it up bigtime. And after all the fuss, most of the guests finally began to relax. They took the time to chat with the out-of-towners like Professor Williams, Suzy Denim, Professor Einfinger, and Corpsina and Vampyra, the Sinister Sisters. To calm her nerves, even Meg Snoople nibbled on some cake, though she felt ill-tempered about how poorly she was achieving her professional objectives today. Her mood wasn't improved by noticing her co-anchor, Chad Hunkley, chatting up Widow Wendell over by the punch bowl.

Emboldened by the delicious wedding cake, the children marched in a tight cluster out to the tennis court. There they gaped at Amos, who was resting on his belly with his front paws crossed. He seemed neither friendly nor deadly—just very quiet, very wise. He regarded the children with one eye. The other he kept trained on Doozy Dorking, his stepmother.

"Wow," said the kids, one by one.

"Amos," said Thud. "You've grown. You've changed. A *lot*."

Amos opened his mouth, trying without success to stifle a small polite yawn. The kids looked at the thick folds of his dignified wattles; they flapped over each other like a series of saddlebags. He could fit a loaf of bread in each one. Assuming he liked bread. What if he still wanted to make a sandwich out of Ms. Earth-Grass?

"We've got to get you out of here, Amos," said Thud. "You're too big to hide in Hamlet."

"I'll take him to the starship," said Pimplemuss. "It'll make close quarters for the rest of us, but he'll be safe there. I hope he isn't gassy or anything."

"We should be honest," said Thud. "We don't know if Amos is safe. He's had a troubled childhood. He might trap you in a cocoon and save you for supper."

"Oooh. He'd get a curried Fixiburger," said Pimplemuss, burping discreetly behind her gloved hand. "I know I'm tempting too. But what other choices do you have?"

"That's awfully nice of you," said Thud, "and brave."

"You catch me feeling decent," said Pimplemuss. "Don't push it, though."

Amos flexed his claws. They were wonderfully complicated digits complete with retractable nails. The dexterous claws looked as if they could manipulate knitting needles or tie a sailor's knot. They seemed capable and dangerous both. "I hope you know what you're doing," said Thud.

"He'll be protection against that scary spider, if it ever shows up," declared Pimplemuss. "Isn't that arachnid on the loose around here somewhere? My fellow Fixipuddlings and I have been patrolling the margins of this tennis court, but a spider could sneak near at any moment while we're busy peering into the shadows."

The mention of Hubda's being abroad reminded the children to make plans for the parade tomorrow and then hurriedly say goodnight and rush back inside. Now that Pimplemuss was apprised of the problems, she could walk back to the *Loiterbug,* and that strange family of chicken and stepchildren would follow her to safety. With luck everyone in town would linger at the reception, and no one would see Fixipuddlings and Flameburpers, including one that looked like a medieval dragon, marching along the edge of a Vermont road.

When people left the gym to start home—helpfully late—they took a good look over their shoulders. They didn't want any spider lunging at them in the dark. But when nothing threatened them immediately, they relaxed. Hadn't it been a wonderful wedding, a memorable wedding? And hadn't lovely Germaine Earth and kindly Timothy Grass deserved just such a sendoff?

To tell the truth, the newlyweds weren't going far—not yet. They were spending their first night as a married couple in a bed-and-breakfast in Woodstock, not far away. But they had agreed to postpone leaving for their honeymoon (a three-day holiday trip to Quebec City) until the fifth of July. After all, even as a married man, the mayor was first selectman of Hamlet. He had some duties to perform in the parade the next day.

Dreams came slowly, when they came at all, to the denizens of Hamlet.

Salim spent the night in a sleeping bag on the back porch of the Mango Tree, with Baby Tusker hovering nearby, a sleepless blanket of warm mist. Salim was realizing that Baby Tusker was as good as invisible to most people, like a film of sleep over their eyes. So hiding Baby Tusker wasn't as big a problem as housing the other nonhuman visitors to Vermont.

Fawn took Rhoda home from the wedding, and Rhoda slept in a corner of Fawn's bedroom. Fawn provided some privacy for Rhoda by standing a copy of the picture book *Madeline* on its spine and flapping the covers open.

Where Hubda slept no one knew, but nightmares woke Pearl Hotchkiss. Her mother came running with a glass of warm milk. "Too much excitement," murmured Mrs. Hotchkiss.

Having arranged with Lois about Beatrice's special guest appearance at tomorrow's parade, Pimplemuss hurried her motley crew cross-country toward the slopes of Hardscrabble Hill. Doozy Dorking trailed after her new idol, and her stepchildren, Amos and Beatrice, accompanied her. At the *Loiterbug*, the Fixipuddlings discovered happily that Amos *hadn't* burned through the hatch of the starship. "You must have figured out how to work the lever when you saw your brother outside," said Pimplemuss to Beatrice. "How you prevented the one hundred forty rescued chickens from following you is a puzzle, though. Did you threaten them with a little flame? Did you go, '*One step further and you're instant rotisserie chicken, you'?* Well, you're a smart little cookie, you are. Now, let's everyone have a great big pee and we'll all go nighty-night."

She opened the hatch. One hundred forty pullets exploded out to peck for a midnight snack of grubs before settling back down to their hennish dreams of liberty and justice for chickens.

19. NINE AND A HALF GOOD PROBLEMS

The Fourth of July was one of the town of Hamlet's favorite holidays.

At eight-thirty A.M., both churches joined forces to put on a pancake extravaganza, in this instance at the Flora Tyburn Memorial Gym. That the pancakes had a distinct aroma of curry this year only reminded people of happy times in days of yore, namely, yesterday.

At nine A.M., volunteers helped set out used books in front of the Hamlet Free Community Library. A dollar a hardcover, or three paperbacks. Book lovers could help Mr. Dewey raise funds to buy new Stephanie Queen novels as they came out, seasonally.

By nine forty-five, people from many nearby towns were already lining the parade route. The marchers, floats, dignitaries, and musicians all gathered at Ethan Allen Park, a bit downslope from Fingerpie Farm. Promptly at ten A.M., the parade lined itself up for its triumphal entry into Hamlet. There, since it was a very short parade, it would toot and bleat and tweet its way around the town green not once but twice.

Fully expecting another exposé, Meg Snoople installed her

team on the roof of her van to catch everything on camera. And since her report from yesterday's Earth-Grass wedding had aired at seven this morning, the crowds this year were larger than ever. Everyone wanted to catch sight of the mysterious so-called Flameburper. Genuine genetic mutant? Or show-biz flim-flammery?

Things all went according to tradition. At first.

The parade always led off with the grand marshall—Mayor Grass—driving the town's oldest citizen in the town garbage truck. The most antique citizen for the past quarter century had been Old Man Fingerpie, and he did his job well, tossing hand-fuls of hard candy well away from the margins of the road so small children could safely scramble for them.

Next came some stalwart citizens driving vintage cars and trucks and farm machinery, spiffy with spit and polish and dec-orated with patriotic bunting.

State Trooper Hiram Crawdad, who had more or less be-come an honorary citizen of Hamlet, followed in his official vehicle, every once in a while sounding the siren and switching on the blue revolving lights to give children a thrill.

Cormier's llama farm (Llama-Rama) was featured next. Three llamas looped together at the neck lolloped by with innate dignity and a certain amount of cluelessness.

Then a much-loved segment: the Ladies' Auxiliary Folding Chair Band. (Men were allowed to join in too, but they had to wear skirts.) This was composed of a dozen or so hearty marchers, each carrying a lightweight lawn chair, the type fea-turing colorful webbed nylon strapping slung around an alu-minum frame. The Chair Band was conducted by Mrs. Cobble, the school secretary, who barked her orders with her custom-ary zeal. "March! Halt! CHAIRS UP! And a one and a two and a

HUPDY-WHUPDY-DO!" She led her followers in a carefully prac-
ticed routine. Rhythmically they all swung their chairs, clattered
them noisily opened and closed, bounced them on the ground
right, left, and center. Intermittently the marchers sat down in
their opened chairs and chanted out various lines of patriotic
doggerel.

"Liberty and justice for ALL!" (*Crash crash crash*)

"Amber waves of GRAIN!" (*Crash crash*)

"One o'clock, two o'clock, three o'clock ROCK!" (*Crash*)

"Of the people, by the people,

For the people, five the people,

Six o'clock, seven o'clock, eight o'clock, ROCK!"

It was all in good fun and wildly applauded.

The Ladies' Auxiliary Folding Chair Band was followed by a
fleet of small children on bicycles and tricycles, and parents
pushing toddlers in strollers. Pearl Hotchkiss's sister Ruby
dragged a wagon advertising FREE KITINS! and eight little kit-
tens peered out under the misspelled sign.

Next came the Sinister Sisters' impromptu display. The
funny clown car with square wheels bumped and thumped and
pretended to veer out of control, threatening people on the
sidelines. One of the elephants followed, plodding in deliberate,
stately fashion. In a black-and-white-striped howdah up top,
Senator Pimplemuss waved graciously. She had exchanged her
twin set and pearls for a patriotic outfit in tasteful red, white,
and blue pinstripes.

Finally—and this was the whole point of the exercise—
along came Beatrice the Flameburper, in the full light of
sun, without apology. Since chickhood Beatrice had always
responded well to music. A tape of circus calliope music helped
Beatrice marshal her steps. Lois Kennedy the Third proudly

walked by her side. She and the Sinister Sisters had decided that they would risk not putting Beatrice on a leash—it seemed so demeaning, somehow—and that anyway the effect, for such national press as might show up, would be more persuasive the more matter-of-fact everyone behaved.

In the light of day, with hundreds of eyes and dozens of video cameras upon her, Beatrice was clearly only a little less than a dragon. No one had quite seen it before—it took the arrival of a fully fledged Amos to sharpen their eyes. But now it was unmistakable. Her skin wasn't quite the stunning Polynesian blue of Amos's—more aquamarine perhaps, or even emerald tinged—and her wings seemed more gauzy, less capable of lift. But she was the hit of the parade, no doubt about it.

"Watch Beatrice make a grand exit tonight!" called Vampyra through a bullhorn. "A special encore performance of the Sinister Sisters' Circus, for the benefit of all the crowds who have thronged like maniacal thrill seekers to follow the FAKE NEWS on *Breakfast in America!*"

"You can't say that!" shouted Meg Snoople from the top of her van.

"That's a real mutant!" cried Professor Einfinger. "Arrest her!"

"I'm not a mutant," Vampyra sassed back. "I'm an undecided voter."

"Liberty and flibberty for all!" pronounced Senator Pimplemuss.

"See you tonight in the Big Tent!" cried Corpsina. "Luv ya lots, ya creep!"

"We're getting a warrant for your arrest!" Professor Einfinger called. "Aiding and abetting an escaped mutant! That creature belongs to Geneworks!"

"Last time I checked," cried Senator Pimplemuss, "the Thirteenth Amendment to the Constitution had outlawed *slavery!*"

Everyone cheered. Beatrice did a little arabesque. Pimplemuss looked proud of herself, as if she'd been studying up on the details of government, as indeed she had.

The parade concluded with the stately procession of Engines Number One and Three. Many of the folks of Hamlet hadn't seen the town's new engine yet, and it got more applause than the Ladies' Auxiliary Folding Chair Band and the Sinister Sisters' Circus elephant combined. How glad they were to see it, with its one-hundred-foot ladder and its shining valves and its superbly coiled hoses! Citizens waved their tiny flags till the air was a red, white, and blue blur.

It being a holiday, Professor Einfinger had a difficult time reaching the right personnel to listen to his complaints. But justice never sleeps, even on a national holiday, and Einfinger decided to play a daring hand. He collared State Trooper Hiram Crawdad and demanded that something be done.

"I *could* do something," said Trooper Crawdad, "something I'd rather not do. I could arrest you for violation of your restraining order."

"If you did that," said Einfinger, "you'd be within your rights. But this is our national holiday about liberty and justice for *all*, isn't it? You have an obligation to give Geneworks the benefit of the doubt. If you don't take that so-called Flameburper into custody, you're obstructing justice yourself. And you know it."

"It's a beautiful day in sunny Vermont," said Trooper Crawdad sadly. "Why are you making so much trouble?"

"If you remember," said Einfinger, "that creature hatched out of an egg that had been genetically engineered by a company I work for. In a certain legal sense, that so-called Beatrice should be under *my* stewardship."

Trooper Crawdad thought Einfinger looked more like a wicked uncle than a doting papa. "Come to the circus," said Trooper Crawdad. "I can't deprive the little children of seeing Beatrice do her circus routine. I'll decide then." He looked at the angry face of Professor Einfinger and added, "Professor. I don't have to like you, and frankly I *don't* like you. You're a trouble-maker. But the laws exist to protect the rights even of annoying troublemakers like yourself, and you may have a point. Frankly, I'm off duty, and I'm going to the firefighters' auction in the cir-cus tent. And then I'm going to the chicken barbecue. I hear they have a famous disgusting creamed corn you can hardly stomach, and I can't wait to try it. Finally, I'm going to the cir-cus. And I will take up your concerns then. Meanwhile, may I give you a friendly piece of advice?"

"Try the creamed corn?" asked Wolfgang Einfinger.

"Stay out of my way," said Trooper Crawdad.

The annual auction promised farm equipment, 1970s furni-ture covered in worn brown velour, and broken video record-ers. More trash than treasure always turned up, but the auc-tion drew a lot of friendly residents and summer people who wanted to support the fire department. Since the Sinister Sisters had lent the use of their circus tent, this year the auc-tion was held inside that cool and glamorous space.

The absence of the graduates was noticed. "Where *are* those troublemakers?" Sharday's dad asked Moshe's mom.

"Up to no good," Nina's grandmother opined to Mike's uncle.

"I can hear myself think for once," said Mrs. Mastrangelo, Anna Maria's mother, "and it's disappointing: I'm a lot more boring than I remembered."

The Copycats, the Tattletales, Thud Tweed, and Pearl Hotchkiss were nowhere to be seen—not in town, that is. They were instead convened up on top of Hardscrabble Hill by the swimming hole in the abandoned quarry.

Despite the holiday feeling, it was a dispirited group, to be sure. One hundred forty pullets scratched for grubs beneath the trees. Sixteen children, five Fixipuddlings, one ghost, and one cupid flopped on rocks or leaned on their bikes or pitched pebbles into the swimming hole. No one felt like swimming except Foomie. The Fixipuddlings didn't look humanoid anymore—retaining the disguises allowed them by their particle shower took a lot of effort, and they needed a break from it now and then.

Pimplemuss was trying to be hospitable, and she offered around a plate of freeze-fried grubs covered in candied pepper. She had few takers, except for Droyd and Peppa, who polished off the whole plate.

"I do admire this holiday," said Salim. "In India we also had a display of flags and we sang our national anthem on Independence Day and on Republic Day. But the Fourth of July seems a snappier occasion. I love how we celebrate our forefathers here."

"*Our* forefathers?" said Forest Eugene Mopp. "Salim, you just *got* here from India—less than a year ago."

"I'm here. They're my forefathers now," Salim insisted. "Baby Tusker's, too."

Baby Tusker was busy trying to suction water from the swimming hole to spray Foomie, but his ghostly proboscis had no earthly suck to it.

"Salim is right," said Pimplemuss. "You don't even have to be a citizen to have rights in the United States. You can arrive from Cuba as an illegal alien, you can arrive from Fixipuddle as an intergalactic alien, and the legal rights of the United States obtain. Or this was true the last time I checked, anyway."

"Oh please," said Thud. "School is over for the summer, okay? Can we stop impressing one another and decide what we're going to *do?*"

"Let's list our problems," said Sammy. "One. Hubda the Siberian snow spider is still on the loose.

"Two. Baby Tusker needs to go home."

"Who says?" interrupted Salim. "He's not causing anyone trouble! Live and let live!!"

"He's *dead,*" Lois gently reminded Salim.

"Three," continued Sammy. "We have to decide what's going to happen to the one hundred forty chickens that Senator Pimplemuss liberated from Fingerpie's barn."

"I was Angel Pimplemuss back then," Pimplemuss reminded him.

"Four. Rhoda has an itchy finger and seems eager to discharge that arrow, and she's a danger to us all. One wedding a season is enough."

"She used her arrow already," said Fawn.

"It's still got its juice, because it didn't pierce two living souls, just two plastic ones. Any arrow, single or one of a pair, has to nip at least one living soul in order to work," said Rhoda. "But I told you already I wouldn't use my last arrow for romance, so don't tempt me."

"*Five,* and everyone stop interrupting," said Sammy. "This one is the most serious. Meg Snoople and Professor Einfinger between them have focused the eyes of the nation on Hamlet, and Beatrice is likely to be taken into custody after the circus tonight."

"I hate to interrupt," said Salim Bannerjee, "but exactly why are the Sinister Sisters being so helpful to us? Is their knee-jerk antibully reaction legit? Does anyone wonder if they mean to kidnap Beatrice and use her in their circus act permanently?"

Sammy sighed. "Okay. That'll be problem five-A. Now, six: What in the world are we going to do with Amos? We could hide Beatrice, theoretically—but she might get bigger in time. Maybe she'll build another cocoon in a year or two and dream herself into a bigger, a newer creature the way Amos did. But we can't hide Amos for long. He's magnificent, but he's too big to camouflage.

"That's about it. Anything else we should be worrying about?"

"Yes," said Thekla Mustard. "Seven: Are we going to be a new club with sixteen members, and may I be the leader?"

"Eight," said Lois Kennedy the Third. "Thekla and her megalomania are always worth worrying about."

"Nine," said Thud Tweed. "My creepy dad was released from prison yesterday and is coming home today. He ought to be here soon. In fact, I should be home waiting for him. I might not even be able to come to the circus tonight."

"Bring him along," said Salim Bannerjee.

"Ten," said Hector Yellow. "Does anyone have any suspicions about Suzy Denim?"

Everyone looked at him. "It's just a funny feeling I have," he said. "She doesn't seem to be related to anyone, but she's been peering pretty closely through her dark glasses at everything. She reminds me of someone, but I can't think of who."

"Mr. Dewey's been giving her a lot of attention," said Carly Garfunkel.

"Maybe he's found another reader to discuss Stephanie Queen novels with," said Hector Yellow.

"Everyone under the sun reads Stephanie Queen novels," scoffed Thekla. "Even that coffee lady who liberated Hubda. There was a Stephanie Queen novel in her coat pocket. I saw it in the paper."

"So," said Sammy, cutting through the chatter, "we'll knock out the notion of Thekla as a problem—we're all used to Thekla; she's less a problem than a force of nature—"

"Thank you," said Thekla prettily.

"—like a patch of quicksand or a plague of stinkbugs—"

"Ha ha."

Thekla looked more flattered than insulted, noticed Pearl. Hmmm.

"—so that leaves us with nine good problems. Or nine and a half. Now, anyone. Any ideas on how to solve them?"

They sat in the dappled light and waited for inspiration.

"Why not borrow another WordSearch dial and put it on Amos?" asked Thud. "Maybe he could tell us what he would like to have happen?"

Pimplemuss shook her beaky head. "Didn't you say Beatrice fried the one we accidentally left behind? Amos might have the same response. We can't take that risk. A WordSearch dial is an expensive tool, and we can't replace Narr's until we get home. Luckily Narr is the strong silent type and doesn't talk much anyway. But he hasn't been able to understand a word we're saying since we arrived." She smiled at Narr and waved her feathery wingtips at him, and blinked her column of eyes.

"And we can't hang around here forever," she continued.

163

"We've rescued the pullets and attended a wedding in the bargain, but we're not about to go hiring real estate brokers to buy us a summer place."

"Could you take Amos and Beatrice with you?" Sammy asked Pimplemuss.

"No!" shouted Lois and Thud at the same time.

"I don't think so," Pimplemuss agreed. "Not if Amos is prone to wrapping up dinner when he's hungry, the way you said he wrapped up your teacher. We couldn't take the chance. Who would navigate our starship if we were all eaten?"

They waited for inspiration some more. Glumly.

"I still wonder why the Sinister Sisters are being so helpful," said Salim after a while. "Why are they hanging around instead of packing up and lumbering off into the Great Beyond, or to Stowe, anyway?"

Then he had a little glimmer of inspiration, a shred of an idea.

"I think I may go have a chat with Corpsina and Vampyra," he said. "Baby Tusker, you stay put."

"What?" the others asked. "What's up?"

"I'm not at liberty to say. *Yet.* I informally agreed to maintain some confidentiality. But I'll report back when I know something." He disappeared at a clip. Baby Tusker waved goodbye.

"Salim will be heartbroken once again," said Rhoda to Fawn, to everyone. "Because Baby Tusker's not going to stay forever either."

"How can you tell?" asked Fawn. "Are you psychic, like the Sinister Sisters say they are?"

"You don't have to be psychic to know everything changes," said Rhoda. "That's what growing up *means.*"

20. ENCORE!

Mayor Tim Earth-Grass and his lovely wife, Germaine, were prepared to wait for the evening's festival of fireworks before leaving for their honeymoon. They joined their friends and neighbors and tucked into a supper of greasy roast chicken, gluey rolls, creamed corn (sometimes called screamed corn), limp salad, and delicious pies contributed by Hamlet households. The meal seemed like an extension of last night's wedding reception, except it was taking place out of doors.

And spiders live outdoors. So as the evening sun began to soften and flatten, oranged by the atmosphere of the horizon, people drew nearer to one another and finished their pie, and cleared out a bit earlier than usual.

After all, there was a benefit to being at a circus. Surely that growly lion and those huge elephants would scare away a spider? And, later, the detonation of fireworks would cause her to run for cover. Run all the way back to Harvard University, thought the good people of Hamlet. Bye-bye, Hubda. And *bon voyage*.

★★★

Fifteen minutes before the circus was to start, the children gathered outside the tent. But several of them were missing.

"Where's Thud?" asked Lois.

"More important," said Sammy, "where is Salim? He called me to suggest we meet at the far end of the green when the circus was over, but he gave no further details of his brainstorm."

The big black limousine used by the Tweed family pulled up and parked in a no-parking zone. Harold the chauffeur got out and straightened his cap. Then he opened the door for Mrs. Tweed. Tonight she had left behind her Petunia Whiner persona. She was back to being herself, a demure country matron—rather overdressed by Vermont standards, but then she'd grown up in a tony neighborhood of London. At least she came by her elegant ways and sniffy manner honestly instead of putting on airs.

"Look," said Lois. "That must be Thud's dad."

And sure enough, Mycroft Tweed emerged from the car next. For the dad of someone as big and clumpy as Thud Tweed, Mycroft was surprisingly spry and dapper. He wore a smart seersucker summer suit and a straw hat, and the smell of expensive cigars made those nearby crinkle their noses. "Come, my boy," said Mycroft into the car, "no need to mope! These are your people, after all. For the time being."

Thud Tweed got out of the car. He had been the biggest kid in Miss Earth's class, and he had been nothing less than a bully at first. He had calmed down some due to civilizing influences. But a few months under Miss Earth's watch hadn't done anything like *this* to him. Thud Tweed's eyes were red rimmed and his nose was raw and runny. He'd been crying.

Tears of joy at the reunion with his dad? But Thud didn't

look all that happy. "I'm going to go sit with my friends," Thud was heard to mutter.

"Nonsense, my boy," said Mycroft Tweed grandly, publicly. "I've been out of commission for too many months. We're having a family night out. You'll sit with your mother and me." He squeezed Mildred Tweed's elbow and deftly propelled them both into the tent. Thud tried to squirm around and signal to his friends, but the meaning of his message was lost.

"What is going on?" asked Lois. "Thud looked awful!"

Before they could worry further, though, the Bannerjee family arrived finally in their station wagon. Meera and Meena looked oversugared from too much cotton candy. Mrs. Bannerjee drove. Mr. Bannerjee showed signs of strain from his work as emergency caterer for the wedding yesterday; he lolled his head against the headrest and held a cotton flannel to his forehead.

Salim jumped out. "Sorry I'm late! I had to rush back up to the starship and clue in Pimplemuss about the getaway plan."

"What?" asked Sammy, and the others echoed, "What? *What?*"

The circus fanfare started. They had to lunge for their seats, for once the show started, no one was permitted to enter the tent. Salim gave a thumbs-up. "No chance to explain! Here's hoping my plan works! Meet you afterward on the green!"

It better go well. It just better. Because now the *Breakfast in America* van was simply one in a pack of media vehicles. It was parked by the Hamlet Free Library along with representatives from CNN, ABC, CBS, Fox, NBC, and, for reasons no one could fathom, the Home Shopping Network.

"Whoo-ie!" said Limpy Clumpett as she locked the door of the General Store and headed across the road to the big top. "It's a media circus at the circus circus!"

167

"What, is the president in town and we never heard about it?" said Bucky.

"I liked that Senator Pimplemuss," said Limpy. "I think, in the spirit of runaway Vermont politics, I'm going to start a write-in campaign next fall. Pimplemuss for president!"

"Hey, for which state is she a senator, anyway?" asked Bucky.

"I don't know," said Limpy. "Probably the state of confusion."

"Then she'll do very well as the senator representing Hamlet," said Bucky.

The lights went down. The music began. The crowd tonight was even larger than two nights earlier. So much—so very much!—hung in the balance.

And while the safety and well-being of Beatrice and Amos hung in the balance, the trapeze artists hung in the balance, too—moment by moment—before being caught and swinging on.

"I do love a good circus," mumbled Grandma Earth to her married daughter.

"You should be up there, Ma," said Germaine.

"After I close my business," said Grandma Earth. "I'll take up the flying trapeze as a hobby in my retirement. Speaking of career moves, have you and Tim decided yet if you're leaving Hamlet or staying on?"

"Mother," said Germaine, "I haven't been married twenty-four hours yet. Give me a break. Cut me some slack."

"I only—"

"Give it a rest," said Germaine Earth-Grass decisively.

The elephant came in.

"Who's that sitting with Professor Einfinger?" asked Mr. Dewey.

"I've seen her face in the papers," said Suzy Denim. Though

the tent was dark, she still didn't remove her sunglasses. "I know. It's the CEO of his company. It's a lady named Dr. Elderthumb, the brains of the outfit."

"You follow the news very closely. Are you an investigative reporter like Meg Snoople?"

"You ask the silliest things, Mr. Dewey."

"I'm a librarian. I pay attention to words, Ms. Denim. Suzy. Or should I simply call you Sue Denim?" The way he rolled the words together, it sounded like *pseudonym*. The word, derived from Greek, which means *false name*.

"You flatter my parents with a cleverness they didn't possess," said Sue Denim. But she seemed flustered.

Mr. Dewey changed the subject. "Well, that Dr. Elderthumb must have come to decide for herself if this Beatrice is really a show-biz circus freak or the fruit of her malevolent genetic engineering. Creepy."

It got creepier a few minutes later, when half a dozen of Trooper Crawdad's colleagues came through and stood in the back. They carried flashlights and billy clubs. They looked as if they didn't want to be fierce but would enforce the law if necessary. Dr. Elderthumb rubbed her hands in satisfaction. *She'd* set up this sting! Trooper Crawdad, sitting with the Clumpetts, seemed dismayed and tried to shrink in his seat.

The clowns appeared in their funny clown car. Spotlights went zipping zanily all around the big top. Every now and then a light would stop and zero in, with canny precision, on a single person in the crowd, making the person's face stand out with luminous glare against the surrounding black. It made affectionate fun of the individual faces, as if saying, *Everyone can be a clown!*

The lights picked out Meera and Meena Bannerjee just as

they both were diving their faces into a single cloud of pink cotton candy. Everyone roared with laughter.

The lights settled briefly on Germaine and Timothy Earth-Grass as they were trying to steal a secret kiss in the darkness. "OOOOOOOOOOH!" screamed the crowd.

The lights flickered and revolved and picked out Mrs. Brill, the school-bus driver and lunch lady. Then they found Dr. Josif Mustard, who gave a little wave. Then they settled on Senator Pimplemuss, who had a seat in the back row.

"She's here too? I hope she behaves," Sammy whispered to Thekla. "What if she decides to liberate the lion? Pimplemuss has always struck me as being pretty unruly. Are the others sitting near her?"

"I see three of them," Thekla said. "Narr, Droyd, and Peppa. But where is Foomie?"

Pimplemuss waved to her constituents grandly.

The clowns then raced away, and Corpsina and Vampyra emerged as before, out of the single clown suit. Since the show must go on, on the show went.

The crowd, however, grew impatient, and after a while people began to shout, "BEE-TRISS! BEE-TRISS! BEE-TRISS!" and to stamp their feet on the wooden bleachers. They drowned out the waltz music. The lion tamer stopped taunting the lion with an overturned chair and righted it instead. He sat on it. The lion purred and settled down with his big mane flopping over onto the lion tamer's shiny black boots.

"BEE-TRISS! BEE-TRISS! BEE-TRISS!"

Corpsina and Vampyra came back into the ring and held up their hands for silence.

"And now," said Corpsina. "Never before attempted! The one—the only—incredible flying dragon! BEATRICE! To be shot out of a cannon into the Great Beyond! Let's hear it for BEEEEEEEEEE-triss!"

As ten thousand silver dots of mylar dropped shimmeringly from buckets overhead, in raced the wacky clown car again. Beatrice perched on the back, balancing herself with faint flutters of wings.

The state troopers readied their instruments.

"Steady, fellas," said Corpsina. "You can take her into custody afterward, when she comes back down to earth. I think she's going to bring news of the Great Beyond with her. Our sister Frankenstella. I have this *feeling*," she added stagily, and put her hand on her breast. "Maybe it is just heartburn. What about that Connubial Curry, eh, folks?" She led a round of applause for Mr. Bannerjee.

"Besides," said Vampyra to the troopers. "It'd be smart not to rile up Beatrice. Our cannon is powered by gunpowder, and Beatrice has a natural flint in her throat. You don't want to have to call out Hamlet's brand-new glossy fire engine *again*, do you? So stay back and let Beatrice do her farewell number."

There was a certain logic to these remarks. The state troopers moved forward to be ready to intervene in the event of a catastrophe. With professional pride but a glum expression, State Trooper Hiram Crawdad put down his bag of peanuts and went to stand by his colleagues.

The applause and shrieking died down.

Corpsina said in a sultry voice, "We've never tried this one before, folks. Why would we? But Beatrice is okay, top drawer, a trouper—like you troopers out there! Ya know what I mean? Her wings will add lift to compensate for the drag of her tail! *My* tail drags like nobody's business by the end of a show, believe me! So, maestro, a drum roll, please!"

The circus goers held their breaths. Alone of the citizens of Hamlet, Salim knew what was about to happen. But he was sworn to secrecy and couldn't tell. Magicians never give away their secrets unless they are being tortured, or questioned under oath, or unless they want to.

Beatrice was helped into the mouth of the cannon just as Salim had been two nights ago. Before her little head disappeared, she opened her mouth and blatted out one beautiful stream of flame, ruby embers against the theatrical darkness of the center ring. "*Ooooooh!*" said everyone. There was no doubt that Beatrice was not a fake stagecrafted creature. Whatever she was, she was the genuine article.

Then Beatrice disappeared into the mouth of the cannon.

"The tent's going to go dark," whispered Thekla, "and will someone remove the cannon? Is that how she's going to be helped to escape? What is Salim's plan?"

"I don't know," Sammy whispered back. "I didn't have a chance to hear all the particulars. Shhh." He grabbed her hand.

How peculiar, thought Thekla. Sammy Grubb has just grabbed my hand. What am I supposed to do now? Squeeze it? Bite it? Scream and run away?

She became too absorbed in the entertainment to think of any other options, so she simply said, "Ewwww," and withdrew her hand. But she said it more mildly than she might have done.

The drum roll continued, the lights shifted and spun. Everyone in the tent bellowed out the countdown.

"FIVE! FOUR! THREE! TWO! ONE!"

Just as on the night Salim had been shot from a cannon, there was a smooth blue *whoosh,* with sparkles and afterglow. Then the spotlights stopped roaming the canvas and settled upon the hole in the tent. Only the most hardhearted of repeat visitors allowed themselves to admit that the hole in the tent was exactly the same size—and was in the same place—as it had been two nights earlier.

"She's *gone!*" shouted Professor Einfinger. "They're all in collusion! She's escaping!"

She *was* gone, too. Only Salim knew where, and how. Because Salim, sworn to secrecy two nights earlier, knew how the trick worked.

Salim hadn't shared his plan with his friends. It had taken him a little while to convince the Sinister Sisters it could work. They had agreed on the condition that he not give away any of their trade secrets. Besides, they said, they had a scheme of their own to carry out, and Salim's plan could help *them*.

Like most good tricks, it was pretty simple, actually.

The person to be shot from the cannon climbed inside it, as all could witness. The would-be human projectile was tamped down by a long-handled implement. What really happened next, however, was invisible to those in the bleachers.

The bottom of the cannon was fitted with a trapdoor, a sort of large hinged flap. As soon as the countdown began, roustabouts crouching out of sight under the platform would open the flap and help the volunteer drop into the secret crawl space below. The roustabouts would refill the cannon with a cellophane sack filled with some sort of blue grainy sand made out of glitter and talcum powder. It was the propulsion of that sack that made the blue *whoosh* out of the mouth of the cannon, causing everyone to think that the volunteer had been ejected faster than the eye could see. By the time the eyes of circus lovers had found the flap in the roof of the tent—cunningly ripped in advance, its ragged edges released by the pulling of a string—no one was looking at the cannon anymore.

173

The bowed side of the cannon platform was fitted out with a sliding door that opened from within. Stagehands helped the little volunteer (it was always a child, except tonight when it was a Flameburper) to roll out of the platform and through a portal in the side of the clowns' crazy car, which was parked snugly against the platform. All secret hatches were closed before the lights began to come up again in the center of the ring. The clown car then made its comical way out of the tent. Circus fans never guessed the clown car was actually spiriting away the person thought to have been shot from the cannon.

Outside, Salim knew, circus assistants would help the volunteer out of the clown car. The volunteer would climb up a ladder onto the back of the circus elephant and make a triumphant reentry into the circus tent.

Every night but tonight. Tonight, the state troopers were right. Beatrice was escaping. Hustling across the empty town green to the rendezvous point . . .

At least, that was the plan. But would it work?

"Patience, my dear audience," said Corpsina. "Liberty and justice for all, remember."

"This is a dastardly plot! Arrest these Sinister Sisters!" screamed Dr. Elderthumb.

Corpsina paid her no attention. "And now—ladies and gentlemen and officers of the law . . . the return of Beatrice!"

The flaps of the entrance were pulled back. As before, the circus elephant, in all her spangled trappings, came slowly treading in. The ankle bracelets and belled earrings jingled, and all eyes swiveled to the howdah up top.

In which, indeed, there seemed to be—

Beatrice?

Well, something like Beatrice, anyway.

Enough like Beatrice to confuse everyone except the children, who could guess some of the wonderful slipperiness of Salim's grand plan.

Foomie. Foomie the Fixipuddler disguised as Beatrice the Flameburper.

Foomie, who must have spent several hours in the particle shower of the starship *Loiterburg* trying to perfect Foomie's disguise as Beatrice.

It *wasn't* perfect. Foomie's skin tone wasn't emerald-aquamarine. It was more a kind of dusty olive. Foomie's orange wings were disproportionately large and flimsy. And Foomie was definitely camping it up, waving and gesturing with two claws clamped over Foomie's head in a kind of victory salute to Foomie's self, something that Beatrice would never have done.

But whatever Foomie's failings, Foomie was nonetheless not a real Flameburper. Foomie was a persuasive creature—as always. But the state troopers moved forward uncertainly.

The elephant reached the center of the ring. The applause was dense but slightly confused. Foomie as a dragon looked less convincing. . . .

"What're you waiting for? Arrest that Flameburper!" cried Wolfgang Einfinger.

"I beg your pardon, sir," said Foomie. "You appear to be under a delusion that I am a genetic mutant of your ownership. Can mutant chickens speak the Queen's English? I think *not*."

Foomie had a point. However garish Foomie looked, Foomie's cleverness with language made Foomie seem more human—as if Foomie *must* be a circus performer in a great disguise. What else *could* Foomie be? The troopers fell back sheepishly as the crowd began to laugh at them.

Foomie pressed on. "If you're looking for creatures masquerading under an alias, may I propose you set your sights elsewhere, officers?"

"Have you come back from the Great Beyond?" yelled Vampyra.

"Indeed I have," said Foomie, "and, as I live and breathe, there is no Frankenstella there."

"No?" said Corpsina. "You jivin' me?"

"So our psychic vibes were a bit, oh, ineffectual?" asked Vampyra.

"How could Frankenstella be in the Great Beyond," continued, Foomie, "when she is *right here?*"

The speed with which Corpsina and Vampyra wheeled their heads, and the instant *zap* of the spotlight into the bleachers, was clear proof to anyone who thought about it later that this whole charade was an elaborate setup. The Sinister Sisters were in on the game. But while it was happening, no one could think that fast.

Foomie threw back Foomie's head and performed a fairly creditable imitation of Beatrice's flame-throwing talents. (The particle shower had never done such a good job before!) Sparkles of red, white, and blue spiraled up in the middle of the Big Tent, making a floral bouquet of American spangles.

Then Foomie pointed a digit of Foomie's Beatrice-ish claw, right across the tent to the woman in the dark glasses sitting next to Mr. Dewey. The spotlight constricted to show only her face. "Your psychic vibes weren't so far off the mark, Corpsina and Vampyra," said Foomie. "Ms. Suzy Denim. There she is."

21. THE THIRD SISTER

Suzy Denim gasped and staggered to her feet. She clutched her lightweight jacket close and swept her hair in front of her face.

"You!" yelled Vampyra.

"Yoo-hoo!" added Corpsina, and waved vigorously. "We *thought* that was you! But we needed to send an envoy to the Great Beyond one last time and see if you'd checked outta that dump! Hate to be personal, but as long as your cover is blown, how're ya keeping, sis? Long time no see!"

"Like *twelve years!*" added Vampyra.

Suzy Denim pushed her way past astonished circus goers and fled from the tent with her hands over her ears. "She's ashamed of us!" explained Vampyra, surprisingly cheerful. "Always has been. Took a new name and lit out for greener pastures."

"Oooh, she's a tricky one," added Corpsina. "Tells a good story about herself, I'll give her that."

"Yarn spinner, that she is," said Vampyra.

"Originally there were three sisters, you see," Corpsina reminded them. "Back before we were so sinister."

"Every family has a ghost in the closet somewhere," admitted Vampyra.

"You're wasting our time," called Einfinger. "Officer, arrest that costumed midget for impersonating a Flameburper!"

"I do object," said Foomie. "Decked up in finery I may be, but I hardly find that a reason for law enforcement personnel to be involved. I was only having fun. The good Sinister Sisters thought they'd detected a spy in their midst, and they were right. Their sister seems constantly to be snooping in the cause of research. And every family, it is true, does have a ghost in its midst somewhere...."

The state troopers were busy making their way to the exit. They felt they'd been made fools of and wanted no more of this embarrassment. They had a hard time understanding who was impersonating what. But before they could reach the tent flaps and scurry away, the lights began to flicker and dim once again.

Everyone settled back in their seats. These Sinister Sisters were clever showpeople, and there was another wrinkle! What would it be?

In Fawn's backpack, Rhoda wriggled forward to look.

Foomie was still sitting on the head of the old Indian elephant. The elephant continued her slow and stately progress around the center ring. Up top, Foomie took the position of a placid monk, with Foomie's Beatrice-like legs crossed in lotus position and Foomie's Beatrice-ish fingers held just so. Foomie gave another little blast of fake Flameburper flourish. A fountain of green and white stars, like miniature Independence Day sparklers, sprayed above the back of the elephant and behind her.

As the tent darkened and the spangles gleamed and fell

toward the sawdust in the ring, a murmuring of "*Ooooooh!*" broke out from all sides of the tent at once.

Behind the old Indian elephant was another shape. It was, people later swore, the ghost of an elephant. If every family had a ghost, was this the old elephant's?

"Baby Tusker!" whispered Salim. "What're you doing here? I told you to stay at the Mango Tree!"

But Salim, though a friend, wasn't an elephant. Maybe the Indian elephant in the circus was a distant relative—a grandmother, a great-aunt thrice removed.

Baby Tusker's wispy, smoky trunk was holding on to the tail of the old circus perfumer. As the old dame swayed, Baby Tusker swayed. The effect was mysterious, hypnotic, and, in a way few could verbalize, almost holy. Father Fogarty, who believed in a lot, felt so, and even Dr. Elderthumb, who believed in little, agreed.

It was a *danse de cirque.*

Baby Tusker's outlines gleamed for a moment in diamonds of white and green, the sparkles from Foomie having settled along his murky outline. He reached out a glowing trunk and patted the old elephant.

"It's perfect!" murmured Rhoda. "I can do some good for Salim, and those circles on the old dame's hide make a perfect target!"

"No, don't," whispered Fawn. But Rhoda slapped her arrow to her bow and took her sighting.

Her aim was true and her arrow swift. It lanced the tip of Baby Tusker's ghostly trunk and stuck, quivering, in the side of the circus elephant, who seemed complacent and hardly to notice, or mind.

But Baby Tusker swept his nose away. A ghost can't be pinned by an arrow, even an arrow from a cupid desperate to do good. So once again Rhoda's arrow, though shot in good faith, retained its potency for later use.

It was as if the nearness of the elephant had reminded Baby Tusker of his new family, the ghostly mastodons up north. Baby Tusker had come for a visit, to remind Salim that friends were still friends though they lived far apart. But the message had been given, and it was time, now, for him to leave. Baby Tusker waved his trunk in the air at Salim and nodded his head. The trunk trailed a fading glow of green and white sparks, and as the sparks faded, Baby Tusker began to fade, too.

"No!" shouted Salim.

"Oooooh," said everyone else.

"Whoops," said Rhoda in a small voice. "Didn't work."

Before Baby Tusker faded entirely, a last little surge of green-and-yellowish sparkle ebbed forth. Was it from Foomie, from Foomie's impressions of Beatrice, from Baby Tusker himself? Was it a *real* message from the Great Beyond? Who could tell? Baby Tusker's trunk, which could never manage a sackful of pondwater, managed something more brilliant instead. It gave forth a little font of sparkles that arranged themselves into something vaguely egg shaped. The top of the egg lifted off, like a little domed hat, and underneath—it could be no other—was a little colored outline of a baby Flameburper.

It had to be Seymour. Not Amos, a mighty dragon, nor Beatrice, a dragonette-comedienne. It was Seymour, waving as if still attached to Salim, through all the other creatures who loved him.

Maybe it wasn't improbable as all that. All blessings are connected. The richness of the future grows from the past. Every smile that delights you works, in part, because of other smiles that have taught you how to respond to smiles.

It hardly mattered. Salim, with teary eyes, began to smile

and wave. There was consolation in the glowing cartoon of Seymour, which waved back before it faded.

Then it was done, and like the balloon of the ghost of Frankenstella, the ghost of Baby Tusker took his leave. In shreds and tatters of silvery smoke, he rose like tongues of incense. He drained mysteriously through the opened hole in the roof of the tent. He was never seen again, or not by anyone who had ever seen him before, anyway.

The spell lasted for another thirty seconds, and then everyone began to clap. What a magnificent circus! What a way to end the Fourth of July!

Oh, it wasn't the end, yet. Of course not. There were still fireworks. What was a Fourth of July without fireworks?

"If there's one thing I've learned while visiting among mortals," said Foomie, "it's that there's no business like show business." As the circus lights cut out and the applause began, Foomie dropped from the head of the elephant and disappeared. Foomie did not reappear for a curtain call. Smart Foomie!

Rhoda took advantage of the darkened tent to swoop over and reclaim her single arrow. Romantically, what a dud this trip was proving to be!

The dark was welcome. Salim was swallowing back his tears, ready to learn how to be happy again. But Thud Tweed was none too happy. Before the lights came up and the various clowns and animals and the trapeze artists and the Sinister Sisters took their final bows, Thud Tweed broke away—from his terrible awful mean father, who seemed to have left prison early just to spoil his son's life—and from his dull boring country-western star mother, who was no better.

★★★

181

The little diversion caused by the apparition of an elephant ghost gave the kids time to scramble away from the Big Top. They hadn't had a chance to plan much, for everything was unfolding too fast. They had to rely on their native skill as kids, using the cunning, resilience, and high spirits of their age and station as best as they could.

At the center of the green, Foomie was jumping up and down in excitement, waiting for them, and Pimplemuss and the other Fixipuddlings showed up a moment later.

"Great idea, Salim," said Sammy, "and great job, Foomie. But where is Beatrice?"

"I was supposed to see her safely back to the bushes by Widow Wendell's inn," said Foomie. "I was waiting outside the tent when Beatrice came out in the clown car. That little clown and I helped her out of the secret compartment. But one of those Boykin brothers was testing a firework on the green, and Beatrice got spooked. She dove into the dark bushes, and I couldn't follow her; I had to make my entrance as the fake Beatrice just then. I assumed she'd come right back when she realized it wasn't a gunshot."

"Well, come on," said Sammy. "We better split. We'll find her soon enough, if no one else does first."

"You're right," Thekla agreed. "The state troopers seem to have lost their oomph, but they might come to their senses and show up to start questioning us. If we lie under oath now, we'll never be able to run for public office in the future."

They raced to the far end of the green, under a sky glowing with the electric blue that a clear summer evening displays before it becomes black and spangled with stars. Senator Pimplemuss ran in an ungainly fashion that looked like a postscript to the clown performance, but nobody mentioned it.

Pimplemuss hadn't studied closely the way human beings ran, and her legs tended to spin out sideways in a wheeling motion.

They paused for breath beneath a stand of old white pines at the north side of the village green, just beyond the Lovey Inn. The scene was, you might say, a bit tense. For a moment, no one could speak. Amos was waiting for them there, hiding in the overgrown lilac bushes behind Widow Wendell's clothesline. But Beatrice was nowhere to be seen.

"What's *Amos* doing here?" exploded Sammy Grubb.

"He came with me," said Foomie. "He was supposed to stand ready to guard his sister, Beatrice, in case of a posse. But Beatrice has disappeared anyway. Fooey."

The children glared. "Don't worry, we left Doozy Dorking and her one hundred forty acolytes safely locked in," said Foomie. "What?"

The children's glares got stronger and meaner. "You've taken a mighty risk, Foomie," said Sammy Grubb coldly. "We're trying to explain away the presence of the smaller Flameburper, and you go out for a excursion with the larger one?"

"Don't look at me like that," Foomie complained. "Not to worry, kidlings. Everyone's at the circus. No one saw us."

Amos was complacent. He batted his eyelashes calmly. Then he poked a single nail into one of his jaw pouches and removed a clot of woven weeds the size of a handbag.

"Disgusting," said Lois forcefully. "It looks like a huge hairball. What's that?"

Amos turned it this way and that. The item fell apart in halves, revealing an interior compartment. "Let me see that," said Pimplemuss.

She dug a gloved finger into the hollow pocket and withdrew a glistening glob of what, for lack of a better theory, appeared to be . . .

. . . damp, fresh spider strands.

"Did you build a cocoon for *Hubda?*" asked Lois.

"And did you eat her?" added Pearl.

"Or did you save her from the wallowing pocketbook of Meg Snoople?" concluded Forest Eugene. "America wants to know!"

"Hubda *might* have ventured across the tennis court last night," admitted Pimplemuss. "We Fixipuddlings couldn't be looking everywhere at once! It's so dark here at night, when you have only one silly moon plugged in!"

"If you didn't eat her," said Thekla, "but were saving her from trouble—maybe that's proof you were saving Miss Earth, too—not just storing her till you were hungry, but protecting her from harm."

"But where is Hubda now?" asked Sammy. "In your stomach, or on the loose again?"

"And where is your sister, Beatrice?" demanded Thekla.

Foomie was gushing, "Speaking of Beatrice, what did you think? How'd I do? I didn't feel I was acting Beatrice, I felt I *was* Beatrice. Did it come across? Persuasive? Give me notes. I can deal."

No one wanted to talk to Foomie just then. Pearl changed the subject by saying, "Thud, whatever is the matter with *you?* You look horrible."

"My dad is back," said Thud bitterly. "And he wants to make a new start as a family man. He doesn't want to waltz into some podunk hicksville hamlet where my mom and I have already rooted ourselves without him. He's thinking Coral Gables, or Boca Raton. Or Reno. Someplace without a winter."

"But what does your mom say?" asked Pearl.

"You know my mom," said Thud. "*Stick with your man!* That's her motto. I don't want to talk about it."

"We'll worry about all that later," said Sammy. "Meanwhile, we've got to get out of here. There could be a posse of state troopers and genetic engineers and media personnel after us in a jiffy. We can lose them in the shadows—we're lucky it's not a full-moon night. But they'll hear us if we stay too close."

"What's exactly is going on here?" said a voice from the front porch of the Lovey Inn.

They all turned. They'd forgotten that not everyone in town was still at the circus.

It was that secretive woman in the dark glasses. Suzy Denim. She was sitting on a wicker chair on the porch of the inn, scribbling in a small stenographer's notepad. "Is that a real dragon in the lilac bushes?"

Sammy Grubb's jaw dropped open. He couldn't speak.

Thekla Mustard stepped forward boldly and pulled herself up on the edge of the porch, on the other side of the railing. "Why don't you take off your glasses and have a look?" asked Thekla Mustard.

Everyone gasped. "My father's an ophthalmologist," continued Thekla. "I know that people don't wear dark glasses in the pitch black except for one reason. They're trying to hide their identity."

"Sometimes dark glasses can be a fashion statement. Tell me about the dragon."

"We don't have to talk to spies," said Thekla Mustard. "It's *your* fault the town is overrun with snoops and busybodies, isn't it?"

"Thekla," said Sammy nervously, "I don't know what you're going on about, but can we do this later? We've got to get back to the starship before people find us here. Look, here comes Mr. Dewey. He's headed this way."

"Take off those glasses," said Thekla. "Prove me wrong."

"I don't know what you're talking about," said Ms. Denim.

"He's coming!" hissed Salim. "Thekla, what are you talking about?"

Mr. Dewey arrived at the porch. He had eyes only for Ms. Denim. "I frightened you," he said. "I was too forward."

"There's a dragon in the side yard," said Ms. Denim. "Have you noticed?"

"I only have eyes for you," he said.

Rhoda began to struggle out of Fawn's knapsack. "I just can't let a chance like this pass me by," she muttered. "I've been too good for too long."

Fawn said, "Rhoda!" and tried to push her down the way the Sinister Sisters had pushed Beatrice into the barrel of the cannon. But Rhoda was tired of being pushed around.

The first revelers from the circus were bustling out of the tent—troopers with their powerful flashlights scissoring the roadside with light, and the silhouetted forms of parents and school personnel, anxious to make sure that their disappeared children were all right on this most mysterious evening.

"It's a romance made in heaven," said Thekla grimly. "You better tell him who you are."

"I know Sue Denim means *pseudonym*," said Mr. Dewey. "Are you really Stella Coody?"

Ms. Denim looked distraught. "Say it," ordered Thekla, "or I will."

"This isn't about me!" she said. "Haven't you noticed? *There is a dragon in the side yard!*"

"Vermont is very tolerant of differences," said Mr. Dewey. "Live and let live. Please tell me your real name."

When Ms. Denim paused, Thekla blurted, "Oh, we don't have *time* for this! Mr. Dewey, don't you realize? I figured it out a while ago. Who bothers to use a pseudonym? Only two types: a spy and a *writer*. When I saw the newspaper photo of the fake coffee vendor carrying *Sabotaged in Schenectady* in her coat pocket, I put it all together! Sue Denim is Stephanie Queen! She's the famous writer! *And* she's the one who stole that coffee trolley and crashed into the spider cage, releasing Hubda into the wild, and brought down all this attention upon us just when we don't want it."

"It was an accident," cried Stephanie Queen. "I wanted to do a book in which Spangles O'Leary got bitten by a Siberian snow spider. It was going to be called *Comatose in Cambridge*. But Professor Williams wouldn't let me see the spider. He said he thought my work was cheesy. Supermarket fiction, he called it!"

"No!" cried Mr. Dewey.

"*Reeeeeeaaaaaady*," said Rhoda.

"But Stephanie Queen's not my real name, either," said Suzy Stephanie Denim Queen. "Stephanie Queen is my *nom de plume*—the name I use while I'm writing. It's really a feminization of Stephen King, see?"

"You're Stephen King behind those glasses?" shrieked Pearl.

"Oh, dear," said Mr. Dewey, and gulped to steady himself. "Well, this *is* Vermont."

"*Aaaaaiiiiim*," said Rhoda.

"I am not Stephen King, you clowns! No, my real name is Stella Coody."

"So the Sinister Sisters were telling the truth. Stella Coody."

"Yes," said Suzy Stephanie Stella Denim Queen Coody. "But don't you agree that that's a horrible name for a writer? Stella Coody?"

"Frankenstella Coody is sort of cool," said Sammy. "I'd read a book by a writer named Frankenstella Coody."

"I wouldn't," said Suzy Stephanie Frankenstella Denim Queen Sinister Coody. "By the way, my friends call me Bubbles."

"*Fire!*" said Rhoda. But she didn't let her arrow fly. She was pointing at Amos, whose breath had set the sheets on Widow Wendell's clothesline on fire.

Meanwhile, Mr. Dewey was gripping the hand of Bubbles Suzy Stephanie Frankenstella Denim Queen Sinister Coody. "You have too many names," he said. "Let me call you sweetheart."

"No one has ever done that before," she gasped.

Rhoda put her arrow away. She didn't want to waste it.

Sammy Grubb said, "This is getting dangerously mushy. Worse than the older rutabagas we had to sort the other day. Come on, kids. Everyone will be up here in an instant, thanks to the flaming laundry of Widow Wendell. We've got to find Beatrice. Where could she have gone?

Thekla said, "Somebody better see that Amos gets safely back to the starship before he's discovered. And the rest of us better split up and comb the highways and byways for Beatrice. We have to find her before Einfinger does. Where shall we meet?"

Pimplemuss said, "It's time we Fixipuddlings were on our way. We want to take the notion of Independence Day home to Fixipuddle with us. We're ready. We'll fire up the starship, and when we're ready to say goodbye, we'll drop by your school-yard. We remember where it is from last time."

"You're going to leave us with all our problems?" asked Thud.

"You're a sassy one," said Pimplemuss. "Actually, I like that. There's never a day without problems, Thuddy. Hurry, little ones. It's time to go."

"We can't move as fast as you can," said Droyd.

"We put our legs on backward, I think," said Peppa.

"So you did," said Pimplemuss. "I was trying to be polite and not mention how stupid you looked. Well, we're in a hurry now, little ones. You better hide out somewhere, and I'll come back with the starship for you. It'll save time. Amos can't take all of us at once."

"Okay," said Droyd and Peppa. "Where will you meet us?"

"Can't come back here—it's too public," said Sammy Grubb. "How about underneath the covered bridge? No one ever looks there."

Lois added, "You, Foomie, better stay out of sight too. In that getup, you still could be picked up as a stray Flameburper. You and Narr better go with Droyd and Peppa and wait under the bridge."

"Good idea," said Foomie. "I'd hate to be captured and prodded in embarrassing ways."

"We'll escort you to the bridge, and stand and defend you if attacked!" promised Sammy.

"This all sounds very Independence Day to me," said Foomie agreeably.

"I'll see Amos back to the starship," Thud told Sammy.

"You don't trust me to get him there safely myself?" asked Pimplemuss.

"No, I don't," said Thud.

"You're smarter than you look," said Pimplemuss. "All right, then. Back to the starship, the three of us! We'll fire 'er up for the big departure. We'll stop first at the bridge and pick you up.

Second stop, schoolyard, and hugs and kisses, and autographs in our keepsake volume. But we better hurry."

"That leaves us Tattletales to scour the town for Beatrice," declared Thekla. "Come on, troops."

Thekla and the girls—Pearl included—fanned out back toward the green. The boys and the four Fixipuddlings ducked sideways, to circle around behind the Lovey Inn and begin to pelt toward the covered bridge.

Not a moment too soon, any of this. The crowd had noticed the fire and was beginning to head their way.

22. THE DRAGON TAKES WING

"**A**re you ready to go?" said Pimplemuss.

"They'll see Amos on the road," said Thud.

"We're not taking the road," Pimplemuss explained. "Mount your steed, Thuddy-boy."

Thud slung his arm around Amos's neck and hauled himself up. The skin of the dragon was slick, like a leather-covered carousel horse. Thud had to clamp his thighs tightly to keep from slipping to one side or the other. "I hope you understand enough English to know what we want you to do," said Thud to Amos.

"Shift up a bit," said Pimplemuss. "I have a bigger butt than you and I need more of the spinal column to rest on." She clamored aboard, clumsily, and settled herself sidesaddle for the sake of gentility. She had learned that senators try hard not to appear gauche in public. Then she made a little adjustment to the WordSearch dial and spoke a sentence or two in another tongue, then adjusted it back.

"You speak dragon?" asked Thud wonderingly.

"No, actually it's a language from the planet known as Slooooomp," said Pimplemuss. "I'm guessing your Amos might be able to recognize a little basic Slooooompish grammar. He has a Slooooompy sort of look to him."

"He does not," said Thud, affronted.

"Well, in that case, avast and away, me hearties! Up, up, and away! To infinity and beyond! Let's slip the sultry bonds of Earth! Look, up in the sky! It's a bird! It's a plane! No, it's a bird that looks like a plane! No, it's a plain bird! No, it's a birdbrained plane! No! It's a—"

In her enthusiasm, Pimplemuss's carefully cultivated aspect of a senator began to wobble, and her features to melt and slide. Thud was glad he was sitting in front of her and facing straight ahead. He could tell what was happening just by watching the human fingers turn into feather-fringed limbs, rather lumpy and outsized, like the gloved hands of a Walt Disney character.

But her voice stayed the same as she talked Amos through his first flight. As she spoke, she lifted her own feathered limbs to demonstrate. Amos's head swiveled on his elegant and mobile neck to regard her seriously. He seemed to understand.

"And up, and flex, and bucket those wings, and pump, and *pump,*" said Pimplemuss.

Amos flexed and bucketed and pumped and pumped. The dragon rose in the air, four feet, six, ten, until they were hovering about the height of the second-floor windows of the Lovey Inn.

"I can't believe my eyes," said Sue Denim. But she was still looking into the eyes of Mr. Dewey, and her dark glasses had fallen on the floor of the porch.

"She needs new glasses," said Pimplemuss, and off they flew.

Fawn Petros was with the other Tattletales as they raced through the backyards and summery dusky meadows, climbing fences, trampling flower gardens, scaring small meadow creatures into their holes. Looking everywhere, everywhere, for Beatrice. Where had she gone? Rhoda was jouncing and bouncing up and down in the knapsack. "Ow! Darn! Take it easy!" Rhoda shouted, but Fawn couldn't pause for breath or to apologize.

Sammy motioned his crew to melt into the shadowy woods on the side of the road. Old Man Fingerpie and Flossie were driving by. The oldest citizen was too ancient to stay up for the fireworks, apparently. Once the truck had passed, heading up Squished Toad Road toward Fingerpie Farm, Sammy put a finger to his lips and beckoned. The Copycats and their Fixipuddling companions crept back to the edge of the road and hurried along toward the bridge.

"This is very exciting," said Foomie.

"I hope we get attacked!" said Droyd.

"I hope *you* get attacked," said Peppa.

"Shhh," said Sammy.

The flight on the dragon was everything Thud had hoped it might be. Quickly Amos learned how to govern his strength, how to adjust his direction, how to work with thermals of air, how to bank for a turn, how to glide. All of Vermont seemed to be holding its breath beneath them. The air, ninety feet up, was bracingly chill.

"Oooh, this takes me back to my childhood!" shrilled Pimplemuss. "We used to have rides like this at the campsite on Snorple Fuzz Mountain."

But Thud didn't answer. He just thought about how much the world looked like a series of waves. The world carried on and on. Mountains, of course, and waves of cloud in the west— the travelers were high enough to catch a surprise glimpse of the sun that had already set some time ago, and was setting now over some more western state.

The world was waves, all waves, just like the history of the world, and the history of individuals, too. Now up, now down, now good, now bad. Riding the dragon, riding the waves of the wind—that was the goal, wasn't it? Not staying in one place, stuck, immobile, but learning that the *up* of it, the *down* of it, was the point? Was the exercise?

And the *up* of it might always make you go *whoa!* in surprise and delight, and the *down* of it might always make you slightly sick to your stomach, in grief and surprise. And the element that was the same, in both the up and down of it, was surprise. What a paradox: Surprise was the only thing you could count on.

Now I hate Vermont, now I love it. Now I want to leave, now I want to stay. Now I miss my father, now I hate him, now I have to love him again.

"There's only one rule," said Pimplemuss, snuggling up to him as if she could read his thoughts.

Though he didn't ask her what the rule was, she answered anyway. "Hang on."

Thekla had instructed her Tattletales to split up into ones and twos. Whether they found Beatrice or no, they would meet at the schoolyard in half an hour, to say goodbye to the Fixi-puddlings.

Lois Kennedy the Third made it her business to scope out the circus grounds. The Sinister Sisters and their colleagues were finishing up their interviews with the state troopers. Meg Snoople had led a pack of television people up to the Lovey Inn, but the sheets had burned themselves out, and Mr. Dewey and Sue Denim had made themselves scarce.

So round and round the darkening village green Meg Snoople went, pointing out places of interest. It became clear, however, that many of her colleagues on other stations felt that they had been had. CNN packed up and cleared out. ABC and Fox did the same. Folks from CBS and the Home Shopping Network started asking about local sightseeing for tomorrow. Mayor Earth-Grass kept his arm around his new wife, and Ms. Earth-Grass kept her arm around her new husband. They were tired of the holiday festivities. They wanted to be on their way into their new married life at last.

But first, and finally, were the fireworks. The Boykin brothers, in addition to being chicken pluckers extraordinaire, also specialized in pyrotechnics. Every year they came over the hill from Puster Center to set off the grand display. Colored pinwheels and dimpled stars, bright chains of deep-throated bass thuds, loud falsetto squeals, yellow and green punches, red and blue asterisks that gave birth to purple and salmon asterisks, and the most dazzling whites.

Like the CIA operative she hoped one day to become, Lois slipped by the circus personnel without being noticed. She found the square-wheeled clown car and, making sure no citizens were peering over her shoulder, she dropped to her knees and slid open the trick door that Salim finally, reluctantly, had told them about. Maybe Beatrice had come back to hide here, once the coast was clear?

The space inside was empty. So where *could* Beatrice be?

She looked around. The fireworks would begin shortly on the far side of the village green, in the space between the Hamlet Free Library and Clumpett's General Store on one side and the Congregational/Unitarian church across the way. Much of the glitz of the circus was already gone, stuffed into trunks and rolled up on flatbeds and trundled away on dollies. The circus folk had been eager to get their animals safely penned, in case the loud noises scared them, and the circus tent removed, too, to make sure falling fireworks didn't set the canvas afire.

Lois began to move a little faster. She ran up onto the porch of Clumpett's General Store. On the bench sat Widow Wendell listening to the most handsome heartthrob ever seen in Hamlet, Meg Snoople's co-anchor, Chad Hunkley.

"We're about to call it quits," he was saying to Widow Wendell. "It was all circus trickery after all—the razzmatazz of advertising. It makes you sick when you realize you've been snookered. Look, let me ask you one more time."

"Chad," said Widow Wendell, "it's true I've had been waiting for another offer of marriage since a month after my husband, Will Wendell, was buried. But: No."

"Let me take you away from all this!" said Chad Hunkley.

"Chad," said Widow Wendell, "I *am* all this."

"You won't marry me?"

"I can't believe I'm saying this," said Widow Wendell, "but you're right. I won't marry you. You're slick and shallow and not very bright. You're built like the statue of a god, of course, but statues have cold dead marble for brains, and so do you. I don't mean to be rude to a lodger at my own bed-and-breakfast, but take a hike, brainless beauty boy."

Where's Rhoda when you need her? thought Lois dully. She sprinted on.

She glanced back across the green. The Big Top was now, technically, a big flop: It was sinking down onto the grass, its tense skin relaxing in airy folds as the ropes that held it taut relaxed, the pegs pulled out of the ground.

The Hamlet House of Beauty, above which Fawn Petros lived with her folks, stood on the corner where the Ethantown Road joined the village green. Just beyond the back of Fawn's house was Foggy Hollow, not so deep here as farther on, but deep enough for a concrete bridge to be required to carry traffic entering and leaving Hamlet from the interstate.

On the ground was a trampled Flameburper feather. . . .

"Beatrice?" whispered Lois. "Oh, not you, too!"

She remembered what had happened a few months earlier. Seymour, the little Flameburper chick that Salim had cuddled in his own hands, and taken to his own heart, had died. If Beatrice had wandered off and come to grief, Lois would feel just as horrible as Salim had. How cruel could life be?

She couldn't stand not to know, though. She rushed to the edge of the overpass and looked down. "Beatrice?" she called huskily.

"Looking for someone?" This time it was the school secretary, Mrs. Cobble.

"Haven't got a flashlight, have you?" asked Lois.

"I do," said Mrs. Cobble. "I never go walking at night without one, in case some joyriding nudnik from Ethantown is plowing along too fast to see me in the dark." She took out a fairly good-sized Maglite.

"Look there," said Lois. "Look there. Turn it that way, look there."

They saw Beatrice, a little thing for a dragon, more crocodile from this angle, with her wings folded against her side. "She's just napping," said Mrs. Cobble unconvincingly.

"No," the school secretary added, reading Lois's mind, "don't go down there. You're not to go down there. I forbid it."

They both saw Hubda appear from under the folded wing

of the smaller Flameburper. Hubda twitched a little in the sharp circle of light, but she didn't flee. She looked stunned.

"Hubda's bitten Beatrice," said Lois.

"I'll go," said Mrs. Cobble. "You stay here. That's an order."

While Mrs. Cobble was neither Lois's parent nor her teacher, Lois felt compelled to obey. A monstrous weight of sadness fell over her. She watched as if at the inevitable sad end of an inevitably sad movie she had seen a number of very sad times. "I should call Hamlet Rescue, I guess," said Lois in a thin, wobbly voice.

"Not yet," said Mrs. Cobble calmly. It took her just a moment to scramble down the slope, while Lois kept the light screwed tight against the form of Beatrice. "You know, Hubda may have bitten Beatrice. But Beatrice is something new in nature, just as Hubda is something old. Maybe Beatrice isn't as susceptible to the poisonous antigens of a Siberian snow spider as a human being is. And maybe, just maybe, there's something in Beatrice's altered DNA that isn't so pinky-rosy-healthy for spiders to taste, either."

With the selflessness that characterizes the best school secretaries, Mrs. Cobble lifted Beatrice up and held her carefully and close as if Beatrice were a sleeping four-year-old. Then with her left hand the secretary scooped up Hubda the Siberian snow spider. Carrying her burdens, Mrs. Cobble made slow and cautious progress back up the slope.

"Now think fast, Lois," said Mrs. Cobble. "I'm going to have to get this spider to Professor Williams, if he's still here. What shall I do with Beatrice?"

"I can take care of Beatrice. Give her to me."

"She's too big for you to carry."

"Give her to me."

There was a sound of sneakers squeaking in the darkness,

coming toward them. "Is that you, Tallulah?" came a voice. It was Principal Buttle.

She saw Beatrice. Her principal's instincts kicked in. She reached out and lifted the ailing Flameburper from the librarian. "We'll get Nurse Pinky Crisp to look at her. The school is the safest place. No one will think to look there, since school is out for the summer. I have the keys in my pocket. There's no time to waste. Hurry."

"But—" said Lois. The Fixipuddlings were going to land their starship in the schoolyard.

It was no use, though. Principal Buttle had begun to hurry away. Lois had to follow her.

"Be careful of that Siberian snow spider, Tallulah," Principal Buttle called over her shoulder.

"I'll be gentle, and Professor Williams will know how to make her comfy," said Mrs. Cobble. "He's staying at the Lovey Inn. I can't wait to show him his Hubda has been found. He'll dance with glee."

"I mean be careful of the *poisonous spider*," the principal explained.

"I'm a school secretary. I've been exposed to everything already," said Mrs. Cobble, though she did store the sluggish spider in her alligator purse for safekeeping—her own safekeeping.

At the top of Hardscrabble Hill, Amos came down with an inelegant thump. Pimplemuss and Thud both fell off into a bed of soft pine needles. The starship *Loiterbug* was hidden in dark shadows. Pimplemuss found where she'd hidden the ignition key under a rock, and she went in and fired up the old jalopy.

"Remind me of the plan," she said.

"First we go to the covered bridge," said Thud, his heavy heart still refusing to lighten. "Narr, Droyd, Peppa, and Foomie will be hiding there with the Copycats. Then we go back to the school, where you can say goodbye to the Tattletales. If they have managed to find Beatrice by then, you can say goodbye to her, too. I hope no one sees us." He scratched his head. "Can you fly this thing without lights?"

Pimplemuss shook her noggin. "First, it's not safe. Furthermore, it's against your country's aviation code. Finally, it's unethical. Any home-flying duck might crash into us, and that would be the end of said duck."

"End of a duck," said Thud, "end of a dragon. End of an era. End of everything."

"Not end of a dragon," said Pimplemuss. "Look, since Amos has given evidence of being protective of life instead of merely a hoarder of future snacks, I've retired my reservations. We'll take Amos with us to Fixipuddle. We'll take Beatrice too, if they find her in time. They'll be safe on Fixipuddle. We treasure oddities there. They make life spicy."

"You're not sure Amos didn't eat Hubda," said Thud.

"I take my time in coming to a conclusion," Pimplemuss objected, "but once I do, I stick with it. He didn't eat Hubda. I'm sure of it. Hubda was small enough for him to gobble down as a midevening snack. There'd be no reason to preserve her for the future unless he was protecting her. No, I'm willing to take a risk on him. He's a good one.

"And so are you," she added. "I've changed my mind about you, too."

It took some doing to get Amos up the ramp and into the *Loiterbug*. But with his supple spine, he could coil himself around the central bank of controls, and he settled down nicely enough, grunting a bit. Doozy Dorking and the pullets all greeted him with clucks of joy.

"That's a nice dragon," said Pimplemuss, scratching him behind the ears. "Well, close up the hatch, Thud. Our mission here is nearly done, I think."

"This is fun," said Thud, slamming down the door and locking it.

"You'd enjoy intergalactic travel," said Pimplemuss. "You might think about it as a career."

People in the village waiting for the fireworks heard a *swoosh* and a *shush*, like a kind of sudden, localized rainstorm over on Hardscrabble Hill. It was the starship *Loiterbug* powering up. With a few jerks and shimmies, it lifted off.

Then, looking like a giant tempered-steel hamburger, the *Loiterbug* began to swoop and tack across the southern slope of Hardscrabble Hill and over to the town garage.

Thud pointed out the landmarks.

Of course everyone in town saw it.

"It's a meteor!" shouted Widow Wendell.

"It's a sign of our love," shouted Chad Hunkley.

"No, it's a meteor!" shouted Widow Wendell, and moved a few inches away.

"It's a shooting star!" shouted Norma Jean Mustard.

"You need new glasses, dear," said her husband. "It's clearly some advertisement for a science fiction movie about a flying saucer from outer space. Very lifelike, too."

Perhaps because of the sense of impossible glory that seems to descend upon American towns as dusk falls on the Fourth of July—for a moment the witnesses seemed paralyzed by the glowing trajectory of the *Loiterbug*. Against the purpling sky, it left a firebird's fiery tail of gold spangles and silver sequins: It was almost as good as a firework.

"Where's it going?" people murmured.

The *Loiterbug* landed to one side of the old covered bridge. The four Fixipuddlings and the Copycats all scrambled aboard.

Across a field, Old Man Fingerpie and Flossie stood agape at their windows.

"Is it Ezekiel's heavenly chariot coming for to carry me home?" asked Old Man Fingerpie. "Oh, Flossie, it's been a great life! I love you." He kissed her, not for the first time in his long life.

"Stop, you old boyfriend," said his wife. "Anything for a smooch! You never change. I don't know *what* that contraption is. The latest gas guzzler out of Detroit, no doubt. And I thought skimobiles were the worst that could happen."

She peered. "Hey, look," she said. A cloud of chickens was being ejected out of a chute. They squawked louder than the engines and fled in panic across the open space to their old home at Fingerpie Farm.

"The prodigal chickens!" said Flossie, and went to feed them.

"Shoot, my time isn't at hand yet," said Old Man Fingerpie, as the starship blasted off for the second time. He glanced at his watch. "Must be something wrong with this thing. Oh well, might as well go have a midnight snack, even if it's not time yet. I might be dead by midnight."

The impossible apparition of colored lights arced up from the direction of Squished Toad Road, and it crossed the town green at an altitude low enough for sets of landing lights to clearly be seen in the hull of the vessel. The *Breakfast in America* film crew was ready now, and caught the whole thing on film. There was nothing that the brave and clever Sinister Sisters could do to pretend *this* was part of a circus act. "They're heading toward the school!" shouted Ms. Frazzle.

"Call out the engines!" cried Mayor Earth-Grass. The volunteer crew began to sprint toward the town garage, while virtually everyone else in the vicinity hot-footed it onto Crank's Corners Road, and toward the Josiah Fawcett Elementary School.

23. THE FINAL FIRECRACKER

At the school, the Tattletales had convened on schedule. There they found the school door wide open, and Principal Buttle and Lois inside, bent over the limp form of Beatrice.

She had a puffy look to her eyelids. Her feathers rattled against one another with a dry clicking sound, like thin ivory wafers. "Oh, my dear creature," said Principal Buttle. "I do remember the antidote that served Miss Earth so well, the time she was bitten last fall. It was the sweets of local produce. But who's to say this is the solution for you? No one knows how your unique system works. No one can predict what to do for you."

"If Beatrice dies," said Anna Maria Mastrangelo, "they'll dissect her, and they'll *learn* how her system works. But it'll be too late."

"If she lives," said Thekla Mustard, "perhaps she'll be a carrier, and infect dozens more. What is to be done?"

"First things first," said Principal Buttle. "Make her comfortable. I've called Nurse Pinky Crisp on her cell phone, and she ought to be here in a jiffy." She plumped up the little pillow on the nurse's couch. Beatrice turned her head and breathed in and out in evident distress. Her breath was ill judged and the pillowcase caught on fire, but only a little. It smoked itself out almost before the eight girls had a chance to fling at it eight small paper cups of water from the water dispenser.

"I'm here," said Nurse Pinky Crisp, looking less than her usual professional self, since she was wearing a seven-pronged foam rubber Statue of Liberty headdress to help celebrate the holiday.

Still, she set to work with a will. To the best of her ability she assessed Beatrice's vital signs. "There's a pulse. That's good. Her eyes are tracking. That's good. Her blood pressure is 480 over 12. That's peculiar. If she were human, she'd have died about five times by now. But maybe this is normal blood pressure for a dragon. How do I know?"

"That's the whole problem," said Principal Buttle. "Who knows?"

A siren wailed in the distance. "Sounds like Trooper Crawdad's got a bulletin to answer," said Nurse Crisp.

"Or maybe Mrs. Cobble alerted Hamlet Rescue," said Principal Buttle.

"What, they think I don't know how to do my job?" Nurse Crisp was miffed.

The siren from the second fire engine began its raucous alarm, and as the noise drew nearer, those gathered in defense of Beatrice looked at each other.

Principal Buttle bit her lower lip. Then she reached out and flipped off the light switch. The nurse's office was plunged into darkness. "They don't know we're here," she whispered. "Everybody, keep down, in case they shine lights in the windows."

The fire engines inched their way around the green—the crowds on the road made the going slow. Many visitors from out of town failed to realize that this wasn't just another demonstration of local civic pride but a real emergency.

"I wish I had the nerve to cut the lights on landing," said Pimplemuss. "But I am a responsible pilot and I just can't do it. We might land on some poor cow that couldn't see us coming. I'm afraid we're a big fat advertising campaign announcing our destination. We're going to have to be pretty quick on the ground here, folks. Get your hankies out and start sniffling."

"This is just so cool," said Thud. "I would love to come into outer space with you, Pimplemuss."

"You'd need a permission slip," said Pimplemuss.

"I can forge one," said Thud. "I've done that many times before for hall passes and the like."

"Works for me," said Pimplemuss, who had done such things herself in her own misguided and highly entertaining youth.

The Copycats gaped at Thud. It fell to their Chief to speak. "You can't possibly do such a thing!" said Sammy Grubb. "Leave home? Leave your parents? What about your dad? Your mom?"

"Look, Sammy," said Thud. "I'm not a Copycat. Really, I never was. So remember that. For one thing, what I do is none of your business. For another thing, don't talk to *me* about people leaving people. My dad left *me*—by committing crimes so serious, he had to go to prison. My mom leaves me on an extended concert tour every time Petunia Whiner tunes up her whiner. And all kids have to grow up and leave home sometime. So I'll do it sooner than most. Leaving Hamlet, leaving the planet—what's the big dif?"

"Well, you can hardly come home on weekends to do your laundry," said Sammy.

Thud shrugged. "I was never that big on clean laundry."

Pimplemuss landed the *Loiterbug* clumsily, crushing the jungle gym in the process. Luckily, for once there were no teenagers smooching on the swings.

"Whoopsie," said Pimplemuss. "Now, listen. I hate to interrupt, but it's nearly time for us to go. Look, there are flashing red lights heading this way, and if I'm not mistaken, an angry mob is rushing behind them singing some national anthem or other." She flipped the switch that began to open the hatch.

"They probably think this is an alien invasion," said Sammy.

"It's an alien retreat, actually," said Pimplemuss, "so I think we'd better say goodbye to you kids. And this time, it's for good."

The boys all shook hands with Narr, Foomie, Droyd, Peppa, and Pimplemuss. Privately they were relieved that they were old-fashioned Vermont boys from a rural background, and that hugging and kissing weren't part of the Yankee way. Admire the Fixipuddlings though they did, the boys didn't want to hug and kiss them, or be hugged and kissed back.

"We'll take good care of Amos. Promise," said Pimplemuss.

Amos, who was already knitting a pullover for Pimplemuss out of old shredded intergalactic faxes, seemed okay with the plan. In any case, his stepmother, Doozy Dorking, roosted on a computer monitor and made deep-throated, contented noises. She'd keep him in line if he began to turn sulky like an adolescent.

One by one the Copycats climbed out the lowered hatch.

But Thud lingered on the ramp, indecisive. He wouldn't leave, and he wouldn't move inside so they could close the ramp, either. He was a passive resister, because he didn't know what to do. So he did nothing.

★★★

Principal Buttle was peering out a front window, eyeing the approach of the fire engines. With a thermometer, Nurse Pinky Crisp was trying to find a respectable way to take Beatrice's temperature. Thekla Mustard was the one who saw the dark shape of the *Loiterbug* descend upon the playground equipment out back and destroy it. "Whoops, another fund drive, and just when we've got the fire engine to finish paying off." She watched the hatch open and the silhouettes of the Copycats emerge. "Excuse me," she said to the others. "We've got company. The aliens have landed."

Principal Buttle said, "Yikes. We're more or less surrounded, I think."

"What're they going to do to us?" asked Nurse Crisp.

"We've got to get Beatrice out of here," said Principal Buttle. "Whether she's ill from Hubda's poisoning or not, she'll be discovered soon. And that won't be any good for her. Is there a way to get Beatrice on board that ship?"

"She'd be all alone," said Lois Kennedy the Third. "You can't make her go against her will. It wouldn't be fair."

"She'd have the—what do you call them?—the Fixipuddlings. They're very kind," said the principal.

"Yes, but they're a bit lunatic. I'd hardly trust them to know what to do in an emergency," said Lois. "Principal Buttle, Beatrice hatched out of the egg that I found. I've tended to her. She's my responsibility. I refuse to let her go on an intergalactic outing without a trustworthy chaperone. And she won't go with just anyone. She's picky and she doesn't trust other people easily." Her lip trembled. "Maybe I should exile myself into space to save her. Oh, Beatrice!"

Principal Buttle put her wrinkled old mug down near Beatrice's beaky dragon face. "My dear dragon Flameburper," she said, "don't you want to go into outer space? It has been my chiefest dream of all. I would be proud and honored to be the first principal in space. If I went, wouldn't you come with me?"

"You can't do that!" cried Pearl.

"Why not?" said Principal Buttle. "My taxes are paid. I have no husband and no children. I've been a school principal for a third of a century. I could do with a change of scenery."

"It's admirable, Principal Buttle, but it won't work," said Lois sadly. "Beatrice only has eyes for me. Me and her stepmother, Doozy, I mean."

Principal Buttle took Beatrice's wingtip between her fingers and began to stroke it lovingly. "Think about it, Beatrice. And, I might add, think fast. The walls are closing in on you here. If we've learned anything from the wedding of Miss Earth and Mayor Grass, it's that when love sweeps you away, you have to be ready to be swept. The farther stars are quite beautiful to behold this time of year, I understand. Wouldn't you allow yourself to be tempted to make a visit?"

And then Principal Buttle concluded her tender soliloquy by adding, "Ow. Bloody hell!"

"Oh, Rhoda!" yelled Fawn.

"Bull's-eye," said Rhoda, grinning.

Rhoda's one-and-only arrow had finally met its mark. Shot at excruciatingly close range, it had pierced the very tip of Beatrice's left wing, skewering it briefly but definitively to the padded flesh of Principal Buttle's index finger.

"A two-for-one special!" cried Fawn.

Perhaps the love potion concocted on the slopes of Mount Olympus was itself a natural antidote to the poison released in the bite of a Siberian snow spider. Or maybe Beatrice had all the necessary antibodies already, and had merely been feeling poorly. Or it might be that a fletched arrow of love never hurts anyone on the road to recovery. No one could ever be sure.

The new fire engine made its cautious way around the parking lot and up to the edge of the playground. The volunteer fire crew caught an untroubled front-on view of the starship *Loiterbug*.

Inside the school, Beatrice flexed her dragon wings and gave herself up to a healthy shudder. Then she popped off the camp bed in the nurse's lounge and did a little merengue step, as if to test her own mettle.

Principal Buttle? She seemed no different. If it is the professional character of a teacher to be in love with her students, and thereby to serve them, the diligent and zealous principal is the same, only more so. Hetty Buttle sat up and gathered a few tongue depressors and a bottle of aspirin from Nurse Pinky Crisp's cabinet, and said, "Well, I guess I'm ready, then."

"RELEASE THE BOY!" came the voice of Mayor Earth-Grass through a bullhorn. He was yelling at the *Loiterbug,* where Thud Tweed was silhouetted in the open hatch.

"Our bus is leaving," said Principal Buttle gently. "Come on, Beatrice."

The Tattletales and Pearl flung open the doors to the school and rushed out onto the grass. They joined the Copycats.

Germaine Earth-Grass, on the back of her Kawasaki 8000 Silver Eagle, came squealing around the corner of the school next. She left rubber as she screeched to a stop. Being a new bride hadn't dulled her fine quick-response time. She regarded the scene and got it in an instant, and instantly she acted in good judgment. Well, she was trained as a teacher.

"The crowd is nearly upon us!" she cried. "Who's ever leaving has got to go now, before they get here!" And the Fixipuddlings hardly needed her to tell them: The sound of shouting voices was growing louder, nearer.

But Thud seemed frozen in the doorway.

"Go," shouted Pimplemuss from behind him, "if you're going! Stay if you're staying! But don't stand in the doorway! We can't wait any longer!"

Still Thud hesitated. The *Loiterbug* fired up its auxiliary engines, fouling the schoolyard with stinky rings of blue smoke. Hot air made the ground look imprecise, wavery, as inches began to show between the ground and the open hatch. Then feet showed, and then yards.

"Thud!" shouted Sammy.

"Come back!" shouted the children.

Mayor Earth-Grass barked orders to the volunteer fire crew. They began the process of unlocking the telescoping ladder. Quickly, they slid it up rung by rung, angled shallowly at first, and more steeply as the *Loiterbug* gained inches, then feet.

"Jump!" shouted Thekla. In full view of everyone, she reached out for Sammy's hand.

"Jump!" shouted Sammy. He squeezed Thekla's hand back.

At a certain point, if the *Loiterbug* got too high, the suggestion of "Jump!" could turn from a plea to return to safety into an accidental invitation to die. . . .

But one never knows exactly how high one is, and sometimes one must jump anyway. Jump, or lose one's chance forever.

Thud looked down. Behind him, Droyd and Peppa nuzzled and teased Amos, distracting the Flameburper, proving he'd settle in okay. Below him, his human friends waited. He hadn't known these good-natured kids for long. One way or the other, he might not know them for much longer anyway. He was moving. Fixipuddle or Boca Raton, both were far from Hamlet, Vermont.

The fire engine's lights reflected off the shiny bottom of the starship, illuminating the faces of fifteen friends. Bright as daisies in a summer meadow, bright as stars in a winter sky.

He had never had one friend before, let alone fifteen. And really, they looked like a human welcome mat.

So Thud said, "Geronimo!" and jumped.

The children had made a circle beneath him, holding hands across the void, stitching their arms into a safety net. Boys reached out for girls, and for boys. Girls clutched boys, and girls. Kids clutched kids. They were more than Copycats and Tattletales now. They were not even Empress and subjects, or Chief and companions. They were kids—or maybe, even more than that. They were human beings.

They caught their Thud.

All their legs buckled beneath them and an ankle or two got twisted. Thekla's eyeglasses snapped. Rhoda, back in Fawn's knapsack, squealed in terror. Someone (who never admitted it) broke wind at the impact. But it didn't matter. Thud was safe. If it wasn't quite accurate to say his feet were on the ground, at least his rear end was.

Timothy Earth-Grass gave the order to retract the ladder on Engine Number Three.

"Wait!" said Principal Buttle, hurrying up. Surprisingly limber, she mounted the body of the fire engine and began to scrabble up the ladder.

"Hetty Buttle!" said Timothy Earth-Grass.

"Where are you going?" called Germaine Earth-Grass.

Beatrice was scrambling after Hetty. The smaller Flameburper was clearly on the mend already. Though she didn't seem to have the ability to fly—yet—her wings looked more fluffy, more flushed with light. "Why, it's a little angel," said Pimplemuss from the hatch. Indeed, with the lighting just so, Beatrice did look more like an angel than a genetically altered bluetoe-lizard–chicken dragon thingy.

"Hetty Buttle!" shrieked Germaine. *"Where are you going?"*

Principal Buttle turned at the entrance to the hatch and helped Beatrice in. "You were right to ask me what I was going to do in the fall," she called to Germaine Earth-Grass. "I was wrong to be so sure I would be in the principal's chair. I'm taking a leave of absence!"

"You're taking a leave of your *senses!*" shouted Mayor Earth-Grass.

"Germaine," said Principal Buttle, as the hatch door began to screw itself shut, "I recommend you for the position of acting principal. You'd be a natural. Maybe Norma Jean Mustard can take over your teaching duties in the classroom. Bye-bye, everybody."

The Fixipuddlings were waving madly as the hatch door finished closing. Mayor Earth-Grass ordered the ladder lowered. Then the windows of the *Loiterbug* blazed with light.

There was Amos, his noble head nodding, as Droyd and Peppa climbed all over his neck and played horsie.

There was Foomie, wiping Foomie's tears from Foomie's eyes.

Narr waved solemnly and bashfully. Doozy Dorking was crooked in his arm, and he was scratching the feathers on her breast.

Pimplemuss took a moment away from the controls to

salute the children on the ground. She mouthed some words that may have been, "I commune with nature!" Or maybe she was saying, "I salute the future!" Perhaps it didn't matter what she said. Perhaps from a space traveler's point of view, both sentiments meant roughly the same thing.

Then Beatrice came to the hatch window, healthy as ever, hopping up and down and doing a little jig, while Principal Buttle leaned behind her and took her last look at the Earth.

What a world to see! As much life as you could imagine came flooding around the corners of the school. All the families! All the visitors to town! They thronged around the newly married couple, the fire engine, the children. They gasped, they gaped, they pointed, they roared.

With a flash of light and a pulse of power so fierce that it fried the circuits of every digital camera or camcorder aimed in its direction, the starship *Loiterbug* made its stately exit.

The ascent of the starship against the blackness was something no one who saw it could ever forget, nor ever describe. It was like a compression of a sky-wide aurora borealis into a single *whoosh.* Streaks of mauve and pink and baubles of sizzling white. Threads of midnight blue coiled around jagged stitches of lemon, copper, bronze, titanium. It was more than the rockets' red glare or bombs bursting in air. It was a signature scrawled on the sky. Even to the most hardhearted, most crusty Yankee soul among them—even to the Boykin brothers, who were so entranced by this once-in-a-millennium display that they packed up the town's fireworks to save them for next year—the final firecracker of the Fourth of July signed its promise of love against the night.

It said:

I pledge allegiance to you.

24. READING THE FUTURE

Grade school was over. The wedding was over. The Fourth of July was over. The summer was stretching toward its hottest days. Childhood seemed forever, but one day it would be over too.

A peculiar calm settled on Hamlet on the fifth of July. People spoke in soft voices, as if someone had died. Perhaps it was that Principal Buttle had passed on. True, she hadn't passed on in the final sense, but she'd passed on nonetheless.

The Sinister Sisters sat down around a table in the dining room of Widow Wendell's Lovey Inn. Adele, Dotty, and Stella, a.k.a. Vampyra, Corpsina, and Stephanie Queen. They ate doughnuts from Grandma Earth's Baked Goods and Auto Repair Shop and discussed the past and the future.

"We were a better circus act when all three of us were together," said Vampyra.

"We were dynamite! We rocked. No one trounced us, no one," agreed Corpsina.

"Honeys," said Stephanie Queen, "we were ordinary potatoes. Don't you remember? It was boring. Nobody came.

Besides, I wanted to make a bigger story out of my life. I wanted to write circuses, not act in them. You didn't begin to develop a reputation until I left, and out of grief and disappointment you changed your name to the Sinister Sisters. It defined you. It gave you a better story. You became tops in the field. Don't blame me."

"You could have written anyway," said Vampyra.

"I *was* writing," said Stephanie Queen. "Just not letters. I'm sorry. To be a writer, you need to keep yourself a little secret. A writer is a spy. Now I've been discovered—Stephanie Queen is not the glamorous bestselling author from midtown Manhattan, she's plain old Stella Coody from Brooklyn Heights."

"You could come join us again for old times' sake," said Corpsina. "We'd happily rejig the cannon to fit you, and blow you into the Great Beyond eight times a week."

"I can't go back," Stephanie Queen said. "But I can go forward. I can keep in touch. I'm sorry. I'll be a better sister. I'll try, anyway."

The sisters sighed. Widow Wendell refilled their cups with mint tea. Mr. Dewey came up to the table and said, "Excuse me, ladies. Stella, are you ready to go for that walk you promised me?"

"I'll go for a walk," said Stephanie Queen. "But not right now, please. Can I meet you at the library? I don't want to pull myself away from my family just yet."

"No problem," said Mr. Dewey. "I'll just immerse myself in *Lovesick in Libya*. I have a feeling it's going to be a prophetic novel."

He left. "I've been thinking of setting a Spangles O'Leary novel in the circus," said Stella Coody to her sisters. "What do you think?"

"No giving away trade secrets!" declared Vampyra.

"Can we be in it?" asked Corpsina. "Make us more wonderful than we really are. If that's at all possible."

Lois spent an hour at Fingerpie Farm, helping Old Man Fingerpie and Flossie Fingerpie fix the rails on the chicken run. "I can't believe Doozy Dorking went into outer space!" Lois said to Mrs. Fingerpie.

"Look, honey," said Flossie, "from a certain point of view, Doozy Dorking always was in outer space."

"You're talking about me!" called Old Man Fingerpie from a dozen feet away. "Don't deny it! I'm as sane as the next chicken! Squawk!"

"I'll miss Beatrice," said Lois.

"Of course you will," said Flossie. "And Salim will miss Baby Tusker, and Thud will miss Amos. But you helped Beatrice survive an unlikely infancy, Lois, and whatever planet she becomes Empress of, she'll have you to thank, whether she knows it or not."

They worked in silence for a while. "You know," said Lois, "I always thought I wanted to be a spy when I grew up. But what Thekla Mustard said to Stephanie Queen really made sense. A writer is a kind of a spy. Maybe it was a writer I wanted to be, all along. It would give me a legitimate reason to pay attention to everybody and everything."

"I believe in paying attention," said Flossie Fingerpie, "whether you write it down or not. Life goes by pretty fast, you know."

"It does not!" bellowed Old Man Fingerpie. "This is taking forever. Everyone keeps bleating about Eternal Rest. When the hell is it going to get here?"

Sammy Grubb and Thekla Mustard spent the day together at the swimming hole at the old marble quarry.

217

Oh, thought Sammy, oh. I always wanted to discover new creatures—the Missing Link. And what I'm discovering is myself. There's a whole other *me* inside of me that I never knew about. The *me* that likes Thekla. The *me* that's starting not to be scared to admit it.

"Of course you like me," said Thekla, reading his thoughts. "Who wouldn't?"

Pearl rode her bike over to Thud's house.

"Do you know what's happening yet?" she asked him.

"No," he said. "I'm not talking to my parents yet."

"You will," she told him. "Meanwhile, I brought you a present."

She handed him Kermit the Hermit and almost ten weeks' worth of frog food.

"Are you saying don't be a hermit?" he asked her.

"I'm saying," she said, "I've never been a Tattletale. I'm a loner and so are you. And so is Kermit the Hermit. There's a virtue in that. But maybe we loners can have a loose affiliation?"

She smiled at him, something she'd never intended to do.

Maybe there were other chiefs in the tribe than Sammy Grubb, she thought.

Salim caught sight of Meg Snoople as she and Chad Hunkley were packing up the van for the last time. "You didn't get very much on film, did you?" he asked her.

"Look, little boy," said Meg Snoople. "I'm not wired for audio and the cameras are all stowed in the van. I'm not doing my job right now. I'm just curious. What *is* it about this town? I don't know if America wants to know, but I want to know."

"Sammy Grubb thinks that maybe some native population,

218

long disappeared, laid down ancient ley lines, and they serve as a kind of 'merge' signal to the universe," said Salim. "Myself, I think the whole world is pretty coincidental, and if you look hard enough at it, you'll be pleasantly surprised."

"That may be," said Meg Snoople. "I've had about enough of trained crickets chirping out 'There's No Business Like Show Business.' I'm nearly ready to hang up my microphone and do something new."

"Well, till you retire, you're always on a hunt for a new story, I bet," said Salim helpfully. "Up the road a bit is the Vermont Museum of Interesting Facts to Know and Tell. On your way out of town, you could stop there and get a shot of the famous two-headed chicken from Puster Center. It's pretty neat."

"Maybe I will," said Meg Snoople. "Come on, Chad. I'll snoop till I droop."

She left in the *Breakfast in America* van. Everyone leaves, thought Salim, remembering Baby Tusker and Seymour both. But now he remembered them with joy, and he was eager to meet new friends to add to his collection of memories.

Professor Williams stopped at Clumpett's General Store and bought a Styrofoam cooler and five pounds of ice. He packed Hubda safely therein. He intended to slow down her metabolism until he could get her safely back to his lab at Harvard, where he could take his time deciding how best to treat her. But, having spent several millennia encased in ice as a young spiderling, her system was used to the cold. She went into instant hibernation. Her vital signs were good, but she was checked out in a Deep Freeze.

Maybe it was just as well, thought Professor Williams. Maybe the world wasn't ready for the last remaining Siberian snow spider. Maybe he should just go and put her in the freezer unit of the fridge at the faculty lounge on the third floor and wait a decade or two.

Especially since she now looked old enough to spill an egg sac of her own, he surmised. Any offspring of hers could only be half-breed Siberian snow spiders, but they might still be pretty worrying. He wasn't sure he could be grandpapa to eight thousand partly poisonous spider babies.

Fawn brought peanut butter on a bagel for Rhoda to eat for breakfast. Rhoda was sitting comfortably on Aunt Sophia's knee.

"Rhoda," said Fawn, "your wings look a little smaller. Are you growing?"

"All this good country air," said Rhoda. "Maybe."

Fawn looked more closely. "Do you think you're turning into a human child?"

"I don't know. What does a human child feel like?" asked Rhoda.

"I don't know," said Fawn. "I have to keep living through my childhood to find out."

"Well," said Aunt Sophia, "if you're going to be a human child, Rhoda, you can be mine."

"Then we would be cousins," said Fawn.

"Cool," said Rhoda.

That's how time passed on the fifth of July in Hamlet. It's hard to describe how time passes in a starship, however. When you're stuck in a starship with your relatives, everything is relative, only more so.

At any rate, no matter the distance that the starship had to travel, the first leg of the journey—at least to where they'd been when they got the distress SOS call from the WordSearch dial—was done at something of a clip. They just took the same shortcut forward that they had taken back.

Then things settled into a routine.

The Flameburpers and their stepmother turned out to be good travelers. None of them got space sickness. This was a huge relief to Narr and Foomie, who would have had to do most of the cleaning up. Furthermore, Narr figured out a way to channel Amos's occasional blats of noxious dragon smoke into the fuel system on the starship. With an inexhaustible supply of renewable fuel, the starship could meander almost indefinitely before arriving home at Fixipuddle. They could have adventures along the way, and picnics. It would be fun.

Beatrice kept up her rehearsal schedule and did interpretative dances once a week. The dances were boring but everyone clapped anyway.

Doozy Dorking eventually got used to Pimplemuss's magnificence, though she still rose to her orange pronged feet whenever Pimplemuss came into the room. At night Doozy settled for sleep on Pimplemuss's face, which was inconvenient, uncomfortable, and sloppy for the Fixipuddling, though Pimplemuss was touched in her own way, until she got fed up and flung the hen out the door.

Foomie kept them all laughing by imitating various types they'd met around the galaxy—not just Earth, but other planets—through the agency of the particle shower. When Foomie did a Miss Earth, though, Principal Buttle said, "Enough, Foomie. I've managed not to get homesick so far, but don't push me."

With none of Earth's gravity to drag her sorry muscles down, Principal Buttle began to rejuvenate. Her eye was brighter, her skin tone improved, her voice regained some of the upper register she had once used in church choir. She also exercised her teaching skills, tutoring Droyd and Peppa every now and then.

They learned quickly, and often obeyed their personal private tutor. But they liked to tease her, too.

One day—or one millennium, it was hard to tell them apart—Droyd said, "Principal Buttle, look! I've reprogrammed our galaxy blaster to pick up some migratory electronic pulses. I've hooked up the WordSearch dial memory banks to search through oceans of unintelligible chatter. I think I can zero in on some postcards from home!"

"Your home or mine?" asked Hetty Buttle.

"Yours. Look."

She settled herself in a chair nodule. "I'm impressed with you, Droyd. You've been paying attention, I see. Go ahead, I'm ready."

Droyd input some data and turned the hand crank.

Up on the screen floated some fuzzy blobby shapes.

"Focus," barked Peppa, looking over Droyd's shoulder. He did.

What should appear but a series of—well—you might call them snapshots. Like portraits in a midlife yearbook. There was an elasticity to them—it wasn't that they moved, like movies, or spoke, like a telephone. But they had a certain communicative quality—maybe it was in their lovely complex aromas. (In deep space, Principal Buttle had learned what few human beings had ever learned before: that, really, the most receptive and intuitive organ in the human body, apart from the heart, is the nose. And Principal Buttle had a big one, and it was proving very talented indeed.)

"Why, look." She sniffed. "It's—it's the children!"

One by one they separated themselves into distinct units. She leaned down and peered closer.

"How charming!"

There was Thud Tweed. He was safe and well! Apparently he hadn't seriously hurt himself in that leap from the *Loiterbug*. Thank goodness! It was impossible to tell if he had allowed himself to be persuaded away from Hamlet by his no-goodnik dad and his complicated mother. But here he was, a grownup Thud, very nearly a genuine Thaddeus, standing with a rolling pin behind the counter of Grandma Earth's Baked Goods and Auto Repair Shop. And he had slimmed down some. Though not enough.

Next was Carly Garfunkel, looking like a rather glamorous bouncer in a New York City nightclub. Or maybe she was changing a tape in a cash register at a convenience store; it was hard to tell.

Mike Saint Michael floated up and then floated away. Not much to say about him, apparently.

The next few were a bit clearer. Stan Tomaski and Nina Bueno were—*married?* To each other? Goodness, for how long had Hetty Buttle been traveling? And they hadn't even had a single rest stop yet!

Moshe Cohn had a stethoscope. Good for you, Moshe! He was donating free medical attention to starving children in a slum in Mexico City. He looked happy and focused.

Anna Maria Mastrangelo was performing in a West End theater in London, doing an avant-garde version of *King Lear* as a nun. The notices on the outside of the theater were ecstatic, but perplexed.

Forest Eugene Mopp, who had been the resident Mr. Science, appeared to be happy doing forestry for the Vermont state preserves. And there, at his side, was Hector Yellow, busy designing sets for some community theater to which they both had season tickets. How sweet!

Sharday Wren had made it big as a dancer, a prima ballerina in the New York City Ballet.

And the others—the ones she had known better—here they came. . . .

Fawn Petros was cutting hair next to her mother, Gladys, in the Hamlet House of Beauty. On the counter behind her chair was a big red Valentine's heart. From a secret admirer? A photograph stuck in the corner of Fawn's mirror showed Aunt Sophia and a pretty little girl in a bathing suit. The child looked about ten and was pretty as a cupid. Waving and beaming.

Salim Bannerjee had predicted his own future accurately. He had gone to law school, and was specializing in international adoptions. He was so grown up, with a briefcase, a cell phone, a little potbelly snug behind his waistcoat buttons! And on his desk were photos of grinning children, a bevy of beautiful Bannerjees.

Lois Kennedy the Third. This was harder to read. Had she actually gone into cloak-and-dagger work? She was wearing a belted trench coat with a high turned-up collar. Fashion statement, or the professional uniform of international espionage? Hetty Buttle couldn't tell, but she supposed this was rather the point of being a spy. One wasn't supposed to be able to tell.

Pearl Hotchkiss was . . . hmmm? A hermit? No, an artist. A sculptor in a studio far across a meadow, with no phone, no e-mail, no radio. She was making large sculptures out of bent wire hangers. They all seemed to be of spiders. She looked happy to be alone.

Thekla Mustard. Oooh, even harder to make out. Thekla in a board room somewhere. Thekla slamming a taxi door! Thekla on a stage delivering a major address. Thekla receiving a medal around her neck, a glorious medal the size of a medium-sized pizza. Thekla with TV cameras on her. Thekla in a stadium with ten thousand screaming fans. Could she be the new Meg Snoople? Or was she a member of the government? President Mustard?

"Quite dizzying, really," said Hetty Buttle.

Sammy Grubb was the last. Normal, down-to-earth Sammy Grubb. What had become of him?

Well, how odd!

He was in a lab coat, quietly talking over some findings with an older colleague. The colleague turned. It was Professor Wolfgang Einfinger. Had that scoundrel turned over a new leaf? Or had Sammy . . . gone over *to the dark side?*

She didn't believe that he could, or he would, or he had.

Then Sammy grew two little horns and a tail, and turned red, and stuck his tongue out at Principal Buttle.

"What! Mr. Samuel Lemuel Grubb, I'll wash your mouth out with soap!" huffed Hetty Buttle.

Droyd and Peppa fell to the floor, laughing.

"What has gotten into you monkeys?" said Principal Buttle. "Are you toying with me? Did you make this all up? Is this all some elaborate nonsense you have invented to torture me and torment me? Double lashings of homework for you tonight if it is!"

But they didn't get double lashings of homework, for Droyd and Peppa wouldn't reveal if it was all a trick or not. They just ran to feed Amos and Beatrice.

Principal Buttle didn't press it. She didn't really need to know. She was sure of very little about her students' futures, but she knew one thing decidedly. They had all been very well educated. They would all be doing just fine.

★ *T H E   E N D* ★

★

Gregory Maguire is the author of many books for children and adults, including the best-selling *Wicked* (HarperCollins). He lives outside Boston, Massachusetts.